MY BIGGEST Break

T. GEPHART

Published by T Gephart
Copyright 2021 T Gephart
ISBN: 978-0-6487943-8-7

Discover other titles by T Gephart at the retailer of your choice or on Facebook (https://www.facebook.com/pages/T-Gephart/412456528830732), Twitter (https://twitter.com/tinagephart), Goodreads, or tgephart.com

Cover by Hang Le
Editing by Insight Editing Services
Formatting by Elaine York, Allusion Publishing
www.allusionpublishing.com
Proofread by Rebecca, Fairest Reviews and Editing Services

MY BIGGEST Break

Dedication

To Bec,
I didn't understand why you were so cold and seemed to
not like me when we first met. And I never thought we'd be
friends. Little did I know that underneath the hard exterior
was a heart of gold, whose trust you needed to earn before you
got to see the real her—a careful but beautiful soul who'd do
anything for the people she loves.
I'm glad we got that chance.
#SistersByChoiceNotDNA

Chapter 1

Belle

Shit.

Shit.

Shit.

I wasn't the kind of girl who was usually late, especially not for an audition. But even as I ran—knowing I was probably going to look like a hot mess when I got there—it was becoming painfully obvious I wasn't going to make it.

Shit.

I ran faster, my ballet flats barely touching the sidewalk as I sprinted to the old theatre in Brooklyn and told myself it would all be okay.

Visualize.

See your success and make it happen.

And while there was nothing I could do about being late, I was going to blow the audition out of the water if it was the last thing I did.

I wanted it so bad.

So.

Bad.

The chance to be a lead was something I'd been vying for my whole career, and this part had my name written all over it.

Literally.

As in, I had printed out the sample script they'd emailed me and written my name beside the character's, proudly proclaiming it mine.

In *ink*.

Because pencil notations were for losers.

"Yes!!" My excitement spiked, grabbing the metal handle and yanking the door open. It was still unlocked, meaning someone had to be inside, my thanks whispered to the theatre gods as I threw myself through the doorway.

"I'm here!" I called out, leaping down the stairs to the front. All stages, no matter how small, always felt magical, and the one I was on was no exception. The three men sitting together in the first row, who'd obviously been deep in conversation and hadn't heard my entrance, turned abruptly at the sound of my voice. "I'm so sorry, gentlemen. I know I'm incredibly late," I huffed out between breaths, "but my name is Belle Mathews. I'm ready to go whenever you are."

I was still trying to regulate my breathing when I got to the stage, ignoring the fact my hair was a mess and I was sweatier than an afternoon of Bikkurim Yoga. Dumping my bag at the edge, I took three cleansing breaths as I walked out to the center, the spotlight illuminated, just waiting for me to step into it.

"Ms. Mathews?" The older guy with the kind face looked down at his laptop. "Weren't you supposed to be here an hour ago?"

"Yes, I know." I nodded, knowing how terrible it looked. "But I didn't have a number to call, and I got tied up in a family emergency and—"

I was cut off with the raising of a hand.

Jagger Hartley—the writer, director, and producer of the production—shot me a death glare that was not at all conducive to making me feel welcome.

"We're done with auditions. Thanks."

And then, without even bothering to hear why I was late, he turned back to the other two men. Completely ignoring I was still on the stage, ready to give him the best audition ever even though I was positive I had a blister, and my once perfectly winged eyeliner had smudged at the edges.

I'd heard the rumors.

Listened to how incredibly gorgeous he was.

His face so devastatingly handsome it was hard to make direct eye contact with and a body that was so hot it was a modern mystery how his clothes didn't disintegrate on contact etc. etc.

But apparently accompanying that hot, sexy, smoldering exterior was a cold, unemotional core with zero humanity and even less patience, and I was beginning to think the rumors were true.

Ironic that his last name was *Hartley*, when it was questionable whether he even had one.

"I know I'm late." I hadn't moved from my place on the stage, ignoring my dismissal and my messed-up hair and glistening skin. Running while necessary hadn't done wonders for my appearance, not that I'd let a little smudged eyeliner stop me. "And I don't think my time is any more valuable than yours. But I did have a really good reason for being late and if you give me just five minutes, I promise, you won't be sorry." I kicked up my chin, standing up straighter as I refused to give up on the first decent audition I'd gone to in months.

Lots of side characters, chorus and backup dancers, but no lead. And while I knew it was going to be Off Broadway and I wouldn't have my face on a billboard just yet. It was a start, and it was such a good part.

Even though the stage lights were almost blinding, I could see Hartley's glare turn to me and his eyes narrow. His stare so absent of any warmth it made my blood run cold. "I said, we're done. Please leave my stage." His words leveled at me like a crack of a whip leaving no room for discussion.

Jesus.

I mean, I knew he was a hard-ass, but did he not have *any* compassion? It was five freaking minutes, and we were all still there. It wasn't like I accosted him on the street and was trying to get an audition unsolicited. I'd done all the right things and gone through my agent, and if I hadn't needed to help Hayley, who'd freaked out over Bobbie's fever making me incredibly late, they'd have seen me anyway.

Refusing to flinch even though he was being unnecessarily mean, I tapped my ballet flat on the stage, finding my center and taking three deep breaths. And without being asked, I launched into the main monologue.

"*I'm not trash!*" I cried out, throwing out my arms as per the stage directions. "*I've been a part of this city my whole life and I'll probably die on these streets, but I'm not nothin'.*"

All eyes—including Hartley's—were on me, watching as I clawed at the front of my dress. "*Look at me. Tell me again how much I disgust you. How you can't love me for who I am. Because we both know that isn't true. And the only reason you're walking away is because you're a coward.*"

I had been so into my performance I hadn't even noticed Hartley had gotten out of his seat and was walking away. He didn't even look back, his steady strides taking him closer to the exit while my heart pounded in my chest.

Seriously?

He was just going to walk out?

And what the hell did I do? Keep going, continue with the rest of my audition piece for the two guys who weren't rude and giving me their attention, or chase after the asshole who was the only person actually capable of hiring me.

Goddamn it.

I huffed out a breath, grabbing my handbag and hefting it onto my shoulder as I leapt off the stage. If he thought I sucked and didn't want to sit through anymore then he could at least have the decency to say it to my face. Who even did that? Just leave without even acknowledging a person or saying goodbye. Was he raised by wolves?

"Thanks so much, I'm so sorry I was late," I called back over my shoulder as I ran up the stairs. Hartley had already made it to the door and was wasting no time opening it and leaving, ignoring me and my thundering footsteps.

My captive audience looked on in shock as I flew to the exit, a muffled "goodbye" trailing behind me as I flung open the door I'd opened mere minutes ago and found myself on the street.

The blister on my foot throbbed, protesting against all the running we'd done as my eyes searched the street. He had only been a few steps in front of me, how could he have disappeared.

Swiveling my head left and then right, I spotted a small alleyway to the side of the theatre. It *had* to be where he'd gone, refusing to believe that despite Jagger Hartley having the disposition of one of those Death Eaters from Harry Potter, he could actually dissolve into thin air.

Swearing under my breath—because now it was personal and I was going to give that jerk a piece of my mind—I took off again, making it to the end of the alley just in time to see him getting into a sleek black Lexus sedan.

Perfect, because what else would someone rude and obnoxious drive but an utterly pretentious car.

He looked up, his eyes connecting with mine as I reached the passenger side of his stupid car and yanked open the door. He hadn't even started the ignition, his eyebrows scrunched in utter confusion.

"What the hell are you doing?" he asked, watching as I pretty much threw myself into the seat beside him. "Are you completely insane?"

"Oh, I'm sorry," I mock gasped, putting my hand up against my mouth. "Was I being rude? You know, like you were when you walked out."

The chances of me landing the gig had gone from slim to non-existent. I was well aware I was probably—okay, definitely—

torching any shot I had at getting the role. And while I may have possibly been able to impress one or both of the guys who'd been kind enough to watch me, Hartley probably would have canned me on principle. What that principle was, was beyond me, but it was clear he'd already made his mind up. Which meant I didn't have much more to lose other than letting him get away with being a jerk.

"You were late. You missed your audition, but somehow I'm rude for leaving?" He glowered, his voice laced with disbelief. "Listen, pixie dust, I haven't got time to sit around, rearranging my schedule because you couldn't decide which dress to wear. Here's a piece of free advice, get a watch, be on time. Now get out of my car."

Ordinarily getting into a vehicle with a stranger was a bad idea. Even one as good-looking as Jagger Hartley. But I took Ubers all the time and had yet to be kidnapped so I was going to take my chances.

Plus, I still had a point to prove.

"I own a watch," I huffed back. "And I'm not usually late. But you were *right* there." I pointed to the rear of the theatre. "And I told you, I was sorry, and it had been an emergency. And while I get you don't owe me anything, it doesn't give you the right to be so rude."

His brow rose, the disbelief written all over his face as he looked at me still sitting in the passenger seat. Like he couldn't quite believe I hadn't gotten out of his car like he'd asked, or dissolved into a puddle of goo or whatever evil he was attempting to conjure up with those sexy hazel eyes.

And yes, they were sexy.

Even though I was mad as hell, and there was a possibility he could bludgeon me to death with his tire iron, there was no denying he was incredibly handsome.

"You done?" His sexy chest—yeah, I'd noticed—rising and falling as he blew out a breath. "Because when I said I had to leave, I meant I had to leave. So do us both a favor and get out of my car."

"Say sorry." I folded my arms across my chest, unwilling to leave until I got an apology.

"Excuse me?" He laughed, rearing back in surprise. "When I'd asked you earlier if you were insane, I didn't think I was actually right."

"I said sorry for being late, you should say sorry for being rude. That's only fair."

I didn't budge, meeting his gaze and not making any move to leave. Since I'd already blown my audition and I didn't have any solid plans for the rest of the afternoon, I had nowhere else to be. And I could wait all day if needed, determined to prove a point. It was one of my favorite things to do, next to being positive and spreading happiness.

"No." He turned, folding his arms across his chest, staring me down as those hypnotic hazel eyes darkened. "I'm not apologizing. Now get out."

Uhhhhhhhhhhhh.

Honestly, the smart thing would have been to get out of the car and go beg my agent to find me something—anything—else. I was positive there'd be a cold day in Hell before Hartley would give me a second chance, let alone hire me for the part. But I was already too invested, and I didn't want the jerk thinking he was intimidating me.

"Guess we'll just sit here then." I smiled, confident that if one of us was going to break, it wasn't going to be me.

He had no idea what I was capable of. I'd once spent an entire summer walking on my tiptoes until my parents finally caved and enrolled me at Miss Alyssa's Ballet School. It hurt like hell, my muscles and toes so sore I secretly snuck into the tub every night just to soak for a little relief. But as my parents found out— believing I'd get sick of my showdown within a day or two—I wasn't easily swayed when motivated.

"Fine." He shrugged, apparently not willing to concede. "But we aren't sitting here." His sentence was punctuated by the ignition, the engine roaring to life as he put the car in gear.

Oh, he thought he was going to scare me by starting the car. Ha.

Please.

I reached for the seatbelt, clicking it in as he pulled away from the curb and traveled down the narrow alleyway I'd run down to find him.

He was going to stop.

The minute we got to the main road, and I hadn't flinched. He was going to stop and apologize, if for no other reason than to get me out of his car.

But as we pulled onto the street, he slowed just enough to make sure he didn't hit oncoming traffic and turned. And then kept going, accelerating as much as Brooklyn traffic would allow him, and ignoring that he had an unplanned passenger.

Damn it.

He was good.

But I was better, not saying a word as I settled into my seat and looked passively out the windshield. Guess I was taking a trip, and hey, I loved nothing more than an adventure, so that suited me just fine.

From my peripheral vision I saw him wiggle his phone out from his pocket. I continued pretending to be uninterested, all while trying to use every shiny surface in the car to help me see what the hell he was doing.

Turns out I didn't need my vision, the sound of his Bluetooth connecting to the car sound system telling me everything I needed to know.

"Call Dane," he spat out, the robotic feminine voice repeating his instruction before dialing the number.

Dane?

He was calling his brother?

While I'd never met Jagger Hartley before, I knew a lot more about him than just the *hot-but-an-asshole* rumors I'd heard. He was the eldest—and only biological—son of Kirk Hartley, a NYC painter and poet who'd been revered as a national treasure.

He could still sell out an exhibition, his paintings commanding at least five figures, and that was for his less popular work. And his mother, Jane, had once danced in the New York Ballet as a prima ballerina. She was not only Kirk's muse, but a champion for art programs in schools, the Hartley family name linked to numerous scholarships. Dane was their adopted son—and Jagger's little brother.

All of that learned without a Google search.

"You better not be calling to cancel, Jagger," the voice—Dane I assumed—responded, without the obligatory greeting. "It's one lousy night."

"I'm not," he spat back, seeing his reflection in the windshield tilt toward me before he continued, "I'm just running a little late. Got tied up in auditions with a bratty actress. I'm just leaving now, assuming traffic isn't bad, I'll be there in two hours."

Bratty actress?

"Asshat," I coughed out under my breath, committed to ignoring him and not wanting to be the first to cave. But I had a real problem with holding my tongue too.

Also, *two hours?* Where the hell was he going?

"What was that?" Dane asked.

"Nothing." Hartley yawned. "I didn't hear anything."

My head swiveled, abandoning my quest to stare aimlessly out the window as it became clear I wasn't the only person in the car who could be stubborn.

There was a sigh on the phone, Dane taking a breath. "Okay, well get here as soon as you can. And Jagger, I know you're only doing this because of me, and I appreciate it."

"Yeah, got to go, bye." He'd barely gotten out the words before he ended the call. Either he was continuing to live up to the asshole nametag or he didn't want me to hear what sounded like a personal conversation. Normally I'd suggest the latter, but since it hadn't been proven he had feelings or even gave a shit what people thought, I had my doubts.

"You know," *fine, I was going to be the first to break the silence*, "if you're planning on crossing state lines, kidnapping becomes a federal offense."

He cocked a brow, barking out a laugh. "You're the one who wouldn't get out. If anyone is being held hostage here, it's me. We can call the cops and let them sort it out, see which one of us they believe. Either way it's going to have to be from Connecticut because I'm already late."

Connecticut?

He was taking me to Connecticut?

"I can't go to Connecticut. Just pull over already." An adventure was one thing, but I was in a car, leaving New York, with an asshat who was possibly more stubborn than me.

My father—veteran criminal prosecutor—would have a heart attack if he knew, and probably try to ground me despite me being twenty-six. Zara, my older sister, would also have something to say. And Hayley and Bobbie might need me.

"Not stopping. You had your chance," he offered with zero apology.

Seriously, what the hell was wrong with this guy?

And had I not been so pissed off, I might have been impressed. There weren't many people I couldn't sweet talk and get my way with, but Jagger Hartley was a worthy adversary.

But come on, already.

"Why the hell didn't you just say sorry?" I huffed. Wondering if he was planning on stopping for gas or something. I could catch a cab or Uber back, but throwing myself from a moving car wasn't happening.

"Why didn't you just get out when I told you to?" he shot back accusingly, like it was somehow *my* fault.

Fine, maybe I was partly to blame, but not entirely.

He was just.

Just.

Ughhhhhhhhhhhh.

"I'm not a brat!" I took a deep breath, knowing he probably didn't want to hear my reason, but I wasn't giving him the choice either way.

"My best friend recently became a new mom, and is totally being a badass raising her newborn daughter on her own. She's turned down the offer to move back home with her parents in Vermont, deciding to stay in the city and refusing to give up her Broadway dreams. And considering she'd actually been a lead multiple times, it isn't some pipe dream either. But Bobbie had a fever—her first—and Hayley had been freaking out. And there was no way I could leave her alone at Urgent Care until I was positive both of them were going to be okay. I just couldn't. Even if it meant I was throwing away my shot."

It was an excuse I was sure wasn't good enough, positive Hartley hated kids, as well as rainbows and sunshine. But whether or not he believed it was reasonable or not, I refused to have him berate me and treat me like some spoilt princess who was late because her flat-iron wasn't working.

Hartley swallowed, shooting a look in my direction before turning back to the road. "I'll get someone to give you a ride back to New York when I get to Connecticut. Try not to be too much of a pain in the ass until then."

Well, I guess that meant he wasn't stopping. And I was taking a road trip whether I wanted to or not.

"You should take your own advice." I folded my arms across my chest, huffing out a breath.

The rumors were true.

Jagger Hartley was the worst kind of human there was.

And I was stuck in a car with him.

Great.

Just Great.

Chapter 2

Jagger

How someone so small could be such a big inconvenience was still a mystery.

She had to be what? Five-one, five-two? I was over a foot taller and at least eighty pounds heavier. But despite our varying height-and-weight ratio, she didn't give a fuck.

Not even a little.

And I wasn't sure if I should be pissed off, or impressed.

I'd seen my fair share of entitled actresses.

Beautiful, somewhat talented, with vision boards full of pictures of Tony awards and billboards. And I swear, if I heard one more asshole try to sell me on the idea of *The Secret* and manifesting that shit into real life, I was going to punch someone.

So I'd assumed it was more of the same when the pint-sized firecracker stepped onto my stage over an hour late for her audition and demanded to be heard.

Hell, I hadn't even been that surprised when she followed me out, no stranger to the less-than-subtle tactics employed when drama was literally their job.

But getting into the car *and* refusing to leave was one I hadn't seen yet.

She had to be crazy.

Because that wasn't the kind of stunt that would get her hired. And had I not already been late to my parents' stupid anniversary dinner, I'd have called the cops.

But Dane was already annoyed I hadn't taken the day off, and as much as I didn't give a shit how much it displeased Kirk and Jane Hartley, I hated disappointing my little brother.

"Can we have some music? Or would that be too much cheer?" She lolled her head to the side to face me, her smile too bright considering our circumstance.

Definitely crazy.

"No, I drive in silence." I didn't bother adding that I usually used my time in the car to think. Not like it was any of her business, and I didn't need to explain my preference.

"Fine," she huffed back, shoving her hand into her bag and pulling out some ear buds. "But I don't have to."

And without any further discussion, she shoved the buds into her ears, and then hit some buttons on her phone, the activated playlist making her let out a contented sigh.

"Fucking crazy," I huffed under my breath. "It's going to be a long two hours."

As for her reason for being late, I'll admit it was admirable. Hayley Easton was an up-and-coming star with every director in town taking notice, until she found herself unexpectedly in the family way. But to her credit, she didn't use her pregnancy as an excuse, working until she almost delivered. The costume department of her latest show had to get creative at hiding her bump, but she didn't miss one show time or rehearsal. Lots to be said about that kind of commitment, and while I'd never heard of her apparent BFF currently sitting in my passenger seat, I was wondering if they shared other traits other than being dedicated and incredibly beautiful.

Yeah, I'd noticed.

A little hard not to when you were forced into a confined space with not much else to do.

But beautiful women weren't exactly uncommon in my line of work. Blondes, brunettes, redheads—all with killer bodies to match. But more often than not they bored me, their stale off-stage personalities being a little too much wash-rinse-repeat for my liking.

But I would hedge a guess there was nothing predictable or stale about Belle, and that spelled all kinds of trouble.

Firstly, I didn't need the distraction.

Fighting to have the industry take me seriously on my own merit was my primary focus, most people believing any doors that had opened had been on account of my last name. Having a famous mom and dad wasn't all it was cracked up to be, especially when you wanted to be seen for your talent, and not because you happened to be someone's kid. And don't even get me started on the money. I'd turned down every single offer of cash from both of my parents since college. I'd done it completely on my own, eating ramen noodles and peanut butter sandwiches trying to keep my lights on, fundraising for my first major play without the help of the Hartley checkbook.

It was important to me that it be my achievement and mine alone, sick of the expectation that the only talent I had was because of the family I happened to be in.

The bullshit that came with the legacy of my last name was something that was thankfully ignored when I attended NYU. And if I had it my way, would continue now I was actively working.

But secondly, I didn't date actresses.

It only led to complications, hurt feelings, and all kinds of expectations I had no interest in. I had my own shit to deal with, let alone the ego and very real drama that came with someone who lived their life mostly on stage.

Of course there was the added complication of them assuming I'd cast them in everything I wrote. You know, sort of like my dad used my mum as his fucking inspiration for almost every woman he ever painted. Sure, it was romantic if you were into that whole true love bullshit, but mostly it was boring.

Seriously.

One fucking woman?

And it wasn't that I didn't know how to be monogamous; I could keep my dick in my pants better than most. But creatively? Like hell I was getting saddled with one flavor for the rest of my natural life. So actresses, dancers, singers—basically anyone who would find their way onto my call sheet—were collectively out. No matter how beautiful or intriguing they seemed to be.

Ignoring the well thought-out and reasonable argument I'd just made, my eyes flicked over to the passenger side where she sat. She didn't look even slightly vexed, enjoying her ride to wherever I was taking her like I was her Uber driver and it had always been her plan.

Wow.

The nerve.

I bet she was listening to some bullshit over-processed pop song, saturated in autotune and mixed within an inch of its life, her eyes closed in a serene bliss that made me both irate and jealous as freaking hell. How the hell did she do that? Was she not even remotely concerned I could be a shady lowlife with criminal intent? Because surely having famous parents and a healthy searchable history didn't disqualify me from being a serial killer.

"Something you want to ask?" Her eyes fluttered open, connecting with mine instantly. I turned my attention back to the road—where it should've been—and cursed myself for getting caught watching her.

Unperturbed by my shift in focus, she pulled one of the buds from her ear and twisted to face me. "Go on, ask me anything you want. I could feel you looking at me."

"I wasn't looking at you." Fine, I *was*, but the last thing I fucking needed was for her to get the wrong idea. "I was just wondering how you could be so sure I'm not going to hack you into tiny pieces and dump you in the woods somewhere. You're so small there's hardly any chance they'd find you."

She laughed—not the reaction I'd expected—pulling the other bud from her ear and placing them in her lap. "Oh, and how do you not know I'm not going to tase you, steal your car, your wallet, and then ask your family for ransom?"

The fuck?

I scoffed, unable to choke back the chuckle. "Yeah? How much you going to ask for?"

Her finger tapped her lips, like she was giving it some serious consideration. "A million should do it."

"A million, huh?" I shook my head, slightly annoyed I wasn't hating the conversation. "That just an arbitrary figure you came up with, or is that some going rate? And I hope you have an accomplice or two, Belle." I looked down at her tiny hands, trying to imagine them restraining me.

"I said I'd *tase* you, silly." She rolled her eyes, hefting up her gigantic handbag. "The more people involved, the more likely to get caught. Besides, everything I need is right in here, no accomplices necessary."

Judging by the size of her bag, she no doubt had a taser, duct tape, and everything else listed in the *Kidnapper's Handbook* tucked inside. "Guess we'll just have to wait and see then." A grin creeping its way across my lips.

It wasn't like me to invite conversation, especially not with people I didn't know. But I wasn't in the habit of harboring stowaways either, so I guess it was all new territory.

An uncomfortable silence settled between us, and I didn't like it.

"This isn't going to change my mind." I felt the need to add, not wanting there to be any misunderstanding as to what it was or wasn't.

"About?" Belle asked, seeming to be honestly perplexed.

"Your audition," I added without qualifying.

"Please." She waved her hand dismissively. "I've got bigger plans for my future now. Especially after I get my million dollars."

Not sure if she'd felt the chill of the silence too or if she was just genuinely trying to keep the joke going, but either way I was surprised. Not a lot of people would have rolled with the punches as easily as she did, or not made it weird. But five minutes with Belle and I could tell she was anything but regular.

And that was probably what made me most uncomfortable. That it was a situation I wasn't sure I was in control of.

And for someone who was addicted to control, it was both unsettling and surprisingly addictive.

Not sure I'd ever been so intrigued by anyone while simultaneously unsettled. And part of me liked it.

Not good.

"I'll pull over at the next gas station. Call you an Uber so you can get back to New York." After all, I was already late, an extra twenty minutes wasn't going to make much difference. Not to mention it would let us both off the hook.

"Dane is already annoyed you're late." She shrugged like it was no big deal. "You wouldn't want to piss him off more than you already have."

I bit my bottom lip to stop myself from wincing, Belle oblivious to the nerve she'd hit.

Dane had spent the last few years trying to play mediator. Trying to stitch our family into some bullshit tapestry that matched the American ideal. The doting parents with their two adoring, loving sons, living in the fantasy that my father would have everyone believe. The rhetoric was old and tired, recited every single opportunity he was asked about his family.

But the tension went both ways, their inability to understand me and my need to do shit on my own, making both my parents beyond frustrated and impatient, worried I might fall on my ass and screw up their legacy. Ironic it was the kid they didn't share biology with that they were most proud of, Dane taking over the family trust and guaranteeing the Hartley name was not only famous, but profitable as well.

And while it would be easy to hate him, there just wasn't a part of me that ever could. He was so *good*, a human with a big heart and admirable ideals that I was positive was only possible because he wasn't really from the Hartley bloodline. And he was the only one who accepted me exactly how I was.

So yeah, while I really didn't give a rat's ass if Mom and Dad were disappointed—again—I didn't want that from Dane.

"Fine." I rubbed my neck, keeping my eyes on the road. Last thing I wanted to do was launch into a discussion about my family with her, or say shit she could potentially use against me later. "But don't say I didn't give you a choice."

"I'll be sure to tell the judge I was here of my own free will." She reached out and touched my arm. "And for my compromise, I promise not to tase you."

Well, at least there was that.

"Generous of you."

My hand instinctively hit the stereo, forgetting I'd said I didn't listen to music as I turned up the volume. I was sure most people assumed I listened to jazz or classical, or something else equally highbrow, but my choice was heavy metal, the loud guitars and angry vocals spilling from the speakers.

I liked the madness, the loud, chaotic noise that seemed fueled by emotions. And for someone who lived their life on a knife's edge of control, I enjoyed the release. Almost like therapy, if I believed in that kind of thing. Which I didn't.

I waited.

Expecting some sort of commentary as to my music choice or my initial position denying her a playlist. But she didn't react at all other than packing away her ear buds into that monstrous bag filled with God knows what and relaxed into her seat.

It was going to be the longest drive to Connecticut ever.

Chapter 3

Belle

I'd be the first to admit I don't always do what I'm supposed to.

Or even what was sensible.

Because if I did either of those things, I would've taken up his offer and asked him to stop at the next gas station. Or perhaps gotten out of the damn car before we started driving out of state.

But since it was clear I wouldn't be doing what would make sense, I was staying in the car, and reaching our final destination, wherever that may be.

Oh, I could rationalize he was already late, and I didn't want his brother to be any more annoyed than he seemed on the phone. Or even that I didn't want to inconvenience Hartley. But all of that would be a lie since the real reason was more that I was curious as hell, and had an affliction of getting involved in business that probably didn't concern me. I say probably because there was always a chance someone *needed* my help. And if there was one thing my criminal prosecutor father and social worker mother always taught us it's that if you see somewhere you can make a difference, get involved. Of course, they were probably thinking more social injustice and that kind of thing, but a need was a need, and I wouldn't be told different.

And Jagger Hartley was definitely a need.

How or why, I hadn't worked out yet. But he was wound up so tight and so devoid of cheer, I had to wonder whether he ate misery for breakfast. He was totally going to ruin that flawless skin nature had given him—I bet he didn't even moisturize— and end up with worry lines and a permanent scowl. And his general disposition could definitely use an overhaul.

Plus, I was nosey.

Fine, it was probably a lot more about that than anything else, but I was doing a good deed and that's all that mattered. The fact he was gorgeous didn't hurt either.

What?

Not like I could pretend he wasn't thirteen different versions of delicious, just because he was acting like an asshole. And not just his hot body, gorgeous eyes and ridiculously handsome face. There was something else that was appealing, an underlying smolder that exuded sex appeal unlike any man I'd ever seen. Like he wasn't even trying. I could appreciate the fancy wrapping without wanting to play with the present inside. And Jagger Hartley had very, very nice wrapping.

Wonder when he found time to go workout at the gym? A body like that didn't get all that toned and muscular splendor simply by being broody. And if I could tell how impressive it was *with* his clothes on, he would be a real treat with his clothes off.

Not that I was thinking about him naked.

Fine.

Maybe just a little.

Okay, okay, a lot.

But he was hot, and imagining was totally allowed.

If the angry music blasting out of his speakers didn't give me a hint he didn't want to speak, his body language clearly spelled it out. His hands were choking the steering wheel so tight I was surprised it hadn't squeaked out a safe word already. And his body—all six-foot whatever—was coiled like a cobra ready to attack. Actually, I think a cobra might be more relaxed, Hartley barely making eye contact as we passed interstate markers taking us farther away from the city.

"Should you stop and buy a present?" I offered, unable to keep my mouth shut even though it would have probably been wiser.

"Huh?" He turned his head, treating me with the attention of those beautiful hazel eyes.

Okay, so maybe I noticed he had nice eyes too, but we were literally sitting inches away from each other, what else was I going to do but catalog everything about him. I thought it might be useful someday, or if he really did intend to be a jerk so I could give an accurate description in court.

My eyes dropped down to his phone sitting on the console between us. "You know, for whatever you're late for. Bottle of wine? Flowers? I always find that people are so much more receptive to forgiveness if you sweeten it with a gift. I can help you pick something, I'm really good at choosing presents."

"What makes you think I need forgiveness?" he answered smoothly, his brow rising as he turned his attention back to the road.

"You know I heard the phone call, right? And that's not because I was being rude and trying to overhear your conversation, but it was literally on speaker."

"And because you heard a three-minute conversation, you assume you know what that was all about?" He shrugged, not angry per se but not overly pleased either. He was like a vault, all his emotions locked up so tight I wasn't sure he had them. Other than annoyance, which he seemed to dish out freely.

"Listen, if it's one thing I know it's people. And Dane," I pointed to the phone, "was upset. He was expecting you to cancel, which by the sounds of it, you do a lot, and you obviously didn't want to go."

"Wow, sounds like you know everything."

I didn't miss the sarcasm.

I should've left it.

Should've read the cues that it was a topic he didn't want to talk about and asked him why we were listening to angry music. If he genuinely liked the noise? Or if the screaming distortion recharged his dark energy like a comic book villain.

But . . .

"No, not everything, but as much as you want to blame it on me, I wasn't the reason you're late. You didn't look like you were in any kind of hurry when I walked in. If you wanted to be on time, you'd have left already."

Shit.

And I'd obviously hit some kind of trigger, or he was just tired of the conversation because I felt the interior of the car cool by at least ten degrees. Oh, and I was no longer sure he was joking about hacking me up into tiny pieces, the murderous vibe he was throwing so intense, he didn't even have to speak for me to pick up on it.

What the hell was I doing?

It was obvious I'd blown whatever chance I might've had with the audition, but I still hoped to work again. Hartley had all kinds of connections, and as big a city as it was, Broadway wasn't big enough for me to survive the mark of the damned.

God, I hoped I didn't get stuck doing infomercials for the rest of my life, or playing uncredited parts on every other network series. I was too talented to be relegated to the Coffee Shop Girl 1 or Shopper Number 2.

"So . . . flowers or wine?" I ignored the boundary I'd probably overstepped and instead went for smiling sweetly. I was only trying to be helpful.

Hartley just shook his head, dismissing whatever he was going to say and turned up the volume. It was clear our conversation was over and if I thought there was an awkward silence before, it was nothing compared to our new situation.

I'd never gone so long without talking.

And other than texting Hayley to check in with her and Bob-bie and make sure they didn't need me to run back to the city—which didn't really count as conversation—I kept my mouth shut.

Literally saying nothing until we pulled up to a large sprawl-ing property in Greenwich. It had a big black gate that opened with a code, surrounded by trees and hedges so you couldn't see the house—or most likely mansion—from the road.

Hartley barely acknowledged me as we drove down the driveway, the road lit with old-fashioned gas lights more appro-priate for old world Europe than New England.

The sun hadn't even set yet, the reflection on the glass brighter than the flame inside the ornate light boxes, noise from the house starting to spill out the closer we got to it.

Oh, and it was totally a mansion.

Huge by anyone's definition, there was no way this could be anything other than the Hartley compound.

Shit.

And double shit.

I'd assumed we were going somewhere to meet his broth-er. A restaurant. An apartment. A public place that didn't allow for shallow graves and body disposal. Instead, I was on private property which I'd probably still get lost on even with the use of my GPS.

Not good, Belle.

Not good.

"Is there some kind of party?" My vow of silence—or career preservation—expired as I took in the cluster of cars scattered around the main driveway. There were no neat valet-inspired rows, vehicles of various makes and models parked haphazardly like snoring drunk frat boys after a kegger.

"I'll call you that Uber." His only response as he unhooked his seatbelt and opened the driver's side door.

Uber? He was calling me an Uber? We'd just arrived at what was clearly some sort of celebration at his massive family home—with, I assumed, his entire family inside—and he wanted me just to get in a car and head back to New York? Oh, there was no way I could just turn around and leave without finding out enough information to satisfy an FBI investigation.

"Jesus, Jagger, Mom has been asking where you've been for the last hour. Did you turn your phone off? Oh, sorry didn't see you'd brought a date. Hi."

The new guy—who I guessed was Dane—had apparently materialized from thin air and was standing right beside us. And wow.

Just wow.

He was only an inch or two shorter than his brother, but impressive all the same. He seemed to spend some time at the gym too, if the way his suit curled around him was anything to go by, sporting adorable sandy light brown hair and a pair of piercing blue eyes. But what was most noticeable was his smile, so warm and lovely, lighting up his whole gorgeous face.

I held out my hand, ready to make my own introduction. "Hi, I'm—"

"Just leaving." We were rudely interrupted by an angry-looking Jagger Hartley. "She's not my date. And I switched my phone to silent."

Each word was sharp, efficient, and deadly, like a bullet with the exact amount of warmth as a gunshot.

"I'm sorry about my brother." Dane eyeballed him hard before turning to me. "He forgets his manners back in Manhattan from time to time. I'm Dane."

"Belle."

He took the hand I still had extended and gave it a polite shake. "So nice to meet you, Belle. How do you know Jagger?"

I waited, expecting *Jagger*—had I ever called him by his first name?—to interject. But he didn't, watching with interest as he waited for me to explain.

"I was auditioning for him," I answered honestly. "I'm an actress."

Jagger—it still felt naughty, even saying it in my head—snorted, actually looking amused.

"What?" I shot back, not willing to let some guy with an inflated ego and a superiority complex say that I wasn't. I might not have had the accolades of Hayley or the resume of some other actresses, but I was just as freaking talented. And eventually my time would come. Annnnnnd how dare he even try to judge me, considering he saw like barely a minute of my audition and had no idea what I was capable of.

"What were you going to say, *Jagger*?" I smiled, wondering if he was going to demand I call him Mr. Hartley or sir or some other bullshit to make me feel inferior.

He huffed impatiently, looking between me and his brother. "I was going to suggest that it was more a hostile takeover than an audition. Would you disagree?"

Oh, so it wasn't my talent he was disputing, okay. And even though he was wildly coloring the circumstances of how I came to be there—fine, maybe he was right, but I'd never admit it—I wasn't all that upset about it.

"So I held you at gun point and forced you to drive me here?" I batted my eyelashes and smiled.

He shrugged, the tiniest smile just barely cracking at the edge of his lips. "You said you had a taser. You mean, you lied?"

Whoa.

Was Jagger Hartley actually making a joke? And why was it so goddamn sexy?

"Errrr . . . does one of you want to explain?" Dane's eyes flicked between us, his voice a little less bright than when we first met.

"I'm not a crazy person," I qualified, positive Dane was building a picture that might have been less than flattering. Crazy actress hijacks his brother, forces him to take her to the family home—all of which would probably have him calling for their personal security—if they had them—or dialing 9-1-1.

"But Jagger," *I liked the way it felt the more I said it,* "was so rude and I just wanted an apology."

Okay, so it didn't sound a whole lot better.

"I mean—"

"You were rude?" Dane grinned at his brother, raising a brow. "Noooo. That doesn't sound right. You've always been so warm and welcoming."

Jagger rolled his eyes, flipping him off before leveling his gaze on me. "You were late."

"Yes, I know. Should they stone me in the streets now or later?" I tilted my head to the side. "Maybe we can ask Dane's opinion?"

Dane chuckled. "Oh, you're fantastic."

"Yes, well fantastic or not, we need to get Ms. Mathews back to Manhattan where she belongs." Jagger pulled out his phone. "Where would you like the driver to take you?"

"You're not just going to send her off, Jagger." Dane shook his head, his eyes still on me. "At least let me offer you something to eat or drink, perhaps use the restroom before you head back. That is, if you have the time?"

I wasn't sure exactly why the invitation was extended, but I was interested all the same. Whether I was the casualty of some weird sibling skirmish or if he was worried I might talk to the press. I'm guessing there were people like that, willing to sell half-truths to the paparazzi to get their fifteen minutes of fame. Or maybe a quick payday. And since I had a real sickness in wanting information, I didn't really care what the motivation had been.

Hayley was fine, Bobbie's fever had broken and she was sleeping as per the latest text she'd sent while I was in the car.

Zara and Lincoln—my sister and her fiancé—would probably be doing boring lawyer stuff like eating takeout while going over law briefs and likely wouldn't even notice I wasn't home.

And since I'd blown the only audition I had for the week, I didn't have anything to prep for. I did some voiceover stuff to help pay the bills, but I'd already filled my quota for the day, so technically had nowhere to be.

"Why thank you, Dane." I smiled brightly, shimmering with excitement. "I would love a chance to have something to eat before I go home. Are you sure I won't be an imposition?" I glanced over at the cars. "It looks like you're in the middle of an event."

"Our parents' anniversary dinner. And trust me, you're no imposition. There are so many people here, the more the merrier. They love company." Dane answered with such confidence I chose to believe him. Also, if the traffic in their driveway was anything to go by, they weren't even going to notice me. I was small and could totally blend in, and people generally loved me.

"Dane," Jagger warned, a silent dialogue passing between them. "I think it would be better if Belle left."

Was that the first time he'd said my name? I couldn't remember if he'd said it in the car, and before he'd called me Ms. Mathews.

"Jagger, don't be silly. Let's go inside, Mom and Dad will be excited to see you and I'll keep Belle entertained." Dane tipped his head to the front door, not giving Jagger a chance to argue.

And while I was positive Jagger could easily heft me over his shoulder, bundle me back into his car and drive me back to New York himself, something told me he wasn't going to make a scene. Not in front of his little brother, which was interesting because from everything I knew about Jagger Hartley, he didn't care what anyone thought.

Dane smiled at me with expectation, his handsome features lighting up with genuine interest. And while I wasn't sure he was flirting, I was curiously uninterested. But it did give me an opportunity to stay a little longer, and that *did* interest me.

"Thanks so much." I took a step toward the ornate entrance way, the front door, ajar. "I'm so excited."

Jagger didn't share my enthusiasm, shooting me a death glare that would have killed me at least three times. "I should've left you at the gas station," he muttered under his breath, going on ahead of us and leaving me outside with Dane.

Dane looked at me apologetically, before gently taking my arm. "So Belle, tell me more about yourself. I'm positive you are fascinating."

Chapter 4

Jagger

I was going to kill Dane.

Kill.

Him.

What the hell was he thinking by inviting Belle in, treating her like one of his new dates? Firstly, we knew nothing about her, other than she had boundary issues and little regard for her own personal safety. She literally got into a car with a man she'd just met, whose intentions weren't clear, and then left the city with zero issue. Nothing. Not even a hesitation or question. Who does that?

Also, as much as I wanted to hate what she'd briefly done on the stage, even I had to admit she was talented. I'd seen veterans not able to center themselves and dive right in, especially given the circumstances. But Belle hadn't even blinked, took a second to get into character, and given what ordinarily I'd have called a decent performance.

If she'd been on time.

And not been a thorn in my side.

But as talented as she might be, that didn't say much else about who she was and what she was capable of. And I'd made the mistake once of bringing a girlfriend home I was seeing on the casual side when I was in high school. She'd taken photos of our house on her cell phone and stolen a soap dish from the bathroom, all ready to sell to some dumbass reporter hoping to get the insider scoop on the *Hartley Compound*.

It's what everyone called it, my dad giving it the stupid moniker when *Time* magazine came to interview him back in the 90s. But stupid or not, I didn't like the idea of people I didn't know snooping around what had been my sanctuary for most of my childhood. It was our escape from the city, spending weekends and summers away from the noise of New York, away from prying eyes and where we could just be kids. My parents eventually sold their condo in the Village and moved to CT fulltime when Dane went away for college, and suddenly it wasn't an escape anymore. Still, Belle could just be another Wendy, looking to make a fast buck and/or use it for leverage.

Fucking little brothers.

And fucking family gatherings.

And while we were at it, fucking beautiful actresses as well. Damn it.

Damn both of them because I was already on edge and the new development had only made it worse.

"Jagger." My mom almost threw herself at me—for a dancer she sure was big on theatrics, then again, we did have an audience. "I'm so glad you made it, tonight wouldn't have been the same without you." She did her best to pull me into a hug even though I was double her size. "Tell me, have you eaten? There's plenty of food laid out on the dining room table."

When she said there was plenty of food, she wasn't kidding. My parents loved to entertain and spared no expense on making sure their guests were taken care of. But I wasn't hungry, and while I'd chase down the agitation gnawing in my gut with a beer—or six—I couldn't shake the need to know where my brother was, and what he was doing with Belle.

She was supposed to go.

To get in a car, head back to New York, and leave me to deal with the charade. It wasn't that I didn't love my parents—the opposite actually, I loved them very much—but their addiction to attention, constantly being in the company of others, made my skin crawl. Every action felt contrived, like I wasn't sure if the hugs were because they thought it would make a good photo op, or if they genuinely wanted the contact.

"I'm good, Mom." I gave her a kiss on the cheek, squeezing her back. "I think I might go say hello to Dad, and then find out where Dane got to."

Her eyes brightened, the smile on her lips getting wider. "I really am glad you came home, Jagger. We've missed you."

I nodded, giving her a final squeeze before heading off, feeling a little irate with myself for losing control of the situation outside. Never should've left the two of them. Who knew where Dane and Bell were and what they were doing. And considering the woman needed little encouragement to get herself involved in trouble, that didn't make me feel good about her wandering around with unfettered access to me and my personal life.

My dad usually held court in one of the main rooms. He liked to be sitting—or standing—fifteen-year-old whiskey in one hand, and a well-rolled blunt in the other. Yeah, my parents smoked weed, part of the creative process apparently, and whether or not that was socially acceptable meant little to them.

Well lubricated, with a decent buzz happening, was when he did his best work. Telling stories, reciting poetry or randomly breaking out his easel was how *he* liked to entertain.

So I moved through doorways, waving to people I wasn't interested in talking to as I looked for Kirk Hartley. Of course, I was also searching for the current banes of my existence which were Dane *and* Belle. They'd literally disappeared in the few moments since I'd left them, not hard to do in the *Compound*—and its labyrinth of rooms—especially when it was full of people.

I wasn't sure who I wanted to find first—bullshit, I knew exactly who and it wasn't my dad—but as the minutes ticked by, my agitation was growing into something else.

Seriously, where the hell were they?

Jesus.

Fucking.

Christ.

It seemed the concern over who I'd find first wasn't something I should've been worried about, more that if I found them together.

Belle was beaming, laughing at something while my dad looked on absolutely enthralled.

"Son!" my dad called out, waving me over to the shitshow while Dane looked anything but apologetic as he stood beside them.

Killing him.

"Jagger, come meet this charming young lady." Dad took a swig from his glass as his head angled to Belle. "She's an actress, maybe you could use her in your new production."

Oh no, she fucking didn't.

Hijacking my attention and hitching a ride was one thing. And not that I'd endorse the behavior, but it mightn't have been so bad. Using my dad for leverage was something else.

My jaw creaked as I ground my molars, careful to keep my temper on a leash as I got closer. Big displays of emotion in front of a crowd weren't on my agenda, so losing my shit was going to have to be sidelined till later. But trust me, I'd definitely be losing my shit.

"Hey." My lips tightened into a smile, I'm sure wasn't convincing, as I eyed Belle. "An actress? Huh, looks like you need better security, Dad. They're just letting anyone in."

Dad laughed, slapping me on the back. "Don't be silly, Son. This is Dane's friend, Belle. And I do say, she's a real treat."

Dane's friend?

DANE'S FRIEND?

Belle was a lot of things, but she was *not* Dane's fucking friend.

How could one tiny woman be so much trouble in such a small amount of time?

How?

I was literally trying to grasp how a woman I hadn't even met until a few hours ago had now become my brother's friend, and was being enthusiastically endorsed by my father.

"Belle, nice to meet you, I'm Jagger." I played along, waiting to see if this was part of her sinister plan or if Dane was enjoying watching me squirm. "And as *charming* as I'm sure you are," *I did my best not to choke on the words*, "all my roles have been cast. Although," I took a breath, trying to make my smile more sincere, "there's a rare opening at Ellen's Stardust Diner for a singing waitress. Can you hold a tune? They've got a pretty high standard."

Her eyes heated, pretty, pouty pink lips slamming shut as her hands anchored on her hips. "Wow, thanks for the tip." Her voice laced with as much sweetness as she could muster. "I love Ellen's and as much as I'd like to audition, I've already got a job. And as *wonderful* as I'm sure your production is, I'm not really into vanity projects." She lifted her delicate hand to her mouth, pretending like she hadn't meant to say the last part. "Sorry, how rude of me."

Are you fucking kidding me?

I wasn't sure who I wanted to strangle first, Belle or my asshole brother who was grinning like a fucking idiot.

"Oh, I can understand how you might assume that." I tried to laugh, the chuckle getting stuck in my throat. "But unlike some people, I've earned my stripes on Broadway. Something you might've known if you'd been around the industry. So, um, sorry, what exactly have you been in? I don't watch reality T.V. and not up-to-date with the latest YouTube sensations."

Checkmate, sweetheart.

She wanted to go head-to-head, then I wasn't pulling any punches. And fuck the *vanity project* bullshit, I'd been refining that script for over twelve months. No one gave me a free pass, and they sure as shit wouldn't have invested their hard-earned cash so I could stroke my own ego.

Belle glared, her little fists balling at her side. "I was in *Phantom,* asshole. And—"

"Drinks, we should all go get drinks." Dane put his hand around Belle's waist—which pissed me off more than it should— and then hooked his other around my arm. "Dad, we'll catch up soon. Don't smoke too much, Mom will be pissed if you're passed out before dessert."

And before anyone could argue, he dragged us both away from Kirk who, had he not been so high, might've been bewildered.

"Wow, Jagger, you're even pricklier than usual. Play nice until we get to the kitchen." He tipped his head to someone trying to get his attention. "Hey Steve, tell Moira and the kids we said hi."

"Me? She started it." I huffed impatiently as he almost tossed us into the secluded kitchen and shut the door. "Not to mention, she shouldn't even be here."

"She? *She*?" Belle waved her hands dramatically like she was waving down a bus. "Do you practice being so arrogant or rude or does it come naturally? It's Belle and I'm here *because* you—"

"Because you can't take no for an answer," I finished for her, my agitation rising even though I wasn't entirely sure what I was angry at.

That she was in my family home?

That she was talking to my dad?

That my brother was clearly attracted to her—I knew what that dopey-eyed look meant—and fell in love with almost every pretty woman he ever met?

Or was it that she was so . . . so, ughhhhhh . . . I don't know. . . something.

"You know what, Jagger." Belle got in close, jamming her finger into my chest. Her attempt at being aggressive downright comical because she was so small. "All you had to do was say sorry. One word. One small word, which I'm positive hasn't left your lips maybe ever, and I wouldn't even be here."

"Guys, can we take it down a notch?" Dane grimaced, looking between us. "Whatever the reason, Belle's here, which makes her our guest. And Jagger, I know this might hurt your rep if I say it, but Belle, he's not usually a hateful bastard."

My mouth had barely opened, the words not even out when Dane raised his hand. "I'm not done." And while I wanted to argue, I was mildly curious what he was going to propose. "So, here's what we're going to do. You two," his finger pointed squarely at Belle and then me, "are going to do whatever it takes to make sure you can be civil to each other. You just have to get through an hour. By that time, we'll be onto desserts, and I'll personally drive Belle back to New York."

Of course he would.

I'm sure he couldn't wait to get her into his car, drive her back to NYC and pick out their fucking honeymoon location. Okay, that was probably an exaggeration and more to the point, why did I even care?

"Wow, Dane, you don't have to go to all that trouble." Belle's voice sweetened on a dime, smiling at my brother like he'd offered to carry her all those miles on his fucking back.

He gave her an equally saccharine smile. "No trouble. It will be my pleasure. Now, work it out. I'll be back in a few minutes or if I hear yelling, whichever comes first."

And with his instructions dished out, he stepped hesitantly toward the door, giving me a warning look before leaving.

"Look, we don't have to be friends." Surprise, surprise, Belle was the first one to speak, the ability to *not* say anything probably beyond her.

"Well, that's the first thing you've said, I can agree on." I nodded, leaning against the kitchen counter. As the party had been catered, the room was ridiculously bare, with all of the action happening in the basement where the alternate kitchen was.

I pulled open the fridge door and pulled out two beers, twisting the cap off one and handing it to her. "Beer?"

She narrowed her eyes, examining the bottle even though she'd just seen me open it, before she wrapped her slender fingers around it. "I wasn't done talking."

"There's a surprise."

She rolled her eyes before continuing, "I was going to say that we don't have to be friends to be civil. I'll admit this is a strange situation—"

"Noooooo," I mock gasped, opening my bottle and taking a swig. "Getting into a car with a stranger, hitching a ride to the home of his parents and wandering into their anniversary dinner is *strange*?"

"Okay, crazy even. But surely you don't think we're still strangers now. There was the car ride. And the audition, and I told you all about my friend Hayley. And if it makes you feel better, my dad, my sister and soon to be brother-in-law are all attorneys, so if I ended up being a criminal psychopath, it would be a huge embarrassment. Not to mention my mom is a social worker and is literally the nicest person ever, but would probably disown me. Which is saying a lot. So you see, if you're worried about me using any of this stuff against you, or acting crazy," she caught herself, "*crazier* than I already have, you don't need to."

Those were pretty big calls, and honestly, I didn't feel like she was a stranger anymore. Weird considering we'd barely spoken in the two hours we were in the car, and the conversation in the theatre barely even counted as an interaction. But even though I didn't know her, she had an insane warmth about her. Like sunshine. And it all felt ridiculously genuine.

"What is it that you want, Belle?" I dared to ask, because as nice as she seemed to be, she surely had an agenda. Everyone did. "You want another audition?"

"You think I did this for an audition?" She looked confused, like it had been the furthest thing from her mind.

"Why else?"

She took a deep breath, tilting her chin to look at me. "Do people do that a lot? Expect things from you? Is that why you're such an asshole?"

"Now you're calling me an asshole?" I laughed, mildly perturbed she was so perceptive while being impressed she hadn't backed down.

"Am I wrong?" she asked, unapologetically.

I swallowed, feeling a lot more exposed than I liked. "No, you're not. I *am* an asshole. Now, if it's all the same with you, I'd prefer to be the one to drive you back."

Chapter 5

Belle

Jagger was a complicated man.

I knew that before I'd even met the guy, but seeing him home with his family just punctuated an already obvious point.

"You want to drive me home?" I asked, convinced I must have heard him wrong. One, because he seemed to fluctuate between tolerating me and being extremely annoyed. Neither a sentiment I was used to. And two, we'd just got there. And while it was fine for me to slink off, disappearing before all the fancy-pants stuff I was sure was going to happen, *he* was their oldest son. His absence would definitely be missed.

He looked to the door, either anticipating Dane's return or hoping for it. "Well, seems fair since I dragged you out here that I be the one to take you back."

Sure, it sounded logical if we were dealing with a normal person, but Jagger Hartley was far from normal. Not to say that I was either, but it didn't change the point.

My hand rested on my hip, narrowing my eyes as I tried to work out his angle. "You don't think your parents aren't going to notice you going AWOL like five minutes after you got here? Or are you so terrified of me being around your family you would risk pissing them off? Or," I took a breath, a third and most unlikely option rattled around in my head, "are you worried I might end up friends with your brother?"

Could you imagine? Not that I believed for a second that Dane's interest in me was anything other than platonic, but I'll admit that taunting Jagger a little gave me pleasure. Why? Well, I wasn't entirely sure, but I wasn't used to people not liking me—especially for no good reason—and I wasn't able to just let it go.

"Other than you being beautiful, and he's a sucker for a pretty face, you and Dane have nothing in common. But if you did, why would I care?" he responded coolly, his icy tone hinting that he wasn't as "okay" with it as he'd have me believe.

"So you think I'm beautiful?" A smile edged across my lips.

Oh, I wasn't fishing for compliments and honestly, whether he found me attractive or not was the least of my problems. Although, yes, there was a small vain part of me that hoped he did because I thought he was incredibly hot, and reciprocation, while shallow, was kinda nice. But more importantly, it was like the first positive thing he'd said about me . . . at all. And I had a hunch Mr. Show-No-Emotions probably hadn't meant to say it either.

His eyes flared with recognition, realizing his slip. "Don't pretend like you don't know you're beautiful, Belle."

I laughed, happier than I should be at rattling his cage. "Of course, I know. And I'm aware that isn't what women are supposed to say, instead pretending to be all bashful and coy like they haven't seen their reflection in a mirror recently. Not that I let something as trivial as society's beauty standards dictate my worth, especially since I'm a really good person and that will always be more important than my face."

His mouth dropped open, his lips searching for words that didn't come before he closed it again. Which was why I thought I'd continue.

"Not what you expected to hear? Let me guess, you figured I'd be some vapid airhead who needs to constantly have her ego stroked and is scared of wrinkles and gaining a few pounds?" I shook my head, fairly accustomed to being underestimated. "But ugliness goes to the bone, Jagger, and it has nothing to do with what you look like on the outside."

And if I had to guess, he was more familiar with ugly beauties than someone who honestly cared. Which was probably why he asked what I wanted. Like he was expecting me to have fifty ulterior motives for being around, just waiting for me to weaponize it for personal gain.

How sad for him, to expect the worst from people. For that to be his default.

He moved in closer, his intense gaze studying me like he was looking for answers. "Are you always like that? Just say whatever the hell you're thinking without worrying about consequences?"

"I'm not unnecessarily cruel." Not always, believing honesty was the best policy. "And I don't like hurting people's feelings, especially if I care about them. But I think the world would be a lot better of a place if people said what they meant."

I'd told my share of white lies.

Bent the truth.

Even skewed reality a little here or there.

But never at anyone else's expense.

His tongue darted briefly across his beautiful lips, his eyes snagging with mine. "Yes, Belle, I think you're beautiful. And while I will probably regret this later, the truth is, I *want* to drive you home."

"Why?"

He still hadn't said, and while I assumed it was to get me the hell out of there with minimal invasion and as quickly as possible, I wanted to hear it from him.

"For lots of reasons, Belle. None of which I want to get into now."

"Because?"

"Jesus," he laughed. "Do you ever stop asking questions?"

"No, not usually," I admitted. "But not to be a brat, it's because I am genuinely interested," I went on to explain. "How about this? You can drive me home if you promise to talk to me on the way back. I'm not interested in sitting in silence for two hours, hypothesizing on why you're doing what you're doing."

"Are you really trying to negotiate with me?" A mix of disbelief and excitement danced in his captivating hazel eyes. I was trying not to like them, or even look at them directly, because he was already sexier than he needed to be. But they were more expressive than he probably knew, and I was a sucker for working out a riddle.

"Jagger, you're probably going to drive me to New York and never see me again." The city was a big place and the chances of me ever landing an audition with him again was slim to none. Plus, since it was the first time I'd met him, I was positive we ran in very different circles. "So what's the harm? Who am I going to tell? Do you think I'm going to blog about it? Post on social media? Take out an ad?"

A slow sigh eased out of his lips, like he was having his own negotiation. "You wouldn't be the first."

And that one sentence said it all.

He'd been burnt.

Probably a few times, and he wasn't going to trust me no matter what I said. And while part of me was slightly hurt, I knew it wasn't personal.

At least, not for now.

Because for whatever reason, I was compelled to get through that thick exterior and show Jagger Hartley good people did exist.

And it had nothing to do with me wanting to sleep with him. Not even a little.

Okay, okay, so maybe I hadn't entirely forgotten how hot he was or how sexy I found him, or how I'd love to find out if he—

No. It was not about sex.

It was a personal mission, and proving humanity was alive and well was so much more important than anything else.

"Okay, new plan. You will drive me home and spend the evening with me."

He coughed, raising a brow.

"Wow, that was *not* what I meant." I laughed, seeing how he might've misinterpreted my intentions. "But no. I mean, spend the evening with me like a regular person. If you think you can be *regular*. I know it might be a challenge, but I promise it will be worth your while. Two people, in the city, no expectations, just for fun."

"Belle." I could see the excuses, all of them ready to shoot me down and tell me why it wasn't a good idea.

But he was wrong.

"Just for once, Jagger, don't overanalyze everything. What is the worst thing that can happen?"

"Ummm, you really want me to list them for you?"

"It's one night. You can go back to being broody and I-hate-the-world tomorrow."

"I don't," he stopped, my raised brow daring him to tell me different, "fine. But we leave now."

"Don't you want to say goodbye?" I looked at the door, wondering if his parents would be upset. They'd surely miss him. Dane would at the very least.

He grabbed my hand and led me to the back door. "Trust me, it's better for everyone if we just go. I'll call them tomorrow."

I wasn't so positive it would be better, but who was I to argue. Besides, I'd gotten him to agree to give me an evening to prove life wasn't so jaded and kindness did exist, it wasn't the time to be pedantic.

"Okay then, let's go. Our first stop is going to be dinner. I'll tell you where."

He rolled his eyes, directing me outside to the path that snaked around to the front of the house. "I can already tell this is a bad idea."

"Too late to back out now, Hartley." I smiled as we got closer to his car. "Try not to have too much fun."

He popped the lock, opening the passenger side door and waited for me to get inside. "Not something I'm worried about. Try not to be disappointed when your little experiment doesn't work."

Ha, he had no idea.

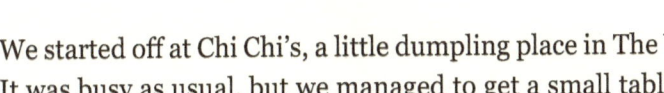

We started off at Chi Chi's, a little dumpling place in The Village. It was busy as usual, but we managed to get a small table at the back, and they were notoriously fast with their food and service, and I was starving.

"What?" I asked, watching Jagger look around at the noisy eatery.

"Nothing. I've just never been to this place. Must have walked past it a million times and didn't even know it was here."

"Let me guess." I tapped my finger against my lip. "You're more a bistro kind of guy. Steak. Beer. Burgers and fries, that kind of thing?" I laughed, thrilled that he was going to be trying something new.

"No, Belle, not burgers and fries. I like all kinds of cuisine. Italian, sushi, fine dining, and even a decent hot dog from a street vendor." He lifted a brow expecting me to be shocked by his response.

"Well, good. But I promise you, you won't have better dumplings than here. I know everyone will tell you Chinatown is better, but they're wrong." I tipped my chin, willing to fight anyone who'd say different.

"They're wrong, are they? You know better than seasoned food critics?" He scoffed, folding his arms across his chest, unconvinced.

"Yes, they're wrong." I didn't bother qualifying, considering in a few short minutes he'd be able to see for himself.

And since I had a point to prove—defending Chi Chi's honor just as important as mine—I didn't bother asking him what he wanted, ordering for the table when a waitress appeared. I ordered drinks too, figuring alcohol might help loosen Jagger up a little, and from what I remembered he only drank half a beer back in Connecticut. Truth be told, I could use a drink too, since my day had been crazier than normal.

He waited until the waitress left, leaning on the table which inadvertently brought him closer. Wowzah, he had such incredible eyes.

"What if I wanted something else?" He looked more amused than pissed off, probably still marveling at my audacity. I'm sure not a lot of people stood up to him, more accustomed to people bending over backward to please him.

"You won't," I shot back, confidently. "And since you agreed to spend an evening with me, we're going to do it my way. Which means, I get to call the shots."

He swallowed, his eyes doing that thing where they rolled a little like he was getting ready to argue. Ironically, even though we'd only met for the first time hours ago, it was the look I was most familiar with. "Fine."

"Oooooooo, *fine*." I chuckled because it felt like a victory to me. "Now stop looking so grouchy and at least pretend to have a good time."

He rolled his eyes again, shaking his head as our waitress returned with our drinks.

"What's this?" He sniffed at the mason jar in front of him, probably assuming when I ordered "Holy Water" it was either a fancy bottle of H2O or a boutique beer.

"It's a cocktail, it's sweet." I swirled my straw through the light blue liquid, pieces of fresh strawberries bobbing to the top.

What I *didn't* tell him was while it looked like a harmless fruit punch, it was loaded with enough vodka and rum that could make even a hard ass like him find a smile. And it was colorful, so what was not to like.

He watched as I took a sip, my lips closing around the straw as I sucked the delicious fruity cocktail that was as lethal as it was pretty. It was soooo easy to get carried away, down the drinks like lemonade—which was the only nonalcoholic ingredient in the drink besides the strawberries—and find yourself drunk dancing in Battery Park. It wasn't all bad though, I made two hundred bucks in tips from people wrongly assuming I was a street performer and ended up buying a new purse.

When I didn't die, or spontaneously combust, he took a tentative sip from his drink, his tongue darting across his lips as he drew back.

"Good, huh?" I asked, secretly wanting him to do that tongue thing again because it was hot. Not what I was supposed to be concentrating on, but I couldn't help if the man was as delicious as he was prickly. I didn't make the rules.

He took another sip, this time a longer pull before answering. "Yeah, it's really refreshing actually. Like summertime in a glass. But I thought this was a dumpling house."

"Yeah, yeah." I shrugged. "The food is authentic, but the owner's granddaughter is running the bar and who says the East can't meet the West in a sexy illicit affair."

"Interesting word choice." He lifted his jar, holding it up toward me. "But I'll agree that so far, I'm not disappointed."

I lifted my jar, clinking it with his. "Wow, you're going to make me blush with all the compliments. Tell me again how *not disappointed* you are." My lips spread into a grin and if I didn't know better, I'd say I was flirting.

Okay, so maybe I was flirting a *little* but that was accidental. He was smiling too and he'd somehow managed to look even more handsome.

In annnnny case, it was harmless, and we were going to get through the night without me thinking about how much I wanted to press my body against his. Or how good he smelled. Or how silky his hair looked and how my fingers itched to run through it.

New plan.

No more drinking until *after* food had been consumed.

Jagger didn't seem to share my same logic, pulling out the straw and drinking from the jar instead.

And shit, I couldn't pull my eyes away from his masculine, sexy throat as he swallowed.

Thankfully our food arrived, the many plates of various delicious offerings strategically placed on the available table surface. I'd ordered big, not having had a decent lunch on account of being with Hayley and Bobbie, and didn't get a chance to grab anything during my brief visit at the Hartley Compound.

We grabbed chopsticks, eating from the communal plates while Jagger waved over the waitress and ordered another round of Holy Waters.

"Ummm, not for me." I shook my head, knowing I needed to pace myself if I wanted to see the night out properly. I wanted to take Jagger dancing, and not the kind that saw us potentially being arrested.

"Wow." Jagger snagged another dumpling, looking sexier than he needed to be as he balanced it expertly between his chopsticks. "Weren't you the one who told me to loosen up?"

"Yeah, *you*. One of us needs to be sort of responsible, and trust me, Jagger, those drinks are stronger than they look."

I wasn't a complete idiot. And while I was happy to let him get his buzz on, hoping he'd lose the uptight attitude so he didn't seem like he ate dissatisfaction for breakfast, I also didn't want him in the ER with alcohol poisoning.

He waved his chopsticks dismissively, shoving that lucky dumpling into his delicious mouth.

"Okay then." I shrugged, figuring I'd fulfilled my duty of care by prewarning him. "Hand over your keys."

"Huh?" He finished chewing, looking at my outstretched hand. "Why do you need my keys?"

"Because Mr. I-Know-Everything, a few more of those and you won't be fit to drive. You really want tomorrow's headline to be *Kirk Hartley's oldest son pulled over for a DUI*? I'm sure the investors for your play are going to love that too. What about Dane? What would he say?"

"Fine." He fished the keys out of his pocket and dropped them into my palm. "But I swear, Belle, if this is a creative way of carjacking me, it won't end well for you."

"Please," I blew out a breath. "If I was going to carjack you, I'd have done it already, not hours after the fact."

And with a promise I'd be careful with his car—it had been a while since I'd driven—we went back to enjoying our dinner.

And drinks.

Lord, I hoped I wasn't going to need some *real* holy water before the night was over.

Chapter 6

Belle

Jagger ended up having *four* Holy Waters at Chi Chi's, but like some modern-day miracle, he didn't seem overly drunk. Definitely more relaxed, and a hell of a lot more agreeable, and dare I say it—really, really fun.

He didn't even fight me when I suggested heading to a club, telling me that he was game for whatever I had in mind.

Dangerous words indeed.

But with a silent promise I'd be good—touching him on the dance floor was allowed because it would be weird not to—we moved our little party to Diablo, a club in Midtown.

There was a line of course, but the security guard spotted Jagger and waved us through.

"Must be nice." I laughed, linking hands—so we wouldn't get separated in the crowd, not because I'd been dying to all night—and walked into the main part of the club.

He huffed out a frustrated breath, squeezing my hand a little tighter. "It's not as exciting as you think it is. And it's mostly because of my dad."

"So? It's not like you're dropping his name, demanding special treatment." I scoffed, accidentally jostled by the crowd. Jagger grabbed my arms as I got pushed in closer, holding me steady as I found my feet. "Thanks." I smiled, liking his hands on me a lot more than I should. "And to continue, I saw you back there, you were willing to wait like everyone else. The guy at the door was the one who called you over."

Jagger breathed deeply, closing his eyes as we stood together in the space. "Maybe." He shook off the rest of the sentence, like he'd suddenly became more aware of spilling more than he wanted to. "So, are we going to dance or do you just like standing in crowded, sweaty places with poor lighting?"

"Awwwww, and I thought the old Jagger had all but disappeared." I laughed, pulling him closer as we moved to the dance floor. "Was almost beginning to miss him."

Jagger laughed, wrapping his arms around my waist. *Wow, that was nice.* And started to move his feet. "Don't worry, Belle, I promise not to turn into a nice guy, no matter how much I have to drink."

I didn't believe him, having seen glimpses of a *nice guy* on the drive to visit his parents, in their kitchen, and while we were having dinner. He'd even spoken a little about growing up as the kid of a national celebrity, listening equally attentive while I told him about my legendary prosecutor dad and amazing saintly mom. It was like there were moments where cracks formed in the asshole exterior he wanted everyone to see, and he was just a beautiful, sexy, and talented guy I was really into.

Our feet shuffled, our bodies moving closer, and before I knew what was happening, I was pressed against him like I'd been aching to be. He was tall and firm, muscles in all the right places, yet my body felt soft against his.

I tried not to enjoy it, closing my eyes for a second as I breathed in his scent and forgot about being good. His hands felt warm against me, my skin tingling as I unconsciously arched against him.

Or maybe it was *consciously*, but either way, I was resolving to give myself the moment before returning to being good.

Just one more moment.

Or five.

Soon.

He chuckled as my head rested on his chest, my hand traveling up his torso of its own accord. "Checking to see if I have a heart?"

"Yes." I nodded, figuring it was as good an excuse as any. "But I won't tell anyone. Wouldn't want nasty rumors that you're human to get out."

I wasn't sure if it was the weirdest thing ever or the most natural thing in the world. Joking with Jagger. Touching Jagger. Just BEING with Jagger.

It felt forbidden and naughty but easy all at the same time, because for all the thorns he had on the outside, I'd bet that heart that was beating against my hand was incredibly beautiful too.

"Don't look at me like that, Belle." His hands dropped to my waist, holding me still. "Whatever you're thinking, you're wrong."

"Oh, so you read minds now?" I tipped my chin, daring to look into his dangerous eyes. "Whatever *you're* thinking, *you're* wrong."

Of course I had no idea what he was thinking, or what he thought *I* was thinking, or if either of us was even thinking at all. Because if I was being honest, what was going through my head weren't actual thoughts. More like how I could get him to kiss me, and what that amazing body would feel like naked, underneath mine.

"I'm not wrong." His hand moved from my waist, trailing up my side as I tried to remember how to breathe.

Was he going to do it?

Kiss me?

Our feet had stopped moving, our bodies still on a dancefloor where no one cared who we were and what we were doing.

"We should go get a drink." His hand dropped, whatever moment we were having all but disappeared as we turned toward the bar.

And while adding more alcohol to the mix did not sound like a good idea, there was no way I was letting him go by himself.

The crowd meant he'd gotten very far, my quick feet able to catch up to him before he'd reached the bar.

"Heeeeeeeeyyyy." I shoved my body between him and his path, making him stop. "What happened back there? We were just dancing, right?"

Oh, we were sooooo not just dancing, but I wasn't going to admit that.

He rolled his eyes, huffing out a breath. "Sure, *just* dancing. And now we're not. Want a drink?"

"Why? Is it because you're afraid of kissing me?"

Yep, I went there.

My sister, Zara, always accused me of talking first and thinking later and this was one of those times. But I never saw any point in holding my tongue. What for? And even though neither of us wanted to admit it—dancing around the issue, we were just . . . well *dancing*—that was exactly what was about to happen.

Jagger laughed.

Actually laughed.

Head back, eyes closed, chuckling like I'd just told him the funniest joke ever.

Which just pissed me off. Because while I could accept him not wanting to kiss me and potentially make it weirder than it already was, it *wasn't* funny.

"Stop laughing, you jackass." I jabbed him hard in the chest. "Don't pretend like you didn't want to."

His chin dropped, his eyes connecting with mine as his lips settled into a grin. "You think I didn't kiss you because I was afraid?"

"Yeah, I do." I shoved my hands on my hips, willing for the crowded dance floor of Diablo to be where I made my stand. "Tell me I'm wrong."

But he didn't.

Instead of the argument I was expecting, he leaned down, pulled me close and before I could work out what the hell was happening, he was kissing me.

A real fucking kiss too. Not some light peck to fulfil a dare or what you'd give a relative.

Hot.

Sexy.

With just the right amount of pressure that I had no choice but to open my mouth and moan.

His tongue slipped in, his hands all over my ass as they lifted me off the floor and held me against him.

Dear.

God.

He was amazing.

Every part of him magic as he kissed me like a Roman soldier who'd been fighting for the Empire and had just returned from war.

"Yes." I arched against him, wanting everything he was giving me and more. "More."

His teeth tugged against my bottom lip, teasing me as he gently pulled away. "Take back what you said about me being scared."

"Huh?" I stood in a daze, barely able to cope with the whiplash of Jagger's moods.

A sexy brow arched as his tongue darted across his lips. "Take it back and I might kiss you again."

"Tell me why you didn't just kiss me in the first place, and I'll consider it," I negotiated. Because if the only reason he kissed me was to prove a point, then he was going to feel my wrath.

And I might be small, but I could get big mad when I was inspired.

"Belle." He shook his head. "You ask too many questions. I didn't because I didn't. Now let's go get a drink."

Great, a riddle that left me with more questions than answers, but on the plus side, his hands were still around my waist as he led me to the bar. And at least he was no longer asking for a retraction—which I had no intention of giving him—and he hadn't ruled out more kissing.

"Okay, Jagger, let's go to the bar."

Shit was bad.

Like *really* bad.

Not just regular bad either, I was talking epic-level catastrophe.

As it turns out, Jagger *wasn't* a modern-day marvel who could consume large quantities of alcohol and be relatively unaffected. No, he was just really good at masking his inebriation, so by the time he looked drunk, we'd passed the point of no return.

Shit.

Shit.

Shit.

He'd been perfectly fine.

No slurred speech, no wavering on his feet, no laughing uncontrollably—nothing. That was until after a few—I lost count, okay, he'd given the bartender his card—rum and Cokes, he looked me dead in the eyes and told me he thought I was the most beautiful woman he'd ever seen.

It shouldn't have been a warning sign, especially since he'd already kissed me, but considering he'd been rationing out details and compliments, I knew better.

Also, his eyes were glassy.

Those beautiful, iridescent orbs that seemed to change either gold or green like the leaves in Maine, were decidedly shinier than they should be.

And had I come to the realization a little sooner, things might not have been so bad. But as it turned out, I was having such a good time watching Jagger relax and tell me about his new projects—something that also should have been a clue—that I didn't.

Until . . .

Yeah, he could barely stand and was mumbling about me being beautiful. By then it was too late, his ability to reason gone while he looked at me like I was a double fudge sundae and he wanted to eat me one spoonful at a time. And considering how drunk he was, I wasn't sure whether or not he actually thought I *was* a sundae.

"Okay, we've just got to get you up the stairs."

Walking him up to my apartment was a hell of a lot trickier than wrestling him into his car. When we'd left the club, he'd still possessed motor skills and a relationship with gravity, two things that had evaporated by the time we arrived at my Greenwich apartment.

Sure, taking him back to his place would probably make more sense especially since I lived with my sister and her fiancé, and I was fairly sure he lived alone. But since I didn't know where he lived, whether he had some fancy security alarm I was bound to set off when we got there, or what the possibility was of him dying from alcohol poisoning when I left, I thought it was better to go to mine. Also, I wasn't a complete idiot, knowing there was no convincing way I'd be able to wipe away all traces of my fingerprints from his car, which would only serve the prosecution too well when they convicted me of his murder.

"More drinks," he slurred—yeah, he eventually got to that stage, batting away my request that he hold onto that banister.

"No. No more drinks. And how much do you weigh? I'm dying here." I tried to use myself as a ballast, planting myself under one of his armpits while I leveraged the rest of his heft against the railing. "Please move your feet, Jagger, there's no way I can carry you up."

I wasn't a weakling, and did Pilates like a boss, but dragging a six-foot-something, hot dude with more muscles than current sobriety up the stairs was a task that was beyond me.

He laughed, failing to see the direness of the situation. "Where are you taking me, Belle? Ooooooh am I going to see your bedroom?"

Shit.

Shit.

Shit.

Deciding to either throw in the towel and camp on the stairs like a vagrant or swallow my pride and ask for help, I gently lowered Jagger down to the ground. It wasn't the most graceful descent, his knees buckling and making his torso pitch forward like a cheap lawn chair, but I got him down safely without breaking him. At least I hoped he wasn't broken; it was probably too soon to tell.

Then, while swearing under my breath, and hoping I'd be saved the lecture until the morning, I called my future brother-in-law who adored me.

"Belle." His gruff voice answered, hinting he'd probably been asleep. "You better be in jail or in an emergency room, it's two a.m."

"Heeeeeeeey, Lincoln." I tried to sound casual even though I was positive he wasn't buying it. "You think you can meet me downstairs? I need some help getting up into our apartment. I promise it's an emergency."

I was deliberately light on the details. One, because I had no idea who could be listening and didn't want any of our nosey neighbors sticking their head outside for a better look. And two, because the sooner he got off the phone and got down the stairs, the better.

Lincoln let out a huge sigh, followed by the rustling of sheets. "Do I even want to know? You know what, don't answer that. Just give me a second to put some clothes on."

"You're the best, Lincoln. I'm just inside the foyer door."

Knowing help was arriving soon, I sagged against the wall and took a deep breath. My feet were killing me and I was exhausted, my day exponentially longer than I'd intended.

"Jesus." Lincoln cursed as his footsteps stopped at the landing above us. "When I said I didn't want to know, Belle, I also didn't want to be an accessory."

"Just help me get him into my room, Lincoln, and try not to wake Zara." Honestly, waking my sister was the least of my problems, although, I really didn't want to deal with her disappointed face.

But more than anything I needed to get Jagger safe, hopefully sober him up, and pray he didn't think there'd been some nefarious plan to get him loaded so I could take advantage of him. The kiss had been consensual, right? He'd kissed me. How many drinks had he had by then? No, it was definitely consensual and other than that one time, we hadn't done anything that would be remotely inappropriate. Other than me shoving him into his car, driving him to my apartment and bundling him upstairs. Okay, so it wasn't looking good for me, but my intentions had not been bad.

Huffing out a breath, Lincoln helped me get Jagger to his feet as we navigated the stairs. It was tight, the three of us not being able to fit in the narrow space, which meant Lincoln had to take one for the team and get him up to our front door all by himself while I followed behind.

"Who is he?" he asked, pulling Jagger into our entrance way.

I locked the door behind us, doing my best to be extra quiet as I secured the deadbolt. "Jagger Hartley, and I thought you said you didn't want details."

"Jagger Hartley? *Jagger Hartley*?" Lincoln repeated, raising his voice louder than the whisper that would've been acceptable. "What the hell are you doing with Jagger Hartley? And please tell me he didn't drive you home in that condition. Because if he did, he's going to have a hard time waking up."

"Awwww, you'd commit murder for me, Lincoln?" I beamed, touched by the gesture.

"Not what I said," he corrected, shuffling Jagger into my bedroom. "I said he'd have a hard time waking up, two different things. Lots of room for reasonable doubt. I probably meant from the hangover and the lack of analgesic I was willing to provide given he'd put your safety in peril."

I rolled my eyes, knowing better than to expect him to incriminate himself even though it was literally only the two of us. "Right, that's what you meant. Just get him onto the bed."

After assuring Lincoln I was safe, not drunk, and had been the one behind the wheel, he left me with a stern warning there'd be more conversation in the morning. I loved that he didn't hover, rolling with the punches, which was necessary when he lived with Zara and me. Also, he probably knew Zara was going to grill me enough for the two of them and he liked watching my sister in a cross-examination. It was like foreplay for those two, and they didn't need any help being all over each other.

Jagger moaned as he laid on the mattress. Lincoln had rolled him onto his side, his big body taking up almost all the room on my queen-size bed. It was strange to see his large, splayed-out body dressed in head-to-toe black against my bright pink comforter. But at least he was safe, and I was home, and I had a few hours to work out my next move.

Not sure if it was a true victory or not, only time would tell, but I was too tired to care.

Longest.

Strangest.

Day.

Ever.

Chapter 7

Jagger

The smell was the first thing I'd noticed.

Floral, like a vase of fresh-cut flowers or springtime in the country.

My head hurt, which was expected considering the hangover, my recollection of getting home, pretty foggy.

Except.

My eyelids peeled open, my vision adjusting to the still relatively dark room. But even in my questionable state, it was clear that it wasn't mine.

Fuck.

Yesterday had been a series of bad decisions, but kissing Belle hadn't been one of them. Sure, I'd tried to avoid it, ignore the attraction and how fucking intrigued I was by her, but when I'd kissed her at that club, I'd wanted to. I wasn't *that* drunk, at least not yet. The real drinking had started after, when I realized I was with an amazing woman who was hotter than hell and nothing more could happen other than that kiss.

And fuck Dane, who'd texted me three thousand times asking why the hell we'd left and why I'd stopped him from driving

Belle home. No wonder I'd needed to drink. Because on top of Belle's beautiful lips spilling never-ending questions, I had to deal with heat from him.

He could have any woman he wanted.

Hell, even if he wanted to date one of my exes, I didn't care. Just not her.

And not because I planned on dating her—because I didn't—so of course it made all kinds of sense why I was screwing up what I was sure would be a happy fucking union.

"Fuck." This time I said it as well as thought it, rolling over onto my back. I didn't even have to see the rest of the room to know it was Belle's, that smell of freshly cut flowers, the exact scent of her shampoo. And as much as kissing her wasn't a regret, coming back to her place definitely was.

Stupid.

I was fucking stupid.

"Are you okay?" The woman in question appeared on the edge of the bed, her hair mussed like she'd just woken up. "Do you need something? Water? Advil? A stomach pump?"

All three sounded like stellar options, especially the water, but I still had to deal with how the hell I'd ended up in Belle's bedroom. And what I'd done when we'd gotten there.

I'd remembered what I'd wanted to do when she'd been dancing with me.

Remembered the feel of her body and the hard-on from hell.

And how much more I wanted to do besides just kissing.

Fuck.

It had been only once.

But I'd stopped.

Because I'd needed to stop.

My ability to taste those beautiful lips only once requiring every ounce of my willpower.

Unless.

"Water." I shuffled up the bed, noticing I was fully dressed, and my hard-on still painfully rock . . .well . . . hard. So while I couldn't be sure we hadn't done other stuff, sex had definitely not happened.

Thank fuck for that.

Belle grabbed a bottle from her nightstand and handed it to me. "Here."

Instinctively I inspected it, checking to see the seal hadn't been cracked. Because as much as I thought Belle was beautiful, and my dick was very much looking to make friends, I still didn't trust her. Especially since my recollection was cloudy and I had no fucking idea what I'd done last night.

"It's still sealed." Her pretty bubblegum colored fingernail pointed to the plastic ring around the cap still intact. "And I'm not trying to drug you. Honestly, I didn't even realize how drunk you were. Because if I did, I'd have cut you off."

Wait.

She'd have cut me off?

I wasn't sure which pissed me off more. That she thought she had any say on what I did or didn't do, or that she assumed I hadn't been in control.

Okay, so I *hadn't* been in control, but that wasn't the point. I could count on three fingers the number of people who'd seen me really wasted, because even when I was three sheets to the wind, I had the ability to keep my shit together like no other

"Maybe drinking wasn't the problem," I spat back defensively.

"Woah, what does *that* mean?" Her eyes blazed with intensity, the caring, nurturing routine dropped.

I untwisted the cap, taking a leisurely sip of the water even though my throat was burning and I was desperate to gulp it. She wanted to see control, I'd fucking show her control.

"Means that here I am, somewhere I'm not supposed to be, with a woman I don't even like. Sounds to me that drinking wasn't my problem."

It wasn't like me to make stupid decisions, and I still wasn't sure what the hell came over me. That ridiculous—but actually delicious—cocktail at the dumpling place had started it. But the rest . . . foggy. And considering how much my head hurt, I'd say my account probably wasn't accurate.

"I didn't drug you. Why the hell would I drug you, and then try and prove I didn't drug you with the water?" Her brows knitted as she pointed to the bottle I was taking another measured drink from. "That makes no sense. Wouldn't I keep you sedated? Or at least pliable until I dumped your body or left you on a street corner for someone else to find?"

"For someone who apparently didn't do anything," I raised a brow, "sounds like you sure gave it a lot of thought."

She pushed onto her feet, pacing impatiently around her small bedroom. It was cluttered but neat, filled with moments of her existence like a time capsule. Books, artwork, photos tacked to her mirror. I'd have loved to study it, see what else it would help me discover about her if I'd had more time, and wasn't so utterly confused by why I was there.

"I did NOT do anything to you. In fact, you should be thanking me because I saved you. I could've left you."

I coughed, trying not to laugh at the pint-sized pixie pointing at me accusingly. "You'll have to excuse me if I'm not filled with the same sense of gratitude. Because if you were as concerned as you claimed to be, you could have easily put me in a cab and sent me home. You know, like a regular person."

"Oh, you—" She caught herself, her cheeks flushed with anger and maybe something else. "Guess you would've preferred I rummage through your wallet for your address. Because *that* isn't crossing a line or anything."

"Ha, a little late in the game to be worried about boundaries, Belle, isn't it?" I laughed, wondering if she'd forgotten about getting into my car and traveling with me to visit my parents. My head was foggy but I'd say that was a bigger imposition. "So, do you often bring incapacitated men home? Or am I your first?"

God, I hoped I was her first.

I knew nothing happened.

Well, I knew we didn't have *sex*.

Other than being dressed, a painful hard-on that clearly hadn't gotten the attention it wanted, and genuinely not believing Belle would do that, I was almost positive I'd spent the night alone. She hadn't even been beside me when I'd woken up, the mattress either side of me, vacant.

But I'd wanted to touch her.

And kiss her.

And feel her sexy little body up near mine, and was sure at some point I'd done at least some of that. Maybe at the club? Or in the car ride over? Or when she laid me on her bed.

But not sex.

Because it would be a cold day in hell when I'd waste sex with someone so exquisite when my memory wouldn't be able to recall all of the details.

Not that I was willing to admit that, especially when it was so much fun watching what I assumed was a perpetual rainbow scramble.

She moved closer, digging her finger into my chest. "I should've left your stupid ass there. I didn't and wouldn't have done anything to you even if you hadn't been drunk."

Ooooooh.

Interesting.

Wouldn't was a very curious word and while I should've embraced my feelings of gratitude and gotten the hell out, I was strangely annoyed.

"Good," I echoed back. "Neither would I."

Great, I was a ten-year-old, poking out my tongue, double-dog daring her. What the hell was I doing? Hungover, in an actress's—who'd auditioned for me—apartment, I didn't even recognize myself anymore.

"Perfect." She pushed her hair from her shoulder, straightening out her crumbled t-shirt that she'd obviously slept in. "The bathroom is down the hall. I put your phone on my charger." She pointed to the nightstand. "You know, because that is what kidnappers do when they drug someone and bring them back to their homes. Also, you have about a million missed calls and messages. Not that I was snooping or anything, but the stupid thing wouldn't stop vibrating and I may have—completely innocently—seen the preview screen when I put it on the charger. You might want to let your parents know you're not dead."

This woman.

Not only was she infuriating and completely lacked any apology, but she was still trying to tell me what to do.

The fucking nerve.

"My *parents*?" I choked back, tempering which part I was most angry about. Either the mention of them or just her plain audacity.

"And how would you know that?" A humorless laugh found its way up my throat. She'd spent like five minutes with them and she thought she knew them? Yeah, she clearly had no idea.

We weren't like that.

We didn't "check-in" with each other, and I'd sooner be noticed as *missing* by the guy I got my bagels and coffee from than by my parents.

It wasn't that they didn't love me, they did in their own way. But they were so self-absorbed. So preoccupied with themselves and their own careers, I honestly questioned if they should've had kids at all. Except every legend needs a legacy, so there I was.

"Dane keeps calling," she corrected, tipping her chin so her unwavering gaze met mine. And even though part of me was still mad, I had to admit she was kinda adorable.

She was so diminutive, delicate features like a master sculptor had created her from finest porcelain. And yet, so utterly unapologetic, with confidence that was at total odds with the tiny, beautiful woman that was standing in front of me. And that contradiction and self-assurance was downright sexy.

"Ahhhhhh, Dane." Well, that made more sense. Though I had to wonder what else she might have seen while she was *charging* my phone. "Well, best not keep him waiting then. I'll get out of here."

Leaving was the last thing I wanted to do. And not just because I felt like shit and I was probably not in any condition to drive.

But as much as I was annoyed I couldn't remember exactly what happened last night, I wasn't as mad as I pretended to be. And being with her, in that room, was addictive in a probably sick perverted way. I liked she didn't back down and wasn't intimidated, and her fiery spark got me hard in a warped and twisted way that would be the topic for a therapist, assuming I had one. But more than anything, I wanted to kiss her again. See if it was as amazing as I'd remembered. Not that I could go there when we were both sober. Nope. Not even a little.

"You can't leave." Belle stood up, her arms stretched out either side of her like she could adequately stop me if she wanted to.

I tried not to laugh, her effort comical if not downright ridiculous. "Errrr, I can and I will." My body straightened, my legs accepting my weight as I stood in front of her.

Only minimal sway, impressive.

She didn't move, her eyes traveling up my body like she was surprised I could stand too. And with no hesitation, her lips let go of a very confident, definitive, "No."

"Excuse me?" I coughed out, wondering what she was planning on doing. Best I could see there was no lock on the door. And unless she was packing a pair of pretty impressive restraints somewhere—uh-hm, okay that wasn't helping—not sure how she was going to back that up.

"You're probably still drunk. And as the person responsible for your welfare, I'm not allowing you to leave. Not until I'm satisfied." Her hands were planted on her hips like she was a superhero, unperturbed by the unbalanced height/weight ratio.

"Don't remember asking you to be responsible for my *welfare*." I took a step closer, confident I could throw her over my shoulder with just one hand. "I'm a big boy, think I can handle myself. Where are my keys?" I looked around the room for them.

Nope.

Nothing.

But I did need to get my phone off her charger and drink more of that water.

"Belle." I held out my hand, hoping she'd drop the keys into it and I could be on my way. "Whatever happened last night is in the past, but I think we both can agree now that it's morning, I need to go."

"No, you don't."

"How is this up for debate?" I asked, positive she was the most argumentative person I'd ever meant.

"You *don't* have to go. And whether you asked me to be responsible or not is irrelevant. Legally, I have an obligation. And you're not getting your keys." Her light brown eyes blazed, the earlier kindness that had been in them was gone, replaced by a rock-solid determination.

She might look like a pushover, but there was little chance she was.

I took another step, our bodies barely an inch apart in her small bedroom. But she didn't move, her eyes locked on mine.

Beautiful.

Not a shadow of doubt in her face or her body, with every—tiny—inch of her filled with so much confidence it was goddamn sexy.

I wasn't sure if I'd ever met a woman like her. Who didn't at least blink at the challenge, or hesitate—something.

"Jesus, you're a nightmare." I chuckled, not wanting to laugh but being unable to help it. "Okay, fine. What do I need to do to satisfy this legal requirement?"

I'd remembered that her dad was a prosecutor, and her sister was a lawyer as well. And I'd already been treated to her ridiculous negotiating skills. So if she needed me to sign a waiver or pass a sobriety test, then that's what I'd do.

"Breakfast. Shower." She held up her fingers listing them off. "Tell me how much you remember about last night."

"Not a breakfast person. And I'll shower in my own apartment. And I remember," *kissing you and wanting to do it again,* "drinking those stupid mason jar things that you insisted we drink and then waking up here," I answered, doing my best to look pissed off even though I wasn't. "Anything else you want to add?" I waited, wondering if she'd fill in the blanks or keep me hostage a little longer.

She held up a finger. "One Holy Water. I insisted you drink *one* cocktail because I was hoping you'd be less of an asshole if you loosened up, but I didn't force you to drink the others or continue drinking when we went to the club."

"Sure, *my* fault. I started all of this." I waved my hands around to demonstrate the very pink room that wasn't mine. "Now, if you're done, I'd like my keys so I can go home."

Again, I held out my hand, knowing I needed to get out of her apartment before I did something stupid. Or more stupid. Because for all accounts I'd been plenty stupid last night in allowing my guard down.

"Count backwards from fifty," Belle demanded, puffing out a breath. "And then walk a straight line heel to toe along the length of the room."

"Are you giving me a field sobriety test?" I choked back a laugh.

She nodded, pointing to the floor. "Since you won't wait until we're positive the alcohol is out of your system and you won't eat and shower, then I need to be sure."

"Oh, I'll give you sure."

I got closer, watching her body react.

I liked it.

The way her pupils dilated and her lips dropped open, the small unmistakable woosh of air on the exhale as I leaned in.

There was zero reason for me to be that close, especially since we'd been plenty close enough before, but I couldn't help myself, especially when I saw what kind of buttons it pushed in her.

She might've thought I was an asshole, but part of her was attracted to me. Maybe she hated herself for it, disappointed in herself that she hadn't woken up with a nice guy like Dane in her bed. Or maybe it was her kink, finding a lost cause in the ultimate DIY fixer-upper.

But whatever her reasons were, I couldn't deny it scratched a part of my ego that I couldn't ignore. And more to the point, *wouldn't* ignore. Which was why getting out of there needed to be my priority.

"Belle." Her name was almost a whisper, the deep gravel of my voice surprising us both. Yeah, I knew what I was doing, and while I knew I shouldn't be flirting with her, I couldn't really stop myself either. Besides, it was well-documented that I was an asshole, so really, I was just going with expectations.

"I'm sure you're used to men doing whatever it is you want them to do. Sit. Roll over. Beg. But I'm not that man."

She swallowed, the bob of her throat so intoxicating and erotic I was worried that I actually was still drunk.

"So, I'm going to ask you one last time. Give me my keys. Please."

Dark lashes blinked around her beautiful brown eyes, the indecision weighing heavily. "Fine."

And with the one word she turned, picking up a large purse and dug out my keys. She slapped them into my palm, holding her hand over the top, stopping me from grabbing them. "Not everyone is trying to hurt you, Jagger."

Her words stung more than they should, especially since I didn't give a shit what she thought.

Or did I?

And more importantly, did I believe her.

"Thank you." My fingers closed, forcing contact as she had yet to move her hand. Her skin was warm and smooth, the size of it so small and petite in mine I almost didn't want to move. "Next time I want more unsolicited advice, I'll know exactly where to come."

"Don't bother." She hesitated, stepping to the side so I could pass. "I know when my efforts aren't needed or appreciated."

"Good, glad we finally understand each other." I nodded, taking a last look at her before stepping out into the hall. "Have a nice life."

And even though I didn't want to be leaving her like that, or go home and deal with the shitstorm from my brother, I knew I couldn't stay either.

That was dangerous.

And I was running out of reasons not to kiss her again.

Chapter 8

Belle

"Want to explain why Jagger Hartley spent the night?" Zara's body filled the doorway, looking more concerned than curious. She'd waited maybe a minute after he'd left, our front door hadn't even completely closed before she was front and center in my current drama. "Lincoln might be okay with plausible deniability, but I want answers. Especially since you *allegedly* had an audition with him yesterday and *apparently* you guys came home drunk last night."

That was Zara, always so careful with language.

"Technically it was this morning. And I wasn't drunk. I was being responsible. I couldn't send him home alone in that state, even if I did know where he lived," I corrected, making it clear that I'd done the right thing.

In fact, why was everyone giving me a hard time? I should be commended, congratulated, celebrated even, for ensuring the safety of a fellow human being. Most wouldn't have been so charitable. Instead, taking the sizeable wad of cash out of his wallet—what? It fell out of his pocket when we put him on the

69

bed. Not like I purposely rummaged through it—and left him in a ditch.

Zara rolled her eyes, planting a hand on her hip. "You can't just bring him home like a stray puppy, Belle. He's *Jagger Hartley*. His dad probably has five lawyers on retainer, please tell me he gave you consent."

"Jesus, I didn't sleep with him, Zara." I rocked back in horror, pulling her into the room. "I slept in my armchair. I wasn't even in the bed with him."

Oh, I'd *wanted* to.

Snuggle up beside him and just enjoy the feel of that big strong body, thinking about how hot that kiss was. But I still had no idea if he'd even meant to do that, or if it had been during some drunk-fueled haze in an effort to shut me up. And I already had too many questions churning in my head about the man, and that was before we'd kissed.

Gah.

He was impossible.

And beautiful.

And so goddamn interesting it made my head hurt, and I hadn't even been the one with a hangover.

Zara visibly relaxed. No doubt she'd been itching to launch her interrogation from the minute she'd found out, but she wasn't going to embarrass me. Even if she was worried I might be bending the law. "Good. What happened at the audition?"

"Uhhhhhhhh," I groaned, sinking into the bed behind me. "Yeah, well *that* didn't happen. Bobbie was running a fever so I was in the emergency room with Hayley and was late. Annnnd big shot," I pointed to the doorway where Jagger had walked out of, "didn't even care. Anyway, I followed him to his car so he could apologize for being rude, and we ended up in Connecticut. And then to prove that he is waaaaay too uptight, I took him out drinking. I think it's safe to say, I didn't get the part."

That was the condensed version, she'd get the director's extended cut edition after I'd sorted it all out in my head.

Zara shook her head, sighing on a deep breath. "Sure, like any of that makes sense. I love you, Belle, but if it were anyone else, they'd probably be in cuffs by now."

"Who'd arrest me? I'm harmless." I scoffed, giving her a smile. And yeah, I knew I had some serious explaining to do later but presently I had more important issues. Like why the hell I couldn't stop thinking about Jagger, and if he was thinking about me.

It wasn't like me to be so obsessed with a guy.

Okay, correction, it wasn't like me to be so obsessed with a guy who showed little interest in me. I wasn't one of those girls who got off on being ignored or turned on by being treated meanly. I got it was a *thing*, women getting some twisted satisfaction out of it, but it just wasn't for me. I liked kindness, consideration and most importantly, mutual and reciprocal attraction. So why I was even entertaining stupid thoughts about a man who had to be drunk to even kiss me was a mystery. I was a smart girl, wasn't I? And at the risk of sounding conceited, I knew I was pretty. I had options. Not like I couldn't get a date if I really wanted to. And yet, instead of forgetting Mr. McGrumpy Pants, and turning my attention elsewhere, I was thinking about what he'd look like naked when he finally got that shower.

Mmmmmmmmm.

"Belle." Zara waved her hand in front of my face. "Can you at least pretend to take it seriously? For my benefit."

"Yeah, yeah. I'm serious. I'm serious about needing some coffee and some clothes."

Not that I was naked or anything, but I wasn't going to sleep in my armchair annnnnd in my clothes. So after I was sure Jagger was settled and not in any danger of either asphyxiating or sneaking out and potentially stumbling into oncoming traffic, I changed. Got into the most conservative pair of pjs I owned, so it didn't look like I was trying to seduce him, and then grabbed a pillow from the other side of my bed. Well, the one that his head wasn't on since his body was taking up most of the mattress.

"Okay, let me know if you need anything. I have to go into work for a few hours but Lincoln is around." She pulled me off the bed and into a quick hug before shaking her head. "And I'm sorry about the audition, I know how much you were hoping to get it."

That was Zara, even when she questioned my life choices, she still wanted me to do well.

Best sister ever.

I hugged her back. "It's okay, there'll be other auditions." And with the confirmation that I was fine and not a liability for a lawsuit, she gave me a final squeeze and walked out the door.

With a huge sigh of relief, and the drama of the morning behind me, I allowed myself to sink onto my mattress, the pillow-y surface cradling my body. My covers still smelled of him, his fresh cologne wafted up my nose as I nuzzled my pillow, rolling onto my side as I breathed in deeply like the tragic loser I'd become.

It was only when I opened my eyes, still inhaling his scent like a cadaver dog looking for a body that my eyes snagged on my nightstand.

His phone.

His freaking phone still attached to my charger where I'd put it.

Shit.

SHIT.

And if that weren't bad enough—which it clearly was—on the other side, hiding behind my ornate pink flamingo lamp, was his wallet. The very wallet that fell out of his pants that I'd so diligently *not* snooped through.

Perfect.

Just freaking perfect, because now I looked like I'd either robbed the guy or was holding his things in a pathetic excuse to have a reason to see him again.

Which I wasn't.

Sure, I'd hoped we'd see each other, but I wasn't so desperate that I'd engineer something as obvious as stealing his stuff.

I'd *told* him about the phone. And had he not been so focused on telling me with his deep sexy voice, "*I'm not the kind of man who is reasonable or even nice,*" he'd have freaking seen his wallet near the charger.

This was totally not my fault.

Not.

And regardless of how hard he would try to spin it—and I'm sure he was itching to find another reason to be annoyed, it was literally his favorite thing—it was on him.

"Uuhhhhhhhhhhh," I huffed out in exasperation. So not only was I going to have to dig through his wallet for his driver's license to obtain his address, invading the man's privacy like I'd been unwilling to do last night. But I was going to have to turn up on his doorstep with his *missing* items like it had been my plan all along.

Like I was a moron and was playing stupid mind games.

Great.

I swear, if the universe was trying to make a point because I'd been so hellbent on being a Broadway actress instead of taking gigs as the *ditzy blonde* in daytime soaps, I'd freaking cave next time my agent called. Work was work, and there was nothing wrong with sugary television content, even if it wasn't my end goal.

"Fine!" I sighed, my eyes lifting to the ceiling. "I'll go, drop off his stuff and look ridiculous because as much as I don't want to, I'm not a coward."

It had occurred to me that I could easily riffle through his things, obtain said address and then pack them up nice and neatly for a courier. But then he'd just assume I was scared of him, which I was not.

"Where do you live, Jagger?"

I snapped the wallet off my nightstand and peeled it open. It didn't even take me long to find his ID, literally only a few items housed between the plain black leather. It was *nice* leather too, Bally, which was ironic considering he didn't seem like the guy who purchased luxury or designer items. I'd expected something alternative or off-brand, handstitched by some unknown, under-appreciated artisan because it was sooooo much more authentic than anything you could buy in a store. I rolled my eyes, maybe he wasn't so different from us regular mortals.

One credit card—really? One? I didn't know anyone who didn't at least have two—no loyalty cards, no flashy store cards, cash—at least a thousand dollars or more, why?—and his New York State issued driver's license.

It was so weird.

He was weird.

But weird or not Jagger Michael Hartley still needed to get his stuff back.

Brooklyn.

Williamsburg to be exact. Huh, I'd assumed he lived in Manhattan, a loft apartment with stark white walls, chrome accents and sparse furniture with literally no warmth or color. So to find he lived in a vibrant neighborhood filled with bars, chic boutiques, hipsters and buzzing nightlife was surprising. But like the wallet, I guess Jagger continued to be an enigma, and not everything was as it seemed. Which of course was my catnip and my intention to never see him again was already in jeopardy and I hadn't even left my apartment yet.

Quieting my overactive thoughts that were bound to get me in trouble, I quickly showered, dressed and made myself presentable. I was careful not to make it look like I'd made too much of an effort, because the last thing I needed was for him to think I was doing it for his benefit. Even though—as much as I hated to admit it—I kinda was. Why? Well, that was anyone's guess and maybe I'd lost my mind in the last twenty-four hours.

But whatever the reason, I was happy when I caught my reflection in the mirror. The perfect blend of casual and stylish, perfect for brunch in Brooklyn. Not that I assumed we were going on a date, please, I hadn't totally lost my mind. But I wanted to look the part, even if I was playing a role. Old habits die hard.

"See ya, Linc! Going to Brooklyn, we're out of creamer again," I shouted from the front door, Lincoln raising an eyebrow as he watched me disappear. He didn't usually ask a lot of questions, but I had no doubt Zara had prepped him with some instructions. I wasn't leaving it to chance, not needing the distraction of explaining my motives to someone else with all their judgment. And besides, Lincoln had made it quite clear he didn't want to know about it, so really, I was just respecting his wishes as well as making it easier for me. Win, win.

And while it had been sort of cool being behind the wheel of Jagger's car, I unfortunately didn't have one of my own. New York City, enough said. Which meant I either had to navigate the subway and bus systems to get me to Brooklyn or spring for a cab. Since I'd gone to the trouble to look effortlessly fabulous, the choice was made easier. Cab it was.

With his ID tucked in my hand, his wallet and phone safely in my bag, I hopped into a waiting taxi and rode to Williamsburg. I had no idea if he'd actually be at his apartment, but I assumed that would be a safe place to start. Plus, I'm sure he couldn't get very far without money, credit card and a phone, so he'd bound to be back if he had gone on an excursion.

When we pulled up to his address, I was surprised to find that it wasn't a modern apartment building with a doorman, but a simple, understated Brownstone. Just a few steps up to a single main door with a small plaque with four buzzers either side. And even if I didn't have his address in my hot little hand, telling me exactly which one was his, I'd have guessed it on sight. Apartment #4—or the top level—which was the only buzzer without a name accompanying it. Not sure if it was for privacy or he genuinely didn't care, but it just added another layer of annoyance to my already growing load.

And yes, I still thought he was hot and wanted to kiss him. But seriously, who did he think he was? Like *anyone* cared where he lived. But sure, let's be all secretive, wooooooo so mysterious.

Eye roll.

It was with great pleasure that I pressed the unnamed buzzer, my fingertip resting on the button a little longer than was probably required as I smiled and waited for a response.

"Yes?" His curt response was one hundred percent expected.

"It's Belle. You—" I didn't get to finish my sentence, a loud pop happening as he unexpectedly unlocked the exterior door.

I'd been ready for some kind of debate. Three to five minutes where he left me on the street, talking through the speaker and demanding I leave it on the stoop. Or we'd pass it through the door with little to no acknowledgement like a shady drug deal.

Inviting me in was not what I'd been expecting. And even though he hadn't explicitly told me to go up, I took the unlocking of the exterior door as an invitation. At the very least, it would stand as a reasonable assumption in court if he decided to press charges for trespassing.

Admittedly, I did take a quick glance around before slipping inside the door, not completely trusting the sudden change of heart. Maybe he was waiting until I got to his apartment before giving me the trademark Hartley controlled wrath. God forbid the neighbors hear! I bet he totally cared what everyone thought of him even though he played it off like he didn't give a shit.

There was an elevator, of course, but instead I took the stairs, walking with purpose up each flight until I reached the fourth and final floor. The door wasn't open even though he was expecting me, the big looming hunk of wood still shut as I rolled my eyes before knocking against it.

Such a douchey move.

The door opened slowly—totally on purpose and he thought actresses were dramatic—filling the gap with his big, hot body. He'd freshly showered, his hair still lightly mussed and damp, a clean T-shirt and jeans replacing the ones he'd worn last night. He hadn't shaven though, the light stubble teasing his jawline in an organized smattering that made him look sexier than he should. His face was impassive, a complete guessing game if he was angry, annoyed or marveling at my bravery—or stupidity—for tracking him down.

"Belle. What a surprise," he deadpanned, the lack of *surprise* evident in his voice.

It annoyed me.

Because while I was probably predictable in that I had a hard time leaving well enough alone, I wasn't chasing after him like he probably assumed. I wasn't pathetic. And I sure as hell could do a lot better than him if I wanted to.

"Don't flatter yourself, Hartley." I grinned, refusing to let him see how much he'd gotten under my skin. "You forgot your phone."

I handed it over without waiting or expecting an invitation inside, the phone lacking any case or personality taken into his palm as he turned it over. Not sure what he was inspecting it for. If I'd wanted to tamper with it or do something else more sinister, I'd have done it last night while he was incapacitated. All that time to play while he was unconscious, he wouldn't have even known the difference.

Assuming I did something.

Which I did NOT.

"Oh, and your wallet." I dug into my bag, pulled out his fancy and rather desolate Bally accessory.

Again he looked at the offering carefully. Taking it from my hand into his before meeting my gaze. "Hmmm, and here I was thinking you were here to check on my wellbeing. Expunge yourself from any liability. But instead I'm left with the question as to why you had my wallet. Especially when you made a big production about not searching through it last night to find out my address. And yet, here you are," he waved at me, "with this." His hand shook the wallet in question.

Gah, why did he have to be so infuriating?

Never had I met someone so . . . formidable.

Usually men just did what I wanted. Well, not *exactly* like that, but a smile went far in getting my own way. But Jagger was different. He was a worthy adversary, unaffected by my charm.

And because I was positive he liked conflict, and got off on it, I refused to be baited. Instead giving him my usual sunny disposition which probably made things worse.

"Well, after I put you to bed, I got bored and thought theft was a nice way to round out my evening." I nodded to his hand. "But you made it so easy for me with that wad of cash, it wasn't much of a challenge. You're welcome, by the way."

I didn't bother adding all the things he should be thankful for because it would take a while to list them. But since my obligation had been met, and items had been returned to their rightful owner, I no longer needed to be loitering in the hall. Which should've been my cue to leave.

Except.

"Any recommendations for brunch locations?"

"Huh?" His usual control and lack of emotion cracked as he eyed me with suspicion.

"Brunch," I said slowly, gesturing with my hand to my mouth.

He propped an arm, resting on the door jamb which of course showcased the delicious muscles I was trying not to think about. "I know what it is, Belle. I was just wondering why you'd assume we were going out to brunch?"

I laughed.

Genuinely laughed because of all the things I thought he'd assume, me asking him out on a date was dead last. He had to be joking.

"Oh!" I stopped laughing, watching his face morph in confusion. "You were being serious?" I tried to contain the giggle as I shook the grin from my mouth. "I wasn't asking you to join me. That would be *ridiculous*." I shrugged. "I just meant it's been a while since I've been in this part of town and since I was here . . ." I waved my hand, "it made sense that I at least grab something to eat before I head back home. And I thought you being a local might have a recommendation. Oh!" My spine snapped more upright as I got more animated. "I bet you're one of those people that leaves reviews."

I could almost picture it.

Jagger at a corner table, carefully sampling everything brought to him before tapping out notes into his phone for future deliberation.

"I don't leave reviews." He huffed impatiently. "I'm not *that* much of an asshole."

"Just a little bit of an asshole?" I circled my first finger so that it was just hovering off the top of my thumb. "Or are you saying that all food critics are assholes? Or just the ones that blog about it? Or that whomever it is—definition unclear at present—is more of an asshole than you are?"

As much as he probably liked to think of himself as smart, he'd walked right into that one. I'd also grown up with a prosecutor father and social worker mother, so I could outmaneuver most people during an argument.

"God." He lifted his eyes to the ceiling, his lips whispering words that were obviously some kind of silent prayer. "You *really* are impossible. I don't think I've ever met a woman like you in my whole entire life. And make no mistake, Belle, I've been around plenty of women."

"Well thank you." I grinned, taking the compliment whether he'd intended it that way or not. "But I will say if you're trying to prove you're not an asshole, mentioning all the women you've been around is not a good way to go." My lips pulled into a grimace. "It's tacky, and insinuating you're a whore isn't as impressive as you might think."

"I am *not* a whore," he shot back defiantly.

"None of my business." I raised my hands in surrender. "Your body, your choice! And as long as it's consensual. You do you."

"Get in here, already." He stepped to the side, a shadow of what I assumed was an invitation.

"I'm sorry?" I pretended I hadn't heard correctly. "Was that some kind of request? I didn't hear a *please* or *thank you,* so I can't be sure. I'd question your upbringing but since I've met your parents, we both know it isn't that."

He sighed heavily, muttering under his breath like it pained him. "Will you please come inside, Belle?"

"Why?" I shrugged, having so much fun with our little game that I was almost feeling guilty.

Almost.

"Because." His voice was tempered, like he was trying to control it. "Since you seem so determined to have this conversation, I'd prefer if we had it inside. Please. Thank you."

"Well, since you asked so nicely." I smirked as I walked right past him. "Of course I'll come inside. But just so it's on the record, I was just looking for a brunch recommendation. The conversation part, that was all you."

Jagger Hartley, you my friend, have met your match.

Chapter 9

Jagger

I was stuck in some wormhole.

The twilight zone.

Groundhog Day.

Some paradox in the universe where a woman, who had no business being in my life, was right in front of me. And worst of all, I wasn't even sure I was mad about it, the annoyance I'd had completely manufactured as I tried to hide the excitement at seeing her again.

And what the hell was up with that?

She was a complete pain in the ass.

Argumentative.

Waaaaaay too positive.

Beautiful.

Ok, the last one wasn't a problem, but all the others were in my top list of traits I tried to avoid in people. And not only was I *not* avoiding her, but I was secretly harboring delight that I'd been an idiot and forgotten my phone.

That had been unintentional, by the way. I'd like to think I was some slick asshole who had planned all of that to lure her to my homefield advantage, but I wasn't. That much of an ass-hole, or that slick. I'd been hung over, irritated, and slightly un-nerved by a woman I couldn't quite define. Add in the fact I was in a strange apartment, and I was slightly—fine, a lot more than slightly—a control freak, and my intention had been to get the hell out of there ASAP.

Hadn't even noticed my phone and wallet were missing. My need to get into the shower and drink about a gallon of coffee, my priorities the minute I'd gotten home to my apartment.

But how fucking wonderful was fate. And that my hangover, mood, and being slightly forgetful had created the opportunity.

And more importantly, that her ability to work my last fuck-ing nerve provided cover to invite her inside. Something I'd been dying to do since she knocked on my door, but I'd stopped my-self because, hello, her lips looked fucking delicious.

She swayed her hips as she walked past me, the bounce of her cute blond ponytail taunting with every step. Her beautiful body was encased in a fitted black dress that clung to her like a body stocking, tamed down by a casual denim jacket and a pair of blinding white sneakers.

Effortlessly sexy, like she was trying to look normal. And I was the pervert for being turned on.

I waited until she turned, drinking in every last delicious drop of her before I had to pretend to be annoyed and unaffected again. I wasn't even sure what I wanted to say, my mouth and mind at odds with which direction to take. Not my cock though. He knew exactly what he wanted, and it started with taking that gorgeous mouth and peeling her out of that cute, yet seductive outfit that must be some kind of sorcery.

"Now you have me here." She looked around, no doubt cata-loging my living room for some kind of analysis later. "What are you going to do with me?"

I can think of a few things, my dick chimed in.

Shut the hell up, cocksucker, no one asked you, my brain answered.

Cocksucker, interesting choice of words, my balls snickered.

And I was not only officially ready to check myself in for psychiatric help but was glad my mouth was being responsible, saving my cock *and* my balls by not articulating any of it.

"Why are you here, Belle?" I didn't really care about the answer, but it felt like something I should ask.

"Uhhhhhh." She looked around, the smile brimming on her face. "Did you forget the part where I returned your wallet and phone? You still didn't thank me for that, by the way."

"Could've organized a courier," I pointed out. "Or left them in my mailbox." Another option I was relieved she didn't take.

"And have your personal belongings fall into the wrong hands or not make it to you?" She clutched her hands dramatically to her chest. "Because you would've been so understanding if it got picked up by the wrong person or somehow got misdelivered." A smirk found its way onto her lips.

"Nope, I wasn't going to risk it. There was no way I was delegating such an important job to just anyone. Which is why I had to come down here myself, and deliver it personally."

I didn't care if she was lying. If she was looking for some morning entertainment and she hadn't gotten her fix, or if perhaps she had some other reason. All I cared about was she was there, in my living room and neither of us was drunk. Oh, and the situation hadn't been one of coercion. The choice to come see me very much hers, instead of buckling herself into my passenger seat and being forced into a road trip.

"What?" She chuckled when I didn't answer. "You can admit I was right. No one is around to hear you and you can deny it later."

"You're not wrong," I conceded, moving slightly closer. "But I think you're here." My eyes roamed over the length of her. "Because as much as those reasons are valid, you secretly like pissing me off."

I secretly liked it too, or maybe it *wasn't* so secretly.

But I wasn't ready to admit it just yet, dying to know if her plans to have brunch had been hypothetical.

She lifted her shoulder in a half-hearted shrug. "You're not wrong," she admitted, neither of us willing to go further to confirm the other had been right. "But you still didn't answer my question about brunch. And I was hoping that since you invited me inside, you'd have some secret place you wanted to share, or at the very least, give me a list of places to avoid. I'm sure you have a few of those."

"For the last time." I took a breath, both loving and hating the benign topic of conversation. "I don't review or rate restaurants."

"Yes, yes, not that kind of asshole. I forgot." She smirked. "Does that mean you have nothing for me?"

Oh, I have a whole lot for you.

"Here's what's going to happen." I shook my head, part of me not actually believing what I was about to say. "I'm going to take you to brunch and then you're going to go home."

Sure, that's what I wanted.

For her to leave.

I was full of shit.

Still, not like I could admit that I was attracted to her but also incredibly intrigued by her as well. And I liked being in her company, which was bewildering because I wasn't that guy who randomly hung out with strangers.

Belle's eyebrows lifted, clearly not expecting the invitation. "Hhmmmm," she pondered, tapping her lip with her dainty pink nails. "Such an enticing offer. Especially with the caveat that I leave right after."

Most of the women I knew would've jumped at the chance.

Either laughing, assuming I was kidding, or not really caring either way. And actresses, the ones I knew would take the face time anyway they could get it.

But not her.

It would be a cold day in hell before she'd let any of my bull-shit slide.

"Well, I assumed that's what you wanted." I changed tactics. "Considering you weren't even looking for the company. I was just trying to be nice, since you made the trip all the way out here to return my stuff."

She laughed, the genuine sound of happiness bubbling out of her mouth making my skin tingle. There was nothing contrived about her, and her laugh was fast becoming one of my favorite things.

"Oh, Jagger. Is that your way of trying to say thank you? I'm not sure what is funnier. That you'd be willing to suffer in my presence for a whole meal or that you'd think I'd just slink off right after, like some dirty little secret. I'm surprised you haven't offered to have food delivered." She looked around my apartment before leaning in to whisper, "You know, so no one sees us together."

Honestly, I couldn't think of anything worse than staying *in* the apartment. Mainly because with no witnesses, I couldn't be sure I could keep my hands and mouth to myself. And because I was clearly messed up, the more disagreeable and argumentative she was, the more I was getting turned on.

Knew I should've jerked off in the shower.

"If I was so worried about being seen with you, why would I take you to visit my parents?"

"Is that what that was?" She scoffed, her smile not dropping for a second. "*You* took *me* to visit them? Then hustled me right out the side door before we'd even had a chance to properly mingle or even eat. Not to mention, I didn't even have time to get Dane's phone number."

The idea of Belle with Dane made me thirty-five different degrees of angry. I hadn't been sure of Dane's intentions, whether he was just flirting with her like he did most women, or if he was planning on asking her out. But obviously he'd shared at least some of those plans with her, talk of exchanging numbers not a precursor to anything good.

"You aren't going to date my brother." The words carried more bite than I'd intended, surprising myself as they came out of my mouth.

"My, my," she tsked, shaking her head. "Not only am I supposed to leave right after brunch like a good girl, but now you're dictating who I can date. Could you be any more arrogant and conceited?"

Not only was she correct, but she had every right to tell me to go fuck myself. Yet, there she was, telling me exactly how much of an arrogant piece of shit I was, and not leaving. And maybe, just maybe, she got off on it too.

Interesting.

"It would be a conflict of interest," I volleyed back, an idea—and not a very good one—forming in my head as I tried to think on my feet.

Belle was going to be the absolute death of me, and in some sick and twisted way, I was actually looking forward to my own demise.

She tilted her head, daring me to continue. "How so?"

"People who work for me, can't date my brother. It creates problems. And I don't like emotional meltdowns. Dane is. . . ." What was I going to say? Not like I could lie and say he wasn't a nice guy, because not even I'd believe that. "Complicated." I settled on, figuring it was open to interpretation. "And so would your entanglement with him."

"Wow, dating went to entanglement in two point three seconds with you, no wonder you've got a reputation for being a jerk." She laughed, the sweetness of the sound hitting me right in the balls. "And when did you hire me? I wasn't the one who was drunk last night, Jagger, so whatever conversation you think took place probably happened in your own head. Pretty sure you alluded that not only did I not make the cut, but you wouldn't even give me the benefit of another audition."

Jesus.

Was I going to do it?

If dating Dane was off the table if she worked for me, I definitely couldn't date her either.

But I also knew walking away wasn't an option. The deadline for that baby had sailed right by when I'd kissed her at that club. Then was further reenforced when I woke up in her room, seeing her beautiful messed-up sleep hair and adorable—and irrationally sexy—pajamas. Her showing up on my doorstep was the nail in my coffin.

"I've already cast the lead female role. She's a headliner, and we need big names to keep our financiers happy."

None of that was a lie, because even if I did have my head up my ass, I couldn't deny she would've killed it in the main role. And as much as it would've chaffed me, hiring someone who'd turned up late to their audition, I'd have done it in a second once I'd seen her on that stage. That was why I'd had to leave, not because I was crazy late for a stupid party I didn't even want to go to, but because I couldn't trust myself if I saw any more of her. And if I couldn't guarantee ticket sales with star power, the money would dry up quicker than shit.

She folded her arms across her chest, pretending to look uninterested. But her eyes gave her away, the sparkle of excitement unable to be dimmed despite her trying to keep it hidden. I loved that about her. The unadulterated elation, and her inability to contain it. Secretly I envied it.

"And?" She nodded her head, waiting for me to continue. "What then?"

My brain was locked in a ridiculous tug-of-war, unable to walk away even though employing her would effectively mean I couldn't have her.

Maybe it's what I needed, because I was struggling the longer I looked at her.

"Understudy. You can be the understudy."

She visibly took a step back, studying me hard with brown eyes that would torture my dreams. "Don't play with me, Jagger.

I think we've both agreed we've had fun with this game, but my career is off-limits."

There was no humor in her voice, the words leveled with such confidence and self-assurance I was amazed she wasn't at the top of everyone's casting list. She was a diamond, uncut, but no less valuable, just waiting to be discovered. And if those few seconds I'd seen were anything to go by, it was only a matter of time before she was headlining.

"I am not playing, Belle." My words a little more seductive than I'd liked, needing to clear my throat so I didn't sound like a pervert. "It's yours if you want it."

What I didn't tell her was that I knew within seconds if an actor was right for the part. It wasn't just the way they read, but their energy, the way they commanded attention. It was in the way they walked, talked, stood. All the things that weren't taught in any kind of school, but innate.

And she had all of that and change.

"Wait, I need to audition." She snapped her fingers, her composure falling for a second as her eyes looked to my living room. "Here, I'll do it here."

Without waiting for an answer, either affirmative or negative, she walked to the center of the room, pushed my coffee table out of the way and took a deep breath.

"Belle, I already offered you the part. This is pointless."

"No." She held up her hand, already in character. "I'm doing it anyway."

And then without asking if I was ready, she launched into the fifteen-minute monologue she'd started on that stage in Brooklyn when I'd walked out.

She didn't even need a prompt, or a script, or even a fucking pause, the words coming out of her mouth so effortlessly like she'd been born to play the part.

Understudy was an insult, but it was the only thing I was offering.

And when she was done—the emotional tempest I'd written sounding so much better coming from her lips—I held my urge to applaud and instead watched her.

Where the hell had she been?

And why the hell had no one discovered her yet?

"Well?" She blinked, the character that had been inhabiting her exorcised as *Belle* returned.

"I—" I cleared my throat, tempering my emotions. "I've offered you the part, Belle. Nothing's changed."

Except everything had changed.

I *thought* I knew how good she was.

Between my gut feeling, the appetizer of her talent I'd tasted right before we went to Connecticut, her fucking *je ne sais quoi*. All of it had been enough to know that giving her the understudy role wasn't a pity move.

But seeing the whole fucking monologue, watching the raw emotion pour out of her completely unrehearsed, and I had no fucking clue what I'd been dealing with.

She wasn't good.

She was brilliant.

And I was in a world of fucking shit.

Chapter 10

Belle

"I've offered you the part, Belle. Nothing's changed."

Wow.

At the risk of sounding as conceited as Jagger, I knew it hadn't been a bad audition. So, even though the lead was no longer up for grabs, I was hoping for a little more . . . I don't know, enthusiasm? I got it. He'd already offered me the understudy and unless I sucked, he probably wasn't going to change his mind. But seriously, did he have a quota for smiles, because even one of his sexy, annoying smirks would have been enough.

Instead, he looked at me blankly, like I'd sung row-row-row-your-boat off-key or given him my bad—if not comical—imitation of Crocodile Dundee. *"Theaaaat's naught a kneighhhh-hife. Thisss is ah knieighhhhife."*

Adorable, but not overly impressive.

But my Lilith had been great.

Give me something, dude!

Should I turn him down purely out of spite?

An understudy for a major part was nothing to be ashamed of. Yeah, you basically had to wait in the wings, hoping the poor girl tripped down some stairs or got a bad case of food poisoning, but your name was still in the Playbill. You were attached to the production. And even if you never stepped foot on the stage, you got street cred, another achievement to list on your resume.

Then on the other side of the argument was my pride.

It shouldn't have even been a decision, accepting the damn thing making more sense than turning it down.

But holy-moly was he making it difficult.

"Can I think about it?"

What was I doing? Because even I knew it was too good an opportunity to sabotage for no good reason.

His eyes widened, the flash of emotion cracking through his steely façade. "You want to think about it?"

"Sure. I need to discuss it with my agent. See if this is the right move for me."

Lies.

So many lies, and it was a tribute to what an amazing actress I was, able to spill them with so much conviction.

"Twenty-four hours," he agreed. "You don't let me know in that timeframe, I'll assume you're passing, and I'll give it to someone else."

Give it to someone else?

Gah, like he was some high and mighty king, bestowing honors.

"Great." I forced a smile. "I'll let you know."

I turned, picking up my handbag that I'd tossed to the floor when I'd started the monologue. "I'll see you around."

"Wait." He grabbed my arm, stopping me from getting any farther. "What about brunch?"

Brunch?

BRUNCH?

Jagger Hartley was impossible.

Like I wanted to go sit at some pretentious, off-the-grid bistro he and every other uptight asshole *loved* because it wasn't commercial or mainstream. Pfft, I could get overpriced whole wheat toast and poached eggs from Himalayan chickens in Manhattan, Brooklyn wasn't so special.

"Wouldn't it be inappropriate?" I tried to keep the sarcasm out of my voice, but failed. Probably intentionally because I wanted him to know he was an ass.

He dipped his head, contemplating it. "Well, since you haven't accepted my offer, there isn't really a conflict, is there?"

Damn him.

Damn him and his stupid reasonable rationalizations.

And damn me too because I was hungry, and was probably going to devour the next thing I encountered that was remotely edible.

"It's my thank you, remember?" He tried to sweeten the pot, confusing me even more. Either he reveled playing with people's emotions or he—like me—was just hungry. The powerplay with an added bonus.

"Ah, yes. The *thank you*. For taking care of you," *and your stupid ass*, "making sure you were safe," *and didn't end up face first in the gutter getting anal probed from a sewer rat*, "and bringing back your belongings," *which you forgot even though I told you they were right there on my nightstand.*

"Hmm, well I guess when you put it like that, brunch is the least you can do." *And this place better have regular food. Not some gimmick bullshit where we pretend to be impressed by a lettuce leaf covered in micro-herbs they pass off as a thirty-dollar salad.*

"Great. I know just the place." The smile I'd wanted ten minutes ago decided to grace us with its presence. "You ready to go?"

"Ready," I answered cheerily, wanting to strangle him and kiss him all at the same time. I'd never been turned on by someone I simultaneously wanted to smother with a pillow, but I guess there was always a first time.

It had to be because he was hot.

And I was hungry.

And clearly sleep deprived.

Or maybe it was charity, because let's face it, he probably had no friends who'd willingly eat with him. Unless you count wild dogs who recognized him as their own kind and probably loved the idea of tearing at some wildebeest with him.

"Belle?" His eyes searched mine, like he wasn't exactly sure what I'd been thinking but had guessed it wasn't pleasant.

"Sorry, zoned out. I get that way when I'm hungry. Let's go." My hand waved with a flourish as I edged toward the door. I accidentally kicked a dog bowl, a few pieces of dried kibble still present.

"Oh, I didn't know you had a dog?" I coughed, unable to imagine him with any kind of pet.

"I don't." He shrugged. "The guy down on three has a Husky that likes to wander upstairs if he leaves the door open. We've become good friends and sometimes we like to hang out."

Your Honor, the defense rests.

Zara was right, I'd have made a killer trial attorney.

Brunch was at a small, boho bistro—gasp, the shock—but thankfully, the food was good. Since it was around the corner from his Brownstone, we walked, the two of us striding in reasonably comfortable silence. Him, probably because he got hives at the thought of casual conversation, me, because I was trying to imagine him being friendly to someone else's dog when he didn't have to. It was strangely endearing, which made my feelings even murkier.

The conversation was exactly as I'd expected at the start. Curt. Nonpersonal. And what I liked to call Broadway table talk. I felt like I was at a job interview, Jagger asking me about my resume, where I went to college, and where I saw myself in the industry. He peppered the conversation with enough nods so he looked like he was listening, but I wasn't entirely sure if he was.

He ordered an egg-white omelet with veggies and whole grain toast—again, shocker—while I got excited about the huge plate of waffles covered in extra syrup with a side order of bacon. It was only when we started eating that I figured I'd ask some questions of my own.

"So you go back and see your family much?" I sipped my orange juice, fairly sure I already knew the answer.

His brow rose ever so slightly. "Here and there. When required."

Wow.

"See, that's just weird." I dropped my fork, mourning the loss of carbs and syrup while feeling dutifully compelled to speak. "I get families can be a 'pain' sometimes but from what I saw, they're great. Are they closet abusers? Make you join a cult?"

Sure, I was more direct than most but since he technically wasn't my boss yet, I could still ask slightly inappropriate questions. Because let's be honest, most of the stuff he'd tell me would be on public record anyway and I'd be able to look for it online if I wanted. Nope, I wanted the juicy stuff, the kind that wasn't available on a Google search.

He chewed his omelet carefully, like he had a required amount of times he needed to pass it through his molars before he was allowed to swallow. "I'm sure they'll be so pleased to hear your opinion, I'll let them know next time I visit."

So guarded.

And, it told me nothing.

He could've easily denied it. Most people would've if it weren't true, hell most would even if it were. Made some joke about growing up with seventeen mothers and getting drunk on the sacramental peyote.

But not Jagger.

Nothing.

Not even a crack about growing up in the compound.

"You know, not saying stuff says things too," I pointed out, remembering something my mom had once said. It was more technical than that, based on some therapy technique, but she was right.

The absence of an answer is still an answer.

He took another careful mouthful, his table manners impeccable, considering he could be such a rude asshole when he wanted. "That doesn't even make sense, Belle."

"No, it makes perfect sense. You constantly avoid anything personal." I held up a finger stopping him from interjecting, which he looked ready to do. "Which I kinda understand, considering your family connections. But seriously," I leaned in a little closer, "who am I going to tell? If I wanted to screw up your life I'd have taken compromising photos and blackmailed you with them while you were asleep. Or refused to leave the party and gotten the inside scoop once everyone got drunk or high—which was probably happening sooner than later." And hey, while my parents were militantly anti-drug use—even marijuana—I was no stranger to taking a sneaky hit.

His fork was lowered by his plate as his eyes met mine. "This was a mistake."

"Wait." I grabbed his arm as he reached for his wallet. "You invited me, remember. To *thank* me. And I haven't been thanked. So if you're thinking of leaving, you can't."

Okay, so it was going to take a lot longer to crack his shell, noted. But I didn't want him to run off either. When Jagger wasn't being cold or aloof, he was actually really engaging. I'd seen glimmers of it in the car, and at dinner, and then later at the club. And underneath that hard exterior, I was positive the real Jagger was amazing.

He eased back into his seat, his hand moving away from his pocket. "And how am I supposed to adequately thank you?"

It felt like a dare, a naughty poke, just begging for me to say something inappropriate. Which I would've, had it not been incredibly obvious he was deflecting.

The flashy smile and charm might work on most women—okay, fine, it worked on me too—but I was nothing if not driven when given a goal. And finding out what made Jagger Hartley tick was definitely a goal.

"Well," I pondered, trying not to think of all the indecent ways he could thank me. "I was going to visit Hayley tonight. Bobbie is not running a fever any more, but Hayley hasn't had a chance to go get groceries since the baby's been sick. You could drive me, save me catching an Uber. Oh, and you could help me carry the shopping bags. Hayley's building doesn't have an elevator, so I have to lug all of it upstairs."

"You want me to come with you." He enunciated every word like he was checking its validity. "To visit a friend—who I don't know—and deliver groceries."

"I'd be delivering the groceries. You're just the helper," I pointed out. "And you know Hayley. I'm sure you've met at some event." Well, I wasn't *sure* but before getting knocked up, Hayley had been listed by Playbill.com as Broadway's biggest rising star. I couldn't even be jealous about it, her talent truly awe-inspiring. It would stand to reason their paths had at least crossed.

"We've met," he confirmed, giving as little as possible. "Doesn't mean she'd want me visiting her at her home, especially if her child is sick."

I waved my hand dismissively. "Pfft, she'll be so grateful for the groceries and the reprieve, she wouldn't care if I showed up with a drug cartel. You've never been around new mothers I take it?"

He looked uncomfortable, seeming to weigh the words carefully in case they divulged too much information. "No, Dane was older when . . . No. I've not been around babies."

"Right. Well, you're in for a treat." I clapped my hands slightly more excited than I should be. "Pick me up around five. You remember where I live, right? Or do you need me to write it down? We can go pick up supplies and dinner and drive it over to Midtown."

"You want me to go *with* you to get groceries as well as take you to Midtown?" he asked, like it was the most absurd thing he'd ever heard.

"Oh my God, Jagger. It's just *groceries*. You worried someone is going to see you picking up some milk and bread and report it to *Deadline*?" I laughed, the idea of someone even caring rather comical.

He rolled his eyes. "I'm not worried about paparazzi, Belle. But I don't consort with my cast."

"Consort?" I fought the urge to snort. "Well since I haven't accepted anything, I'm not part of *your cast*." I punctuated with air quotes. "So we won't be *consorting*." More air quotes.

Honestly, I hated when people did that. So pretentious. But I couldn't help myself when I was around him.

His eyes narrowed, no hint of a smile on his lips. "You're turning it down?"

"I have twenty-four hours, remember?" I reminded him. And I was going to use every last second to my advantage. "Now finish your sad looking brunch." I pointed to his half-eaten beige omelet while I reattacked my waffles. "I'll even let you steal a piece of my bacon if you ask nicely." I pushed the plate toward him. "But only one," I warned.

He looked enviably at my plate of crispy bacon before reaching down and taking two—TWO—pieces. "Thanks." He took a bite and smirked.

Ugh.

He was such a jerk.

Chapter 11

Jagger

I'd spent more time with Belle in the last two days than I had with my director's assistant.

I couldn't even understand how it happened. It was liked some weird fucking parlor of mirrors where no matter which way I turned, there I was again.

Was I disappointed?

Not even a little.

I will say that the idea of going to see Hayley Easton—a woman I'd met maybe twice—and her baby was not something I was looking forward to. It wasn't that I hated babies, I'd just never really met one.

I wasn't the guy you invited to baby showers, something I was glad for. And most of the people I knew were either deliberately childless or had kids that had already moved away to college. Sure, some of the actors had kids, but I didn't really 'hang' with actors.

But I couldn't admit to Belle that being around something so fragile and small was slightly terrifying. Hell, I was in a constant battle of wanting to admit *everything* to her while needing to keep my mouth shut.

She was easy to talk to.

Unarming in a weird and delicate way.

It was so effortless that I could almost forget we weren't actually friends. I wasn't sure what we were, but friends weren't it.

"Why did you leave?"

My younger brother's voice cut through my jumbled thoughts, the phone call I'd been expecting happening sooner than later. He didn't get agitated easily but when he did, it was usually because of something I'd done. Or didn't do. He forgave me of course, because that's how Dane was. But somewhere in that brain of his, he really believed he could make a difference.

"I told you I would make an appearance. I didn't promise to stay." The car eased to the curb as I pulled up to the front of Belle's apartment building. "I saw them both, wished them a happy anniversary, Dane. No one probably even noticed I was gone."

"*I* noticed," he spat back. "Was it Belle? Is it because I offered to take her home?"

I'd successfully avoided his calls and messages most of the day, but I couldn't do it forever. And of course I knew when the conversation took place, it would also include the woman who I was waiting for.

"Did you ask her out?" I hated that I had to ask, or that I cared so much either way. But Dane wouldn't lie, and if he had, I needed to know.

"Is that why you left? Because you thought I was trying to steal your girlfriend?"

"She is not my *girlfriend*," I corrected, not comfortable making the distinction. "And you didn't answer the question."

"Jesus, Jagger." Dane breathed out in frustration. "Is that what you thought?"

"Dad introduced her as *your* friend, and Belle was—" Shit, was I about to say *mine*? Like I fucking found her first and he couldn't have her. Did it sound as fucking pathetic as it did in my head? Because Christ, I couldn't even remember the last time I'd cared enough about a woman to start a fight over her, let alone with my own brother.

"Belle, *what*?" Dane asked, not giving a shit I was acting like a moron.

"It doesn't matter. Look, I need to go, Dane."

"Jagger, I don't know what the hell your relationship is with her, but I think you need to at least be honest with yourself. And for the record, I didn't ask her out. But I do want to see you. You think we can have this conversation in person? I can meet you for lunch?"

I'd assumed he wouldn't be so easily pacified, but I wasn't in the mood to elaborate. Especially when I wasn't so clear on it myself.

I'd just met her for fuck's sake.

There was no fucking relationship.

Except . . .

My eyes looked up at the apartment building I was parked in front of.

Fuck.

"Sure. Dane, listen, I really do need to go but I promise I'll call you tomorrow when I'm not acting like such a prick."

He chuckled and I could hear the smile in his voice. "You're not a prick even if you have everyone else fooled. Call me tomorrow, big bro. Later."

I punched the steering wheel of my Lexus, the engine of the sedan still idling as I waited on the street. It was just before five, like she wanted—not even sure when I became so fucking obedient and punctual—and texted to let her know I was there. Which of course she answered with an immediate call, asking me to come upstairs.

I didn't.

I'd already given this woman way too much rope, and going up there was only looking for trouble. Besides, she lived with her sister and brother-in-law, and I wasn't fond of lawyers. Both apparently highly regarded in legal circles, as was her newly retired dad. I'd done my research in the fleeting hours we hadn't been together, and we couldn't have had more different upbringings.

She'd probably had brownies and milk with her after-school specials. I couldn't bring friends home from school because my dad liked to wander around wearing nothing but a robe as he chowed down on Froot Loops right from the box. To say it was unconventional was an understatement.

Which was obviously the reason I was waiting in my car instead of walking up the stairs to go see the woman I was really starting to like.

"Fuck, Jagger." I punched the steering wheel again. "This girl is not for you."

Great, now I was quoting *Scarface* as well as talking to myself. Could I be any more pathetic?

Not sure if she was deliberately making me wait, but she didn't open the passenger side door until it was exactly five.

"Hey." She smiled brightly. "You could've come up instead of waiting down here like a stalker."

My head rolled to the side, needing a minute just to take her in. Gone was the cute dress from earlier that did weird things to my balls and in its place was a fluffy hot pink top and a fitted pair of black pants that covered her lower body like they'd been painted on.

Fuck.

Me.

I coughed, clearing my throat. "Leather pants, Belle, really?" My head tipped down as I kept my eyes level with hers. I wasn't chancing taking another look, knowing it would be trouble if I did.

She laughed, her hand flying back and hitting me in the chest. "Pllleeeease, no one wears real leather anymore. They're synthetic." She rubbed her hands down her delicious legs. "Aren't they fabulous? And even more importantly, no animals were harmed. Now, let's head to the grocery store, I've got a list."

Oh, I had a list of my own, but it wasn't for the grocery store.

Shaking my head and reminding myself I still had some control over the situation, I put the car in drive and eased away from the curb. All I had to do was keep my hands to myself, ignore how beautiful she was, and get through the night. Then, in the morning, she'd accept the goddamn understudy role and she'd be completely off-limits. And temptation or not, I didn't fuck anyone I worked with. I never crossed the line, even with consent, it was highly inappropriate, bordering on sexual harassment.

She directed me to a small supermarket off the main road, and I was able to find a parking spot. Then, once we were stopped, she unfastened her seatbelt and turned to me.

"Come on, you're not going to just sit in the car again, are you?"

I looked toward the small grocery store, my desire to go in at an all-time low. "Uh, yeah, that's exactly what I'm going to do." I shook my head, drawing the line at roaming aisles with her like we were some fucking couple. "You don't need me to hold your hand, and I've got work I need to do."

She huffed dramatically, tossing her hands in the air before popping the handle of the door. "Fine, suit yourself. Enjoy your *work*."

Then with a quick shimmy out of her seat, she was out of the car and onto the sidewalk. I waited until she was walking away before getting a look at her ass in her not-leather pants. I didn't care what they were made of, they looked sensational and did amazing things for her body.

My eyes stayed on her until she disappeared inside, my attention returning to my phone. I wasn't really planning on working while I waited, but I did need a distraction.

Get your head out of your ass I typed out in my notes. I'd never been big on trying to write shit into existence but since not much else had worked for me in the last twenty-four hours, I was willing to give it a try.

I should probably add **keep your hands to yourself** and **find your balls** to that list while I was at it, instead opening an internet search window and Googling images of Belle.

There wasn't a lot, headshots attached to her website, snaps from performances when she was in college, and a couple of ensemble cast photos. Not one of them did her justice, all of them showing a fraction of how beautiful she was, and none of them hinting at her talent.

I was deep diving her social pages when she returned to the car, the knock on the driver's side door startling me from my stalking. "Fuck." I dropped my phone, glad it fell screen face down.

Her smile was infectious, better than the ones I'd been staring at online, as I opened the door to help with the bags.

"If you'd told me you were going to buy half the grocery store, I'd have come in and helped you carry it out." I popped the trunk, loading the shopping bags into the back of the car. "Jesus, how much did you buy?"

And didn't I feel like a complete cocksucker, sitting in my car like an ass while she balanced three large paper bags.

Belle looked grateful for the assist, watching as she smiled on the sidewalk. "Did you miss the part where I said Hayley had a baby? You know how much stuff little people need? Trust me, this is nothing."

Even just a glance at the bags, and I could tell she hadn't randomly tossed things into a cart. There was bread, fresh fruit, cereal, milk, diapers—stuff you'd expect a mom to buy, not a hot twenty-something-year-old from Manhattan. And while it was surprising, it probably shouldn't have been. Because every time I thought I'd had her figured out, she threw me a curve ball.

"Okay, where to next?" I asked, feeling like a dick for misjudging her. Sure, I wasn't admitting it out loud, but there was no way she was the talentless, self-absorbed, spoiled airhead I'd assumed when she'd walked in late to that audition.

"Dinner. I'm starving." She grinned sliding back into the car.

Confident she'd have a plan for that too, I hopped into the driver's seat and retrieved my phone from the console. Luckily the screen had gone black so any evidence of me being creepy was hidden as I carefully X'd out of any incriminating windows and shoved it safely into my pocket.

We arrived at Hayley's Midtown apartment shortly after picking up a pizza on the way. My stomach churned with a weird energy as I parked, not sure why I was feeling nervous. I'd met the woman before, and while I wasn't practiced being around babies, I wasn't a fucking moron. It wasn't like I was babysitting the kid, so what did it even matter? And more to the point, why did I even give a shit what anyone thought? But as rational as all that was, I had a knot in my gut as I pulled the groceries from my trunk, leaving Belle to carry the pizza.

I let her lead as we climbed the stairs to the second floor, no elevator meant I had a perfect view of her perfect ass the entire way. And even though I was wrangling three paper sacks full of shopping, I couldn't hate a minute of it.

"Heeeeeeeeey!" Hayley's eyes widened when she opened the door and saw me standing next to her friend. "Hey Belle, when you said you were bringing company, I thought you meant Zara and Lincoln."

"Zara had work and Jagger owed me a favor," Belle declared like it was no big deal. "And we come with supplies." She pointed to me holding the bags of groceries.

You'd think having a relative stranger land on your doorstep would be a problem, but other than initial surprise, Hayley just ushered us in. "You guys." Her voice softened. "Thanks so much. Bobbie is still under the weather, and I haven't had a chance to run to the store." She grabbed one of the shopping bags from my arms, giving me a smile. "Hey, *Jagger*."

Ahhh, so maybe she wasn't so casual about it, my name accompanied with a little more interest than a standard greeting.

Hmmm, I'd have assumed Belle would've given her best friend the entire rundown of the saga with a flip chart and Cliff's Notes. And I was more curious than I cared to admit on exactly how much she'd shared . . .or hadn't.

"Hayley." I tipped my head, my hands still occupied with the remaining bags.

If she wasn't going to say anything about me being there, then I wasn't either, determined not to be outwitted by two actresses even if I did feel completely awkward. "You want these in the kitchen?"

"Sure." She waved me to the open-plan kitchen. "Just through there."

A little cry echoed from a baby monitor, Hayley dumping the bag she was carrying on the coffee table and picking up the device. "Sounds like someone heard her favorite aunt was here, I'll go get her."

Great.

There was going to be three of them.

Oh, it didn't matter that one was a baby. I had no doubt that Belle would find a way to recruit the kid and somehow stack the odds. The woman was a fucking marvel, and if I wanted to come out of the night with some semblance of control, I needed to keep my shit together and be prepared for anything.

With Hayley disappearing to where the newest little troublemaker was hiding, I took the time to place the bags on the kitchen counter. Belle followed me in, the pizza she'd been originally carrying left in the living room replaced by the other bag of groceries.

"You're freaking out." Belle smirked, grabbing the gallon of milk from the paper sack and putting it in the fridge.

I folded my arms across my chest, refusing to admit she was right. "So you're wrong when you read minds as well. Good to know."

She chuckled, unpacking the bags randomly and dumping out oatmeal and bread. "I'm not wrong, but sure, we'll pretend I am so you can live in your delusion."

The delusion was that I could make it through the night without kissing her, the impulse made harder the longer we stood in the small space. Her body twirled, pulling out more groceries and putting them where they apparently belonged like a choreographed ballet. Her body lithe but agile, her arms and legs in strong graceful lines as she literally danced around me.

"Freaking out," she whispered, pliéing as she dropped the bananas into the fruit bowl. "Oooooooh, there's my girl!" Her sweet voice rose an octave, abandoning the fruit, the dance, and me.

I hadn't even noticed we weren't alone, Hayley having returned and leaning against the wall. She had reinforcements too, a bright-eyed little brunette grinning at Belle.

"Look at that adorable face," she cooed, scooping her out of Hayley's arms. "Could you be any cuter?"

"Don't think she's old enough to talk." I moved closer.

While Belle's attention was wrapped in the new guest, Hayley's gaze was fixed on me. I was used to it, walking into a room and feeling eyes follow me around. Much like the current situation, most usually expected some kind of reaction.

"Of course, she can't talk, Hartley, she's only six-months." Belle rolled her eyes. "But just because she can't answer, doesn't make it any less true. Now Bobbie, this McGrumpy Pants is Jagger Hartley." She turned to face me, the baby cradled in her arms. "Say hello, Mr. McGrumpy Pants."

Ignoring the title and the sentiment, I put out my hand, letting Bobbie grab one of my fingers. "Pleasure to meet you, Bobbie. So, you're the reason Belle was so late to her audition."

"What audition?" Hayley suddenly became interested. "*Lilith*? The one we ran lines for?" She looked between Belle and me. "I thought that was next week?"

Interesting.

Guess Belle either didn't share everything with her friend or she hadn't gotten around to it yet. Although, considering how close they seem—going to the E.R. with the baby and buying groceries—you'd think Hayley would've been the first person she called.

"It's nothing." Belle waved her hand, obviously forgetting the kamikaze audition and the carjacking later. "Jagger was nice enough to give me another chance."

Ha! That wasn't exactly how it had worked but sure, whatever, I'd correct her later.

Hayley narrowed her eyes, taking the baby that was starting to fuss a little. "What do you mean? You got the part?"

While I was tempted to see what kind of spin Belle was going to put on it, I was tired of the conversation happening like I wasn't there. "No. She didn't."

They both turned to look at me, Belle's eyes widening a little. "Hayley, why don't you go get started on the pizza, and Jagger and I will put the rest of this stuff away. Then I'll tell you all about me landing the understudy role."

Belle didn't seem like the kind of person to deliberately be cagy, and she wasn't fooling anyone. But Hayley was either used to Belle's diversionary tactics or it was some kind of girl code, regardless, Hayley nodded, taking Bobbie and heading back out to the living room. Not that we'd have much privacy, considering most of the apartment was open plan.

Belle grabbed my arm, pulling me to the farthest edge of the tiny kitchen. It was becoming a theme for us, conversations in other people's kitchens.

"Just don't, okay." Her voice lowered, glancing over her shoulder and waiting for Hayley to turn on the television. Music floated in, the distinct noise of some sort of kids show popped in the air before she continued, "Why did you have to say that?"

"Ummm, because it's the truth?" I scoffed, keeping my voice low even though I wasn't sure why we were whispering. Anyone with half a brain would know we were talking about it, even with

that monotonous annoying fucking jingle about a talking uni-
corn playing in the background. "Did you not tell me the reason
you missed your audition was because Bobbie was sick? I didn't
realize it was a secret."

"It's not, but the last thing Hayley needs is to feel guilty and
not call me next time. I made the choice to be late, me. It's not
anyone else's fault. And it's hard enough for her to be a single
mom without worrying she's screwing up stuff for me."

It had been obvious Belle cared about her friend—missing
the audition, the groceries, dinner—even without the confirmation, I'd seen it firsthand. But it wasn't just that, it was the
lengths she was willing to go to so feelings weren't hurt even if
it impacted her. That was something I wasn't used to. Or even
expected.

Who was this woman?

And why the hell did she not even seem real.

"I should go." It was out of my mouth whether I wanted to
say it or not. And thank fuck for that.

It had never been my intention to stay. The deal was pick
her up, help her deliver her shit, and then leave. I'd done that.
I'd even made small talk, which I hated, so the way I saw it was
I'd gone above and beyond.

"Don't go." Belle grabbed my arm. "Stay, have dinner with
us."

It wasn't even tempting, and not because I *didn't* want to
spend time with her.

I did.

But I was already uncomfortable with the feelings I was
having for her and I didn't need more complications in my life.
It was bad enough when I was just attracted to her. Wanting to
have sex with her was one thing, wanting to get to know what
kind of person you had to be to get the kind of loyalty and dedi-
cation she seemed to have for her friends, was something entirely different.

My head shook, determined to get out the door and stop the insanity before it went any further. "I fulfilled my obligations. I'm assuming you're accepting the understudy role?" She'd be crazy if she didn't, but more than that, I really, really wanted her to.

"I'll give you my answer tomorrow like we agreed. And you could stay because you wanted to, not because you have to."

"Tomorrow then. Enjoy your night." And before I did something stupid, like tell her that nothing I'd done since I'd met her was because I'd had to, I pulled out my keys from my pocket.

Without warning she threw her arms around me, pressing her small frame against me. "Bye, McGrumpy Pants."

I rolled my eyes, pretending not to love the contact as I hugged her back.

It would have to stop.

The touching.

But not right then.

"Try and keep out of trouble." My lips hesitated on the top of her head, not daring to get closer. "And call me tomorrow."

She pulled back, flashing one of her breathtaking smiles. "Cross my heart." Her fingers trailed seductively across my chest. "Try to be in a better mood."

I rolled my eyes. "There's nothing wrong with my mood."

Reluctantly, I unwrapped my hands, my eyes tracing the lines of her body before they landed back on her beautiful face. "Goodbye, Belle."

"See ya, Jagger."

And with a wave, I walked away.

She didn't follow, staying in the kitchen as I said a hurried goodbye to Hayley before I left.

Tomorrow she was going to be completely off-limits.

And even though it was irrational and irresponsible, I could've had one night with her.

My feet hesitated outside the door, wanting to be that jerk to see if she'd have gone there with me.

Maybe.

"Fuuuckkk," I huffed under my breath. "Go home, Jagger."

And like it or not, that was what I did.

Chapter 12

Belle

He left.

I can't believe he just left, who did that? Especially when he just got there, and we hadn't even eaten dinner yet.

"Are you going to make me ask?" Hayley looked at me pointedly. "Because I will, but I figure it didn't need to be said that you have some explaining to do."

It was like déjà vu, an interrogation after a hasty exit from Jagger, only instead of the questions coming from Zara, it was Hayley.

"He's so frustrating." I huffed out a breath, taking a seat beside her as my eyes stayed on the door. Intellectually I knew he wasn't coming back, but part of me was still hoping.

"Because he doesn't do what you want like every other guy you've ever met?" Hayley chuckled. "Yeah, can see how annoying that would be."

"Not every guy I meet does what I want," I argued back. Maybe most but not *every* guy. "And what's wrong with being with men who are accommodating and considerate?"

Hayley rolled her eyes. "Girl, there's nothing wrong with finding a good guy." She settled Bobbie on the playmat at her feet on the floor. "God knows I wish I'd been more selective before letting a guy knock me up. But there's a difference between a good, decent man and a sucker. And a lot of the guys you date just give in too easily. How are you going to be in a real relationship with someone who is too worried to tell you they disagree."

I opened my mouth, ready to prove her wrong and then closed it again. Men *didn't* usually disagree with me. In fact, I can't even remember having a fight or an argument with any of them, even when we broke up. I'd always assumed it was because I dated men that were just really compatible, never once believing there'd been no conflict because they were worried.

"You think men are worried to disagree with me?" I asked, the thought taking root in my mind as I tried to evaluate every relationship I'd ever been in. "Oh, my God. Am I a terrible person?"

It was the one thing I never wanted to be, believing that even if I was having a bad day, at my core I was good. The idea that I was some horrible bitch who people were afraid of was distressing.

Hayley laughed, yanking me into a hug. "Bee, you're one of the nicest people I know. Hello, you're my best friend and my daughter's god mommy. But yeah, you're not the easiest person to say no to. And men, especially the ones you've dated in the past, they've not had the strongest resolve when it comes to you. And sometimes, arguing is a good thing. It means they're invested, and not just a passenger."

Why hadn't I ever realized? Why had it never occurred to me that I'd never had an argument, or maybe that was why they all ended the same way. Me feeling bored and uninspired, and like the relationship wasn't going anywhere.

"Oh my god, that stupid woman was right." I shook my head, knowing it was ridiculous but still unable to talk sense into myself. "I'm never going to find love."

"Whoa, hold on a minute." Hayley pulled away from me, forcing me down onto the couch as we both sat. "That silly fortune teller you and Zara went to when you were kids on Coney Island was a fraud. You *know* that not only was she a fake, but an elitist bitch who told people whatever she wanted to in order to get paid. She was wrong about Zara's soul mate, and she was wrong about you. She wasn't even trying, Belle, she admitted to making everything up."

Logic.

Great, I was trying to have my mental crisis, examining every relationship I'd ever had, and Hayley was trying to reason with facts.

"Fine, maybe that woman did admit to being full of shit," I conceded. "But it still doesn't change the fact that I basically attract men who are afraid to disagree with me."

Or maybe it was the other way around, and I was attracted to men who had no balls.

Oh my god, that was even worse.

"Bee! I can see you overthinking it, and whatever it is, you're wrong. Besides, you might have thought you successfully sidestepped the question about Jagger Hartley, but you haven't. You need to tell me exactly what happened and why he was in my apartment helping you with groceries. Which by the way, I'm incredibly thankful for and can't even remember if I said so." Hayley tapped her temple. "My memory has been terrible. I swear, it doesn't stop with the pregnancy. I'm still chasing brain cells I'm positive I lost somewhere."

Bobbie laughed as she kicked at the toys on her playmat, shoving her little hand into her mouth.

"Okay, let's eat and I'll tell you the whole thing."

Hayley grabbed a bottle for Bobbie while I grabbed some sodas. It was the kind of conversation we needed to have sober, especially since my brain was already scrambled.

Then, as little Miss Bobbie enjoyed her dinner, we polished off slices and I explained the whole fiasco from running late for the audition, the unexpected road trip to see his parents, our boozy dinner, taking him home, getting the offer for the understudy, and then convincing him to help me with groceries.

"Wow, that's a pretty intense twenty-four hours, even for you, Belle."

Sure, when she put it like that, it had been action packed. "To think, two days ago I hadn't even met Jagger Hartley and now I've kissed him and spent the night with him."

"Wait . . . you *kissed* him."

Oops, did I forget to mention that?

"It was just some drunken dance-floor kiss, it didn't mean anything." I waved my hand, still not sure if it had been intentional or not. He hadn't tried again, but it felt like he wanted to.

Or maybe I wanted to and it was wishful thinking.

In any case, we'd shared one kiss, and he'd been clearly drunk so who knows if he even remembered. And, if later I found myself on the other side of an assault charge, thank God I had good representation.

She didn't say it, but I knew what she was thinking.

"I know, okay." I shook my head, still confused by the tangled emotions. "It won't happen again. Especially now I'm going to be working with him. And with any luck, he won't even remember we kissed the first time."

Hayley blew out a long breath, Bobbie having fallen back asleep in her arms. "I'm the last person who would judge you, Bee. But if you don't think it's even a little bit complicated, you're delusional. Jagger Hartley isn't just going to play chauffeur for an understudy. Even one as talented as you."

It was *complicated*, she was right about that. But as much as I tried to hate him, I couldn't. And it wasn't just that I was attracted to him—which I was. Or that he was talented—which I'd still yet to admit to him. But he was so incredibly layered and fascinating that I just couldn't help but be compelled.

Compelled.

And I didn't do well with resisting compulsion.

Personal flaw.

"Pfft, I've got this," I lied, determined to get through the rest of the night and not think of him. "Enough about him. Let's talk about my exciting new role as the understudy for the main part! I still haven't decided if I'm going to throw marbles down the stairs or go see that Voodoo woman who hangs out at Washington Square Park."

Hayley laughed, knowing that as desperate as I was to have my chance on stage, I wasn't going to do it by sabotaging someone else. The bad karma wasn't worth it, and any success I got, had to been earned honorably or it didn't count. And even if I did lose my mind and employed underhanded tactics, theatre ghosts were a real thing. And I didn't need to be haunted by some pissed-off soprano who was marauding the halls in her eternal unrest.

"You're going to kill it, Bee." She pulled me in for a one-armed hug careful not to wake the baby.

The play.

She was talking about the play.

Funnily enough it was the only thing I wasn't worried about.

Damn you, Jagger Hartley.

Damn you.

It was ten a.m. when I picked up my phone, ready to dial Jagger's number.

I wasn't going to overthink it, or drag it out more than I already had, determined to stop being ridiculous and accept his offer.

It was a huge opportunity, the chance of me being on stage at least once or twice, better than average. And when I did, the audience would love me, see that I was ready to step out of the shadows of the ensemble and be the star I was born to be.

I could feel it.

The butterflies fluttered in my stomach, my hand hovering over his name for a second and I had to wonder what part I was most excited about.

Saying yes, or having a legitimate excuse to talk to Jagger.

Or that he'd been the one to give his phone number in the first place, an exchange that happened at brunch when I'd returned his phone and wallet.

"Just do it, Belle," I whispered to myself, hitting his name and waiting for the call to connect.

"Jagger," he answered curtly, any other greeting, missing in action.

I'd seen him save my number in his phone and he'd texted me at least once, so unless he hadn't checked the caller ID, he knew it was me.

"Hi, Mr. Hartley. It's Belle Mathews."

Sure, I told myself I was being professional, addressing him the way I would any director, especially on a non-social call. But in reality, I was looking for a response, waiting to see if he'd keep his cool, clipped vibe going.

"Ms. Mathews, I was expecting your call."

Oh, so *that* was how we were going to do it?

Fine.

"Great, well I'm accepting the role of Lilith's understudy. Thank you so much for thinking of me. I'm excited about the opportunity and can't wait to work with the rest of the cast."

It was exactly what I should've said, and had it been any other director, I'd have given myself a gold star. But it wasn't any other director, and while my dialogue was sincere—I was excited and thankful—it wasn't half of what I really wanted to say.

"Cutting it a little close, aren't you?" He might've been trying to hide his emotions, but I heard the smile in his voice.

Which of course got me excited because while he was playing it cool, I bet there was more he wanted to say too.

I cleared my throat, the grin creeping across my lips and I was glad he couldn't see me. "You did say twenty-four hours.

Brunch was yesterday at eleven. Technically I still have six-ty-minutes."

"*Fifty* minutes. Your watch must be slow. Although, if memory serves me correctly, telling time isn't exactly your forte. I'm surprised you weren't late."

I rolled my eyes.

And even though he couldn't see me, I had a hunch, he'd have guessed.

So much for keeping it professional because even though it started off so promising, there was something about him that I just couldn't help myself.

"Maybe you're just early. It's not always a virtue to get there first."

It was his turn to clear his throat.

"I've never had a problem with my timing."

My skin flushed hot even though we'd said nothing even close to sexual. I mean, it *was* sexual, because there was no way he was still talking about actual time.

"That's reassuring." I tried to get my brain out of the gutter and back on the task at hand. I still hadn't signed anything yet, and it would be so Jagger to decide on a whim that he wanted to go in another direction.

"Indeed."

There was a beat of silence, and as much as I wanted to continue with the banter, I very much wanted the job. "When would you like me to start?"

"We're having an informal table reading on Wednesday. The main cast will be there, and you should have your contract signed by then. I assume you'll want your agent or lawyer to go over it?"

"You would assume correct." I might be desperate to get my big break on Broadway, but if I signed anything without proper vetting, I'd be killed by my dad, Zara *and* Lincoln. And if there was anything left of me, my agent Estelle would take her turn.

"I'll send it via courier this afternoon. Be at the Lighthouse Theatre in Brooklyn at noon on Wednesday. That's twelve o'clock, sharp. Any late comers will be locked out."

"I won't come late."

Ordinarily a harmless sentence, but I could hear the small chuckle under Jagger's breath. And even though the context had been completely innocent—for once—I was sort of glad I'd had that little slip.

"We'll see, won't we. Goodbye, Belle."

He'd used my name.

Not Ms. Mathews.

Not just a generic farewell.

He'd said *Belle*.

My heart raced, feeling my skin tingle all over as my mouth opened. "See you, later, Jagger." And with his name fresh on my lips, I ended the call.

Wednesday we'd have an audience, and it would have to be all business.

And while I trusted myself to behave and not act like a love-sick teenager hyped up on hormones, I was super curious what it was going to be like.

If the crackle between us would still be there when we looked at each other. If anyone would be able to tell I wanted to rip his clothes off with my bare teeth and kiss him senseless. And if his eyes would still darken whenever he said my name.

I flopped down onto my bed, resting my hand on my dia-phragm as I breathed in deeply, holding each lungful as long as I could before letting it slowly ease past my lips.

Was he having the same thoughts?

Was there more he wanted to say?

And suddenly I wasn't glad the conversation had taken place over the phone, wishing I'd been able to see his face.

"Uuuuuuuuhhhhhhh." My voice growled deep in my throat.

It was going to be harder than I thought.

Chapter 13

Jagger

There was zero communication with Belle over the last few days.

Didn't need to be.

I'd asked legal to prepare the contract, had it delivered to her apartment, and she'd returned it signed the next day.

Not sure what I was expecting, but I assumed she'd have questions. Or adjustments. Or something that would need a response. But she didn't, turning it around faster than I'd expected. Of course, it was easier when you had live-in counsel at your disposal, a standard boilerplate contract not any different than the others she'd probably signed.

Still, to say I was disappointed was an understatement. The lack of calls or texts from her not only surprising but seeming to be completely out of character.

Funny how I felt qualified to make that judgment considering the amount of time I'd known her. And yet, I'd challenge anyone who told me I was wrong.

So, she was either deliberately not calling or texting me to prove a point or she was genuinely trying to keep things between us professional.

Like I'd asked.

And expected.

And didn't fucking want.

Because nothing said stupidity like saying one thing and meaning another. But when it came to Belle, I couldn't help but be stupid.

While I was going through last-minute stage instructions with the artistic director, the actors filed in and took a seat in a makeshift circle on stage. I purposely didn't look at the door, keeping my attention on the conversation because I knew I'd be distracted.

"You want me to start them off, Jagger?" Joe, my assistant director, interrupted us briefly.

I checked my watch, seeing it was still early. "Thanks, but we're all done. Is everyone here?" My eyes casually glanced at the circle, the crowd chatting amicably to themselves. And there she was, absolutely stunning in a long flowing purple dress that clung to her breasts and hips.

Fucking hell.

Doing my best to try to hide the sharp intake of air, I coughed into my hand. She wasn't even looking at me, her smile lighting up her whole face as she chatted with Serenity, the female lead.

Of course she was talking to Serenity.

While other actors might have been intimidated by their competition, Belle had charisma for days and seemed to be un-flappable. And she apparently had an uncanny ability to make people love her because in addition to being beautiful, she was genuinely warm. She was also talented, which Serenity hadn't found out yet. Doubt she'd be so 'welcoming' of her understudy if she knew Belle could probably outperform her.

She wasn't late. And I wasn't sure if I was glad or angry that I didn't have a reason to pull her aside for a chat.

"Where's Chase?" I asked, wondering where my other lead was. Not that I really gave a shit but concentrating on his absence gave me something else to think about.

"He's going to be late. Called about thirty minutes ago." Joe checked his watch again. "Do you want me to call him, check his ETA?"

I shook my head, my eyes still glued to Belle. "We can start without him. Get Logan to fill in, I've got a meeting with the investors at five and I need time to get my gag reflex under control."

Joe laughed, one of the few people on set who got to see the lighter side of my personality. "I'll grab you some Chapstick so your lips are supple for all that ass-kissing."

"Thanks, asshole, you're a real peach." I discreetly flipped him off. "Now let's get this cast into shape."

Joe brought the group to attention, passing out fresh scripts as the chatter died down. While there was no doubt I was the one in control of the production, I didn't need to flex at rehearsal, which was why I hung back and observed. Belle's eyes floated through the space, landing on me as I raised a brow. For as much attention I didn't want to give her, I couldn't help myself. And she was obviously feeling the same way because even though Joe was speaking, her focus was on me.

The cast started reading, words I'd written acted out in audio as they went down the pages. It was a surreal experience. I had written countless scripts and screenplays before. Put on productions all through college, even a couple in a small theatre or two. But this was my first big deal. The first one where there was real money involved, and not just some one-night-only that wouldn't matter if it sucked.

And even though I should've been reveling in it, soaking up every second, I couldn't quite enjoy it.

Belle.

She was both a blessing and a curse, and I was the sadist who was loving the knife's edge.

"Anything to add, Jagger?"

All eyes were on me as Joe's voice called me out of my stupid daydream. The one where there was no one else around, and I was kissing Belle like I'd done in that club.

I wasn't even sure where they were in the script, if it was somewhere in the first scene or I'd blacked out. Dangerous. Especially since I was the one who was supposed to be in charge.

"That was great." I was guessing but assumed it had gone well. "Let's continue, get through as much of it as we can before a break. Then we can split into groups and work on stage directions."

Joe nodded, scribbling on his notes. "You heard the man, let's pick it up from Lilith's monologue. Serenity, all you."

She cleared her throat, beaming with the attention and launched into an adequate read. Granted, emotion and performance weren't required for a first go-through, but I just knew Belle would've done it better.

Chase finally arrived, apologetic but still got a healthy stare down from me. I'm sure he had a suitable excuse—at least I hoped so—but I absolutely abhorred lateness. It reeked of disrespect and entitlement, like your time was somehow more valuable than anyone else's.

After the minor interruption, the cast continued, working through the first half of the script. Since concentration was starting to wane, I gave the go ahead for us to break.

"Did you notice I was early?" Belle sidled up to me, cup of coffee in hand. While her smile was warm, it wasn't flirty, which was a relief.

"I did," accepting the coffee, "but if you're looking for validation for being on time, you're probably better off speaking to Joe. And you don't have to bring me coffee, but thank you."

She laughed, shaking her head. "I know I don't *have* to, but I wanted to. And I know I impressed you, don't pretend like you wouldn't be giving me a gold star if you had one." She pinned an imaginary sticker to her forehead. "They might be scared of you." She glanced over her shoulder at some of the cast looking on slightly bewildered. "But I'm not. Serenity was even bragging about how awesome she thinks you are. Apparently, her last director had a serious coke habit and barely knew what day it was."

I chuckled lightly. "I'll take being more functional than a coke addict as a compliment, shall I?"

Her eyes widened, realizing how it might have sounded. "No, I didn't mean it like that. You're great. *Really* great. Honestly, I'm really excited to be working with you."

"Good. I'm . . ." I searched for the words, trying to make it as platonic sounding as possible. "I think you're a great addition to the cast."

It was a horrible thing to say, because as much as I believed it, I wanted to tell her how glad I was too. Her eyes didn't dim though, still bright as they always were. "Well, I better get back. I'm sure you have important director stuff to do." And without waiting for me to agree, she shot me a quick wave and headed back to her seat.

I watched curiously as she took out her script and started scribbling furiously. More interesting since we hadn't discussed it, and she hadn't even read. But whatever she was writing, she was committed to, her hand working across the page before flipping to another part.

"Did you have any notes for me?" Serenity looked at me before looking over at Belle, who was ignoring us both. "She's enthusiastic, I'll give her that, but I'm never sick."

I cleared my throat, wondering if that had been part of Belle's plan. She didn't seem vindictive enough to be trying to make Serenity insecure, so I assumed she was justifying our interaction so no one would be suspicious. It had been so seamless I hadn't even noticed.

Oh, she was *good*.

"Actually, I do. Let's go sit with Chase and I'll work through them with the both of you." I gestured to Joe, signaling I was done with the break. "Joe can work with the ensemble."

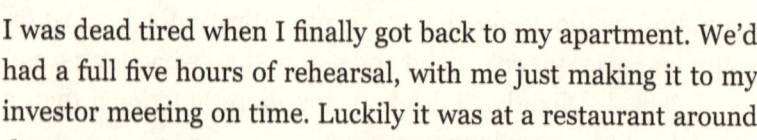

I was dead tired when I finally got back to my apartment. We'd had a full five hours of rehearsal, with me just making it to my investor meeting on time. Luckily it was at a restaurant around the corner, which meant I could literally walk.

It went as expected. Figures, projections, money people looking for promises that they were going to get a return on their investment. And as much as I knew it was part of the business, I hated the feeling of needing to grovel. They didn't care about my script or my vision, just as long as I could turn a profit. So I answered their questions, assured them their money was well spent, and choked down all the *fuck yous* I'd have preferred to have said.

"Jesus, Dane!" I clutched my chest, finding my younger brother sitting on my couch as I opened my front door. "You could've called, told me you let yourself into my apartment so I didn't have a heart attack."

Dane laughed, rising to his feet. "You didn't call me back like you promised. And I didn't trust you not to find an excuse not to come home. Or have some lame meeting you had to be at."

"I *was* at some lame meeting." I sighed, tossing my keys on the sideboard before shoving his shoulder. "You bring anything to eat? I had a dinner meeting, but the food was terrible. I could either swallow their bullshit or the overcooked Alfredo, wasn't capable of doing both."

"I'll order in." Dane wandered over to my fridge, pulling out two beers. "It will give us a chance to chat."

"Come on little, bro." I sighed, tipping my head against the back of the couch as he brought over the beer. "It's been a long ass day, I'm tired and the last thing I want to do is chat."

I wasn't a talker, shocking I know. I didn't like dissecting my problems with company, taking a Gallup Poll on possible solutions. But Dane—like always—missed the memo on my preference. Or he ignored it, something he'd done from when we were teenagers. While Mom and Dad seemed indifferent to my moods, ignoring my withdrawal from their chaotic and unconventional life, Dane never did. Even though he was the younger one, the one *I* was supposed to be looking out for. Which was why he was in my apartment instead of being in Connecticut where he should be.

"Fine, I'll talk. You listen. We'll both eat." He clinked his bottle against mine as he reached for his phone with his other hand. "So what are you in the mood for? Shitty Italian food is obviously off the menu."

"Dumplings." My request was made without any further thought, my mouth craving them since my dinner with Belle. There was a minefield to psychoanalyze had I been inclined to share, but since I didn't, Dane could just believe it was random.

"Sounds good." Dane opened an app on his phone and found a local dumpling place that delivered. "So, how's Belle?" he asked casually without looking up from his screen.

"I thought we agreed I wasn't talking?" I lifted the beer to my mouth and took a swig.

"Ahhh, but you're not talking. You're answering questions. Which you could've done over the phone if you'd bothered to call me back." He pointed his beer at me and grinned. I swear, even after all these years he could still manage to maneuver himself out of an argument with almost no effort.

I threw up my hands, admitting that I had totally blown off calling him. "Fine, I didn't call because I knew what you'd say. And Dane, I don't want to hear it."

"So you're a psychic now?" Dane laughed. "Because if you are, maybe you can tell me who's gonna win the World Series. I'll give you a cut."

"Dane." I closed my eyes, exhausted from the day.

It wasn't just the rehearsal and the meeting, but being indifferent toward Belle took a whole lot of energy. It was fucking hard not to be captivated by her, to watch as she sat on the sidelines, observing, no ego, taking notes of every direction I gave Serenity like she was scribing the word of God. Jesus, if half the actors were as attentive as her, my job would be a cakewalk. I bet she'd be a fucking dream to direct, the idea of watching her on a stage sending a tingle right down to my balls.

"Just ask her out. See where it goes. You wouldn't be the first or the last guy to date one of the people you work with."

"You're not serious," I scoffed, the idea so freaking ridiculous. "Either people will think she only got the part by sucking my dick, or I'm sexually harassing her. Neither is a positive outcome."

Besides not wanting that drama, I didn't want it for Belle. Because as bad as it would be for me, it would infinitely be worse for her.

"So I can date her then?" Dane shrugged with a wicked grin on his face. "We'd make a great couple."

My brow arched, knowing given half a chance he'd date Belle in a heartbeat.

"Oh relax, Jagger." He laughed. "Pack your death stare away for someone else. You know I'm joking."

"Do I? Because I'm not sure I know shit right now." And wasn't that the truth. How this woman had turned my world upside down was a mystery.

Dane relaxed into the couch, looking at me with expectation like he did when he wanted to get his way. "There are ways around it."

"How so?" I asked, curious to see what his workaround would be.

He shrugged, putting his bottle on the table. "You assign her to your assistant director. Technically you don't pay her, the production does, so if Joe's responsible for her direction, you're not really her boss anymore. She's the understudy. So assuming she does eventually get the tap on the shoulder to fill in, at most you'll be giving small corrections and stage directions on the fly. And anyone who's ever met you knows you're impartial, you're indifferent to everyone equally." He laughed, thoroughly enjoying himself.

"Uhhhhh." I scrubbed my face with my hand. He wasn't wrong per se. I *didn't* pay her. And if I was no longer her direct report, then it would *probably* be okay, especially if I came clean and everything was above board. It would look so much worse if we snuck around, assuming she was even interested. And that was a big IF.

"Things were a lot easier when I was the one giving advice." I pushed his shoulder, glad he'd come to visit even if the topic of conversation wasn't preferrable. "Why don't we talk about your love life instead."

"Nah, I'm not seeing anyone. Although I was considering signing up for some dating apps." A smirk spread across his face.

Of course he was kidding. Dane didn't need an app to find a date, he just needed to walk out to the street and loiter awhile. "Great, let me know how that works out for you."

"Well, Mom did say it had been an age since she'd been to a wedding. We both know they'll probably die waiting for yours." He laughed, picking up his beer and taking a sip. "Unless . . ."

"Wow, we went from me dating her to marrying her in not even a minute. The pressure to produce an heir is on you, little brother. Let's be honest, that's who they'd prefer it be anyway."

Dane shook his head, putting his beer back on the table. "Jagger, I know our parents are complicated. And as far as upbringings, ours was a little fucking weird. But they *do* love you. You can pretend you're not part of the family, but it doesn't make it true."

Great, another topic of conversation I didn't want to have.

"Dane—"

"Jagger, look. I get it." He cut me off, not letting me finish. "You have to wear the weight of expectation a lot more than I do, especially since you're biologically theirs."

"Don't even start with that shit!" I pointed at him, not ever thinking about him as anything other than my brother. "You're as much theirs as I am."

As much as I hated giving credit to the self-absorbed people that raised us, they never—and I do mean never—treated Dane like he wasn't theirs. In some ways, I feel like he was more a Hartley than I was. His ability to be a part of their world, forgive their idiosyncrasies, and adapt to it all was something I was a little jealous of. Not that I ever hated him, because I just didn't have it in me. But sometimes I think he was the son they'd wanted *me* to be.

"To us, yes, but to the rest of the world, you're the only real Hartley. Not that I give a shit." Dane chuckled because he had this uncanny ability to let that stuff roll off his back. "But at the end of the day, you can't keep running from who you are. They're part of you, Jagger. Sure, some of it is fucked up, but there's good in them too. And *that's* the part in you. You're the only one who can't see it."

I was saved from further therapy by the buzzer. "Food, thank god." Lifting my ass off of the couch, I moved to my front door and hit the release for the external door. I was starving, and the opportunity to fill Dane's face so he couldn't give me the same speech he usually did was really appealing.

"Just think about what I said. About Belle. And about Mom and Dad." He disappeared into the kitchen to go get cutlery while I waited at the door for the delivery guy and after tipping him, I carried the bag back to the coffee table.

Dane had his phone in his hand, looking . . . fuck, I don't know, concerned, perplexed, confused?

And usually that look meant bad things. Like Dad had decided he needed *both* his sons to be at the gallery opening for a press call. Or Mom wanted to farm me out as a date for a daughter of one of her friends. And I wasn't interested in either.

"What?" I asked, wondering if Hartley Inc. had taken a slight bump in stock prices. "If they're texting you and telling you to—"

"Shut up for a second, will you." He held up his hand and pressed the screen on his phone.

And when he flipped his phone around and showed me, a video started, a powerhouse blonde belting out "Defying Gravity" while standing on top of a chair at some bar.

Belle.

The video was Belle.

"What the hell?" I took the phone, checking the time and date stamp, wondering when the hell it was posted. "Is this old?"

"It was uploaded twenty minutes ago. Mable's Karaoke Bar. Manhattan." He took his phone back. "You're tagged. I have a Google alert for all our names."

I wasn't going to even ask why he had an alert set up for all our names, because the less I knew what the press was saying about me, the better. But why the hell had I been tagged on the video?

"What does it say?" I dared ask, praying some asshole hadn't picked up on the crazy chemistry I was trying to deny. I'd been careful in front of the cast, and so had she, surely no one suspected anything. And even if they did, we hadn't done anything really. One kiss? Hung out a little? Nothing *really* inappropriate.

"Says new addition to Jagger Hartley's new stage show, the best kept secret in town."

Guess I should be relieved it didn't say Jagger Hartley's newest *addiction,* which would have been more accurate. And the reason why seeing her—even on a screen—made me feel crazy inside.

"You said twenty minutes ago?" I ran my hands through my hair. "You start dinner without me, I'll eat when I get back."

He didn't even argue, ask me what I intended to do when I got there, or try to talk me out of it. Instead, he put the bag of dumplings in the fridge and grabbed my keys from the sideboard. "Let's just pick up a burger on the way. And I'm coming with you."

"Dane—" I warned, not sure I needed any additional complications.

"C'mon, big brother, I'll be on my best behavior."

It was pointless arguing, especially when there was no time. For all we knew she could've sung that song and left. Or gotten bored in the time it took getting from Brooklyn to Manhattan and moved to another bar. And even though I was dog tired and starving, I wanted to see her.

"Fine. But I'm driving." I took back my keys. "And if you flirt with her, you're walking home."

"Understood." Dane laughed. "Now let's go see the best kept secret in town."

Fuck.

Chapter 14

Belle

"I have to work tomorrow." Zara eyed the shot glasses in front of her, opting to switch to soda instead. "Not everyone has a noon start time."

"Psssshhhh." I laughed, lifting a shot glass and handing it to Hayley. "We're celebrating. Bobbie's first sleepover with grandma," Hayley cheered, having not had a proper night out in forever, "and my exciting new job as Serenity's backup."

We clinked glasses and downed our shots. I wasn't even sure what we were drinking, something sugary sweet that tasted more lethal than it probably was.

"I can't get too drunk." Hayley licked her lips, both of us only slightly buzzed. "I have to pick up Bobbie at nine from my mom's and a hangover with a baby will suuuuuuuuuuck."

I waved my hand, dismissing her concerns. "I've got rehearsal at noon, I can't afford to be wasted either. Jagger will have a fit if I show up less than bright-eyed and bushy-tailed."

"Ahhh yes, Jagger." Zara smirked, ordering us another round that looked suspiciously like ice water. "How's that all going? Managing to keep your hands to yourself?"

"Pleeeeeeeease." I rolled my eyes with all the drama. "That is nevvvvver going to happen. The kiss was a freak of nature. He was drunk or had an out-of-body experience, I'll be happy to just be his friend at this point."

As much as I wanted to kiss Jagger—which I did, very, very much—I really wanted to be his friend too. I wanted to be in his life, be that person he could go dancing with every once in a while, not judge him. And while I had no idea what kind of people he had in his life, I was positive they weren't anywhere near as fun as I was. And he needed that. Even if he didn't know it, he needed that.

"Well, it's not like he can ignore you." Zara chuckled. "Especially not now."

"Why not now?" I asked, sipping my glass before waving the bartender back over. "We don't have to get drunk, but can we at least do a few more shots before switching to water?"

Zara sighed, shaking her head as I ordered more Jelly Donuts, which was what we'd apparently been drinking. "Because I uploaded the video of you."

I chuckled, not really concerned about a video of me singing being out in the wild. "He probably doesn't even surf the internet. It's too mainstream." I laughed out loud. "I bet he has some ancient typewriter and he reads the newspaper in its original form."

"Oooooh, so retro." Hayley grinned. "That's kinda hot though."

My finger waved at her accusingly. "Not helping."

Who cared if he saw the video or not, it's not like there wasn't a dozen clips of me singing, dancing or doing audition pieces online already. It was literally in our best interest to be seen, hoping someone important would stumble on something and then give us our big break. Or the video went viral, which was just as good.

But none of that had happened for me, despite my best efforts. And it was totally fine because I just knew that when it was my time, I'd get my shot. Serenity was looking a little *peaky* earlier in the day, maybe she was getting the flu.

Zara just grinned, ignoring her Jelly Donut and sticking to water. "Sure. Whatever."

She was being cockier than usual, which might have been suspect except since getting together with Lincoln, she'd picked up some extra smugness from him.

"Just pretend to have a good time, Zara. I know you'd rather be tucked up in bed with your hot fiancé, doing obscene things, but celebrating is important." Besides, she could defile him when we got home, and I was unconscious. Thank goodness we had great insulation, and I wasn't subjected to their debauchery. Lincoln's old roommate Dr. Nate was still traumatized.

"Oooooooh, it's my turn to sing!" Hayley jumped from her barstool as her name was called over the microphone. "Get ready for my triumphant return." She did a pirouette before bounding toward the small stage.

Zara's eyes followed Hayley as she grabbed the mic, ready for her colorful rendition of "Baby Got Back." "I don't say it enough, but I'm really proud of you, Belle."

"Awwwwww." I waved my hand, knowing I'd get emotional if she started with the big sister stuff. "If you're trying to make me cry so we can go home early, think again. I'm wearing waterproof mascara and I have at least one more song on the list."

And since I had no idea when I'd actually get to sing for a paying audience, I was taking my opportunity with the fine people at Mable's. Besides, they loved us here. Anytime someone stepped up and didn't do a horrible white-girl version of Beyoncé or something similar, the crowd went wild. And I had no problem with giving my ego a little boost.

Hayley bounced all over the stage, singing her heart out about liking big butts, and as predicted, the applause was deafening. She curtsied, the smile plastered across her face as she made her way back to where we were at the bar.

"Yay!!" I cheered as she slid back onto her barstool. "See, Jagger isn't the only one who can do retro."

Funny how I'd been actively trying to not think about him, and yet he found his way into my thoughts anyway. Gah. It was a sickness.

"Speaking of Jagger." Zara pointed to the doorway before feigning shock. "I wonder how that happened?"

"What the hell." I tried to swallow, a gust of air expelling from my lungs. "What did you do, Zara?"

Holy.

Shit.

Not one Hartley, but two had entered, both Jagger and Dane looking mighty freaking fine as they stood at the entrance glancing around. Jagger was wearing the same clothes from earlier, his chin covered in some late evening stubble while Dane looked fresh pressed in a designer suit and a mischievous glint in his eye. *Were they looking for me?*

Even though I knew I wasn't that drunk, I was positive I currently didn't possess the motor skills to walk and talk at the same time. And what would I even say, anyway? Maybe it was just some weird-ass coincidence, like how Zara met Lincoln at the hospital, even though he wasn't really the guy she was looking for.

"Belle." Zara waved her hand in front of my face, causing me to blink. "Did you hear what I said?"

"No, no I did not." I shook my head, trying to concentrate. "What did you do and why is he here?"

"I tagged him and the venue in the post. I had a hunch he'd end up seeing it." She chuckled, looking very pleased with herself. "Figured he needed to see what talent he had under his nose."

Interfering was very out of character for Zara. In fact, out of the two of us, it was usually me who pulled shit like that. But I guess after all the years, I had some payback coming. And if she had to sit at a karaoke bar on a worknight, after hearing how much I thought Jagger was soooo beautiful and soooo talented, she was going to entertain herself.

She still thought he was bad news. Warned me not to go *there* especially since we were working together. But true to my darling sister's unending support, she'd encourage me to go for my dreams even if they didn't align with hers. Even if she thought I was making the biggest mistake of my—

"Jagger." It slipped from my lips as he found his way in front of me.

It seemed that in the time I was having my internal crisis he and Dane had spotted us from the doorway and shuffled through the crowd.

"Belle." My name used as a greeting and a response.

The air between us crackled, charged with electricity, or sexual tension, or maybe it was the off-key squawk coming out of the speakers. But I wasn't questioning it, excited, nervous and energized all at the same time.

"I'm Zara." My sister held out her hand. "We didn't get a chance to meet when you were in my apartment."

Her smile was smooth, as was her introduction, Jagger taking the offer of a handshake. "I'm Jagger and this is Dane."

"Yes, Hartley. I'm aware." Her lips smoothed into that knowing grin that said, I know who you are and why you're here. Which meant at least one of us did. Spoiler alert: it wasn't me.

"And I'm Hayley," my gorgeous friend interjected. "Hi, Dane." She completely ignored Jagger and fluttered her eyelashes at his attractive younger brother. It had been a while since she'd been on a date, and Dane was really good-looking. Not in the same sexy, cool way Jagger was, but hot in all the right measures.

"Hi, Hayley, I'm Dane." He reciprocated her attention, the smoldering look in his eyes rolling over her in ways that was indecent for a public establishment.

Ok, maybe I was a little drunker than I thought.

"So, what brings you here? You planning on getting up on stage?" I pointed to the petite redhead murdering a rendition of Celine Dion's "My Heart Will Go On," hoping to refocus the conversation. I was grasping at straws, my mind thinking of all the dirty things I'd do to Jagger if I could push him into a dark corner.

"We saw the video," Dane added, turning his attention back to me. "Belle, you are extremely talented. We had no idea you could sing like that."

"Oh, that." I laughed, glad for the partial buzz I had from the earlier shots. "We were just playing."

Which was partly true. I'd also noticed he'd said "we," which seemed to indicate both himself and someone else. And since he was with Jagger, one would assume the "we" included him. Unless he was talking in rich-person speak where they referred to themselves in third person or plural to make themselves more important. Dane didn't seem like an asshole though.

"Is that what you call unauthorized social media announcements about your involvement with my project?" Jagger's brow arched. "Playing?"

"What would that be?" Zara asked, her words so measured and confident that even I was impressed.

Dane laughed, flipping over his phone and playing a video of me singing.

Zara's brow rose. "Huh, well looks like Belle has a fan. Since her involvement was made public on Monday, it's not really a secret, is it? And considering *she* didn't upload anything, there was no violation. In fact, not sure who posted that video." Zara waved her hand around the bar. "Could've been anyone here."

Ooooooooh, Zara was good.

And as much as I would've loved to see her in an intellectual pissing match with Jagger, I was more concerned about whether he was *actually* mad or just his default annoyance like he usually was.

He didn't look mad.

But I'd lost the ability to be impartial.

Jagger's lips twitched, like he wanted to smile but was worried it didn't fit whatever narrative he had going on in his head.

"I didn't post the video, Jagger." I felt the need to clarify. I stopped short of saying I didn't know who posted it, because I knew exactly who it was, and she shared my DNA.

"Can I talk to you for a minute? In private." Jagger's voice softened, his head tipping to the side.

"We're in a bar, Jagger." I laughed, looking around. "Where do you want to go?"

I mean, there were bathrooms.

A janitor's closet.

Surely someone had an office we could break into.

It wasn't like there weren't private areas around even if they weren't technically available.

But I'd been drinking. And it was hard enough to keep my mouth and hands off him when I was completely sober, I wasn't trusting myself if we went somewhere *private*.

"Outside?" he suggested, his hand resting on my arm. And while at first I assumed he was kidding, there wasn't any humor in his face or his voice.

Maybe he was mad.

"Belle, you don't have to go anywhere." Zara ignored Jagger and Dane, pegging me with a look. "He can say whatever he wants right here."

"It's fine, Zara," I reassured her, confident I could handle myself. "I've got a few minutes before my next song, I can step outside and see what Mr. McGrumpy Pants wants."

Jagger didn't even try to hide his eye roll, but seemed pleased I'd agreed. But if he thought we were going outside so he could yell and be all mad and bossy, then he was in for a shock.

Straightening my spine, I gestured to the exit and then turned and walked toward it. I didn't check to see if he was following, feeling the weight of his gaze on me as I strode to the door.

It was hot and sweaty in the bar, probably intensified by the alcohol and the singing dancing combo, the air noticeably cooler outside.

Or maybe it was just his mood, the steely gaze he had on me making my skin tingle as I turned to face him as we found ourselves on the sidewalk.

"What, Jagger?" I planted my hands on my hips, not giving him the opportunity to speak first. "I didn't post the video, okay. And who cares, anyway? There are a million videos," *okay slight exaggeration but whatever*, "of me out there. Annnnnnnnnnnnd," I continued, "I was totally professional today. Turned up on time. Didn't give you googly eyes, didn't kiss you or touch your hot ass."

Wait.

What?

That wasn't what I'd meant to say, my hand slapping across my mouth as I did my best to shut myself up. For all my declarations of being professional, it was all shot to shit.

Damn those Jelly Donut shots!

"My *hot* ass?" Jagger asked like he hadn't heard me perfectly fine the first time.

Trying to pretend I didn't say it was beyond me, and I was too far in the mess to try to smooth it over anyway. And besides, he did have a hot ass, surely this wasn't news. If he wanted to fire me because I said he had a hot ass, then so be it. That was a hill I was willing to die on.

"Jagger." The fresh air making me feel more alert as I lowered my hand from my mouth. "You." I pointed to his chest. "Have a *hot* ass. Granted, most people are too scared to make direct eye contact with any part of you." I waved to his body like the forbidden vessel it was. "But even risking a horrible fate, there is no denying it."

"Just my ass?" he questioned.

No smirk.

Like he was seriously asking if it was just his ass that was hot or if the parts attached to the ass were hot as well.

I blinked, weighing my options as to whether I was being baited or if this was a valid request and I had an obligation to set him straight.

Shit.

I was terrible at keeping my mouth shut.

Terrible.

Literally unable to bite my tongue and smile politely when I had a lot to say.

My lips pressed together, giving my best valiant effort to not completely blow it.

His brow rose, silently daring me.

"Fine!" I snapped, figuring there was no point trying to stop. "No, not just your ass. All of you," I waved my hands animatedly around him, "is hot. Really hot."

"And you want to touch me?" He leaned in closer, his voice ridiculously erotic and husky.

"God, yes," I admitted, because really, I was terrible at lying. "Am I fired?" I cringed, wondering if it was possible to openly admit you wanted to maul your boss and still expect to have a job.

I mean, surely I got points for honesty.

And we weren't at work.

He pushed out a hard breath, looking around at the people milling around on the street. No one was really paying us any attention, but I probably wouldn't have noticed anyway.

"No. You're not fired."

"Well, that's a relief." My hand fluttered at my chest. Not to say that it wasn't a changing situation but at least currently, I was still gainfully employed. "We should probably go back in." My eyes moved back to the door. "I'm not sure when my song is coming on and Zara will probably come out here and—"

OH.

MY.

GOD.

I couldn't finish my sentence because Jagger was kissing me.

KISSING.

ME.

On. The. Mouth.

Did it only happen when one of us was drunk? Or at a club? Or—shut up brain and enjoy it.

My hands threaded through his hair, leaning into his amazing, well-toned body that was so unbelievably hot. I mean, I had told him I'd wanted to touch him. I figured I might as well do it while I could.

"Mmmmmmm." He hummed his approval.

Great.

I was so getting fired.

Chapter 15

Jagger

I wasn't her boss.

I repeated it at least a million times before I kissed her.

And in the end, I didn't care, because she looked so beautiful, and she'd just told me she wanted to touch my ass.

It was a miracle I'd been able to wait as long as I had, wanting to press her up against the outside wall as soon as we'd cleared the exit.

"Please tell me you remember kissing me before," she mumbled against my mouth, her hands stretching down to grab my ass. "Please tell me you weren't completely drunk."

"Are you completely drunk now?" I managed to get out between kisses, not wanting to waste time on words. "And I remember everything about these beautiful pink lips."

I'd dreamt about those lips, imagined her mouth more times than was reasonable. It was an obsession, an unhealthy addiction that I knew I needed to quit but sought no fucking remedy for. And I promised myself that if I ever got the chance again, it wouldn't just be her mouth that I tasted.

My cock pulsed in my pants, getting harder as she rocked against it and I tried to pull away. "Now how drunk are you?"

"Buzzed but not impaired. I can make sound judgments." She pulled me closer, leaving no doubt she wanted it too.

Her response was so quintessentially Belle and it made me laugh. "Good, because I'm not going to stop at just kissing you, Belle, and I need to know this is what you want."

I'd slept with my fair share of women, some of who I really didn't care much about. They didn't care much about me either so I guess I felt justified in the transaction. But she was different, and regardless of how much I wanted her, I wasn't going to fucking touch her unless she was absolutely sure.

A car horn blared from the road, some asshole hanging out his window screaming something at the car in front of him. And while I hated being pulled away from that moment, the suspended reality where nothing else mattered, I was not going to fucking maul her in the street.

"Don't stop." Her mouth moved against my jaw, standing on tippy-toes as she craned her neck to reach. She was so delicate and small yet resilient and strong. A contradiction I might never recover from.

"Belle, we're outside. I'm not fucking you up against a wall." I tried to rein in my breathing, hoping my balls would chill out because they were just fine with that plan.

"We're gonna have sex?" She blinked back, a little surprised. "Don't say things you don't mean, Jagger."

"Yeah, we're gonna have sex, Belle." My hand grazed against her cheek, unable to stop what I felt was inevitable. I wanted her. Intoxicated so deeply that I was beyond making reasonable choices. And staying away from her was no longer an option. "But not here."

My eyes followed the lines of her throat as she swallowed, her beautiful eyes fixed on mine. "But I still get to work for you, right? You're not going to have sex with me and *then* fire me, are you? Because my career isn't a bargaining chip, Jagger. You're really hot, and I've wanted to sleep with you since being stuck in that car with you. But I'm not some bimbo who will throw away my chance at success for a one-night stand."

It was refreshing to hear, if not a little sobering. But there'd be a cold day in hell before I'd be the reason she'd risk anything. And I sure as shit wasn't interested in a one-night stand either.

"I called Joe from the car on the way over here," I confessed, the stupid drive taking longer than it should and making me thirty-five times crazier than I'd been back at my apartment. "He's going to be directing you from now on. The production pays you, not me. Technically, I'm not really your boss anymore."

It was funny how all the shit Dane had said to me felt unattainable and ridiculous. Stupid even. I wasn't an animal who couldn't control myself. She was a beautiful, talented woman, I was insanely attracted to but there would be others, right?

Wrong!

And somewhere between seeing that video and walking into that club, I didn't feel like I had many other options left.

I couldn't walk away.

Fuck knows, it would be easier.

But Jesus if Belle wasn't impossible to ignore.

"Wait, what does that mean?" Her brows furrowed, her breaths coming out in short sharp bursts and I couldn't tell if she was excited or mad.

And I fucking liked that I didn't know. That there'd always be an element of guessing when it came to Belle.

"It means," I brought her a little closer, my hands anchoring on her hips, "that I want you. But I'm not prepared to fuck everything up because of it. So if you want it too—"

"Yes!" She jumped, my hands catching her as she wrapped her legs around my waist. "I want this."

"Good. But we're still outside," I reminded her, my hands squeezing her ass. "What are we going to do about your sister and friend?"

Honestly, I didn't care about being rude, but I knew Belle did. And since Dane had ridden in the car with me, I guess I was responsible for him too. Shit was a lot easier when I didn't give a fuck.

"Oh, my god!" Belle's hand went to her mouth. "We're celebrating and I have another song."

I nodded, unable to help myself from smiling. "Yeah, I know. Which is why I brought it up."

If I had to sit in the bar for another hour, listen to her sing, and get a stare down from her sister to get Belle at the end of the night, it would be worth it. I'd probably do more than that too. Not to say I was pleased about the idea, but I'd do it.

Her eyes searched mine, a pleading look passing through them for a second before she made up her mind. "We're going back in. You're going to be nice to Zara and Hayley and I'm going to sing. Then we're going to leave."

"That's your plan?" I laughed, wondering how she was going to explain her sudden need to leave with me. "What about Dane?" I teased.

"Shit. Do we need to drive him home?"

As much as I loved my brother, driving him back across state lines would've been my limit. Thankfully he'd driven himself into the city, so that wasn't a problem. And while his car was still parked outside my apartment, he'd be fine saying his goodbyes and then grilling me later. "Dane's a big boy, he'll be fine."

"No, no, no. Just promise me you're not going to change your mind." She grabbed my face with her small delicate hands, holding me still. "No changies, Jagger. You are going to take me to your bed. We're going to have sex."

I'd never had to promise a woman I was going to fuck her before, but for Belle I'd do a lot more than that. "I'm not going to change my mind."

There was still a chance *she* might, but I wasn't going to get hung up on the stupid possibilities. Instead, I enjoyed the feel of her as she dropped her legs and slithered down my body. "If you're trying to make me harder, you needn't bother," I groaned, my dick still on board with sex in the street.

"Oh, am I responsible for that?" She fluttered her eyelashes innocently, her pretty pink lips edging into a grin. "I mean, I wasn't sure that was for me."

"You know it's for you. Now let's go get this over with." My head tipped toward the door.

"Be nice," she warned, giving me a stern finger wave before swaying her ass right back into the club.

Fucking great.

My eyes lifted to the night sky.

My balls officially hated me.

Chapter 16

Jagger

I was fucking nice.

Sat there while her sister gave me the stink eye and Belle sang her next song. It was "River" by Bishop Briggs and not sure if that had been her original choice or she'd changed it just for me. In any case, Belle could've walked out of that bar with any man—or woman—after she stepped off that stage, in what had to be the sexiest, erotic version of fucking karaoke I'd ever seen.

Dane and Hayley were either too busy eye fucking each other or had lost interest to even notice I had my hands all over Belle. And while Zara didn't seem pleased, she didn't say a word when Belle announced she was leaving with me.

Belle of course insisted we drive Dane back with us, even though my younger brother was more than capable of getting his own ride. But I didn't want to waste time arguing, saying our goodbyes to Hayley and Zara, and me pretty much breaking every speed limit between Manhattan and Brooklyn.

"Bye, Dane, talk soon." I didn't even wave as I parked. "Belle, let's go."

Dane laughed, smug that he'd been right. I hadn't been able

146

to stay away, and for whatever reason, he felt he was somehow responsible for the push. "Bye, Jagger."

Fuck it.

I didn't give a shit who wanted to take credit, the debate took up mind space I didn't have while I was anxious to get upstairs and get Belle where I wanted her.

Under me.

Belle was more polite, giving Dane a hug goodbye as she got out of the car. "I'll give you Haley's number if you want. She's super sweet—"

"Belle." I shook my head, unsure of whether she was stalling or genuinely trying to play matchmaker. I just couldn't tell. And as much as I wanted to rip her clothes off, the guessing game she kept me on just made me more turned on. "You can text him later."

Not sure if it was my clipped tone, or the look I was giving her, but their dialogue was cut short as she sidled up to me. "So cranky."

"You know this, yet you're here." I chuckled, kissing the top of her head as we watched Dane leave.

Never had I been so relieved to see him go, praying there were going to be no more distractions as we made our way to my apartment.

"You're pretty quick on those locks." Belle played with her bottom lip as I opened my front door and pulled her inside. "Do you pretend there is a serial killer chasing you, and you need to get inside?"

"You're insane." I pressed her against the wall as I relocked the door. Wasn't going to take the risk of any unexpected visitors, and now I had her alone, I needed to touch her. "The only thing I was thinking about was you."

"Me?" she asked innocently, arching against my body like she didn't already know how turned on I was. "What were you thinking about exactly?"

"How beautiful and sexy you are, and how much I've wanted to do this." I pressed my lips against hers, swallowing her moan.

"Wow, Jagger." She gasped, her hands wrapping around my back. "I think I want to know what else you've been thinking about."

"You know I'm not big on talking, how about I show you instead." I pulled her from the wall and pinned her body against mine. The ridge of my cock strained against my pants, her eyes rolling back in satisfaction as I lined myself up just right.

"Ooooohhhhhh." It was halfway between a moan and a groan, my hands guiding the rock of her hips. Even with the barriers between us, I could tell I was hitting her exactly where she needed, her breath coming out in faster, more desperate bursts.

I could've made her come just like that, fully clothed, rubbing her up against my dick. But I wanted more, to have her on my bed—naked—so I could enjoy watching every single minute of what I'd imagined at least a hundred times.

As her legs wrapped around me trying to find more friction, I lifted her and carried her to my bedroom.

My lips didn't leave hers, kissing her, savoring her, tasting her as I took each step, our mouths only parting as I lowered her onto my mattress so I could look at her.

She was . . . fucking edible.

Her blond hair was sprayed across my dark comforter, dark lashes framing her light brown glassy eyes. "Don't stop," she begged as she tried to pull me down with her. "Jagger, please don't stop."

"Not a chance," I promised, moving my mouth to her neck as I licked her hot skin.

If there was a way I could make her clothes disintegrate without needing to take them off, I'd have done it in a heartbeat. But since eyeing them with contempt didn't do the trick, I moved my hands to her body and stripped off the layers that were offending me.

"Slow down," her hands moved to my face, "I'm not going anywhere."

"You think I'm impatient because I'm worried you might leave?" I kissed her, unhooking her bra and palming her tits. "Belle, I've wanted this since the first moment I saw you, I'm dying here."

It wasn't like me to be so honest, or give anyone the advantage. Admitting I was at her mercy was vulnerability I didn't want to show. But with Belle, whatever I thought I wanted went out the window.

She stretched on my bed, arching her back as she sucked in a breath. "You want me, Jagger?" Her hand trailed down my still-clothed torso, her nipples hardening as I watched her chest rise and fall. "Then maybe you should take your clothes off."

It was a simple enough request but meant I had to give up touching her.

Not happening.

Which is when I decided to delegate. "You do it."

It was one of the few times she didn't argue, getting her fingers busy as I moved my mouth to one of her breasts. I sucked her nipple, feeling it get hard as I rolled it with my tongue, a moan escaping her lips as she tried to concentrate and take off my shirt.

"C'mon, Belle. You can do better than that." I chuckled, moving my hand down between her legs and slipping into her underwear.

She was warm and wet, grinding against my hand as she managed to get my shirt off. I helped by kicking off my shoes, sliding a finger inside of her as her focus moved to my pants.

"So good." She panted, her colorful pink nails wrestling with the button and zip of my pants while my thumb circled her clit.

My dick wanted to be where my hand was, straining against my boxer briefs as she yanked them down with my pants. My cock sprung free, bobbing a few times before she wrapped her small hand around it and gave it a long, firm tug.

"Jesus." My head dropped, sucking in a breath as I looked down between us and saw what she was doing with her hand. She'd edged her body to the side, shifting from under me while I was distracted by the view.

"I want to kiss it." Her tongue trailed along her beautiful full lips, teasing me with promise as my fingers slid out of her panties. "Let me kiss you, Jagger, and then I'll let you kiss me."

Such an innocent request except there was nothing innocent about it. And while I wanted to rip off her panties and 'kiss' her first, she'd already yanked my pants down my hips and pressed her soft plump lips on the head of my cock.

"Fuck," I groaned, closing my eyes as her delicate tongue circled the crown, my abs tensing as her mouth opened wide as she took a slow, deliberate lick.

I was going to lose my mind.

Neither one of us was even fully naked yet, and I was going to come in her mouth like it was the first time I'd ever gotten a blowjob.

Deciding to at least give the appearance I had some control, I grabbed what was left of my clothes and tore them off. She ignored my effort, licking and sucking my cock while I stripped, completely unperturbed by my movements.

It was only when I was completely naked and ready to move back onto the bed when she took my entire length into her mouth.

"Mmmmmm," she hummed against my shaft, pulling me deeper into her throat as my balls drew up tight. And unless I wanted it to be over before it even began, I needed to pull my cock from the freaking paradise that was her mouth.

"You want me to come in your mouth?" I asked, grabbing the base of my dick and sliding it out of her shiny lips with a pop. "You've had your turn, now I want mine."

Knowing arguing was like breathing for Belle, I shifted between her legs before she could protest. My hands traveled up her smooth skin, her thighs parting for me on command as my thumb returned to her clit.

Circling her through the fabric of her panties, I felt her get even wetter, systematically edging down her underwear as I continued to rub.

"That feels . . ." She left the sentence trailing, little contented sighs slipping past her lips as I pulled down the scrap of lace and put my mouth where my hand had been. "Oh. My. God."

The gasp was all I needed, pressing my tongue against her and slowly lapping against her clit.

Her hands threaded in my hair, her hips bucking against me as she tried to fuck my face. I loved how unrestrained she was, chasing her pleasure as I licked, sucked and kissed her.

"More," she begged, one of her hands moving to her nipple and playing with it while my tongue plunged inside her. I was painfully hard, fucking the mattress underneath me as I plunged two fingers inside her.

"Ahhhhh." Her back arched, her inside walls clamping down on my fingers as I continued devouring her. I wanted her to come, to feel and watch her unravel for me and know it was only for me.

"That's it, Belle." I kissed the inside of her thighs, watching the desperate rocking of her hips against my hand. "I can feel how close you are for me."

"I want to . . . to . . ." she stalled out, unable to find whatever word she was looking for as my tongue flicked against her center.

"You can have whatever you want," I assured her, the smile creeping up my face as I felt her get closer. "But for once you're going to let me be in control."

Her lips parted as quick, desperate breaths pushed out, her body writhing against the bed as I kissed her clit one last time. She didn't even need to tell me she was there, feeling the pulsing against my fingers as she tipped over the edge, the trail of "oh my god, oh my god," echoing through her shaky lips.

She coated my tongue, her body convulsing in little waves as I teased out what was left of her orgasm. I loved the way it felt, the tightness around my fingers squeezing me as she came undone.

"You're so fucking beautiful." With one last pump, I slid out my fingers and rolled to my side. I wanted to touch her, kiss her smooth skin from her adorably painted toes to the sexy curve of her neck. "I could look at you for hours."

She turned toward me, her breathing still scattered as her hand wrapped around my hard cock.

My teeth clenched as I hissed, the feel of her small palm against me turning me on more than a hand job ever should.

"I was supposed to be kissing this." Her lips spread into a sly grin, moving her grip slowly up and then down, twisting at the tip. "Is that not allowed?"

"Is that what you want?" I gritted out, prepared to let her slowly torture me to death if it meant I got to watch her do it. "You want to suck my cock, Belle?"

"Maybe." Her shoulder lifted in a shrug, her body rising from the mattress and hovering over mine. "Or maybe I want to do something else."

"Like?" I asked, my dick an iron rod in her hands as she straddled my lap and sat on top of me. I loved my vantage point, resting my head on the pillow as my eyes feasted on every inch of her body.

She was perfect, every part of her flawlessly portioned with curves so sexy she almost didn't seem real. Her skin was so warm and soft, my hands cupping her pert tight ass as she lifted herself and rubbed against my shaft.

"Jes-sus."

I was going to black out.

Feeling her slick, hot center sliding up and down as she jerked me off was almost more than I could take. And if I thought I'd be content to just come in her mouth or hand, I had to be insane.

"Belle," I warned, my hips rocking against her core as I reminded myself I wasn't wearing a condom. "This is a dangerous game you're playing."

"Yeah?" She sighed innocently, like she didn't know she was tossing lit matches at gasoline. "Should I stop?"

In. Sane.

She was going to drive me slowly fucking insane and I was torn between letting her and needing to save what was left of my freaking balls.

"Protection," I groaned out. "Right now, Belle, or I'm going to end up doing something very stupid."

I'd never had sex without a condom.

Never.

Rich parents with a famous last name, and it was a risk I wasn't ever willing to take. But for all my determination never to be some kid's baby daddy or a mark for a girl with an agenda, I'd have tossed all of that out the window for Belle.

"Where?" she asked, rubbing the head of my cock against her opening in what could only be described as sadistic. "Tell me where, Jagger. Because I want you to fuck me."

I loved the way she said *fuck*, that dirty word coming out of her pretty little mouth just did things to me that it shouldn't. And if I'd have thought I'd been able to walk away before, there wasn't a hope now she'd told me she wanted it too.

Lifting my back off the mattress, I kissed her, feeling her grind against me as I maneuvered up the bed. Talking was no longer an option, digging through my nightstand with one hand as she moaned in my mouth.

"Jagger," she panted, her needy, slick center driving me crazy. "I want you."

And fuck did I want her too, my fingers barely functioning while I tore open the packet and sheathed myself with the condom.

Then all bets were off, lining up against her core and pulling her down on me in one swift thrust. It was tight and hot, and felt so good I almost couldn't breathe.

But the pause didn't last long, needing to move as my hands wrapped around her hips. The glide in and out of her started off slow, giving her time to adjust.

"Yeah, just like that," she breathed out, her voice thin and needy as her ass shifted and her back arched.

"Christ, Belle," I gritted out as I picked up pace, "you're driving me crazy."

If my intentions were to be slow with her, then I'd truly screwed up. My hips bucked out of control as I thrust up from under her, guiding her down as I drove in deep.

It was hard, fast and desperate, chasing a high as we moaned each other's name. I wanted to be gentler, but couldn't, the primal urge taking hold of us both as our moans turned to growls as she rode me.

"Belle." I hissed out her name, my spine tingling as I felt her core tighten around me. "That's it, baby. I can tell you're close."

I kissed her, swallowing her screams as she came hard on my cock, the pulses moving up my shaft and pushing me over the edge as I came too.

"Fuck, Belle," I panted out between kisses, unable to stop as I pumped over and over again. "You feel so good."

Her body collapsed against me, her tits pressing against my chest as we both fell back onto the mattress. My arms wrapped around her, our breathing still fast and erratic as I savored the feeling of her warm skin.

"Can't move." She chuckled, her lips nestled against the curve of my neck.

"Don't." I gripped her tighter, wanting my arms around her all night. "I'll hold you just like this."

It was ironic I'd never been much of a cuddler. Not that I didn't enjoy the tactile feeling of affection, but I really appreciated my personal space. Sure, after sex there was non-sexual intimacy, but I'd never really realized that even then, I was careful keeping my distance. An arm wrapped around, a hand on a hip—but generally two people lying side by side in proximity.

But with Belle, it was different. Her body covered me, weighed against me like a blanket as the scent of her filled my nose. I loved it. The smell of perfume or shampoo, something peachy and sweet. And I wanted her right there, on me, while I held her against me, feeling more connected than I ever did.

"You okay?" she asked, her question breaking the silence between us.

"Mmhmmm," I mumbled, kissing her. "I was just enjoying the moment where we're together and you're not being argumentative."

She laughed, her fingers pinching my side. "And wow, you weren't an asshole for that whole time either. Who knew you had it in you?"

"Oh, I'm still an asshole, Belle." I sighed, running my hand down her back. "You're just tolerating it because I made you come twice."

Her head lifted, looking into my eyes as she smiled. "Guess you'll have to keep doing it then."

"Yeah, guess I better."

And while I had no idea what the hell I was doing, I knew I didn't want to stop.

Chapter 17

Belle

I spent the night with Jagger, and it was oddly amazing. Not that I doubted he would be amazing *in* bed—that body had to be built for good things surely—but after would be a different story. Would he even want me to stay? Would I want to? Or would there be regrets on either of our parts? For as much as I liked to see myself as an optimist, I didn't have my head totally in the sand.

But the awkwardness I assumed would follow wasn't there.

There was no discussion. No diagram or in-depth study. He just wrapped his arms around me and cuddled.

The sentence in itself felt like a contradiction, and no one was more surprised than me. I laid eerily still, worried to breathe for a good five minutes, concerned that if I moved he'd spook and revert to the cold, prickly Jagger I was more familiar with. But he was warm, considerate, delicate. A softer side that was truly beautiful and welcoming.

I'll admit that at one part of the night I forgot he was a Hartley, all of my initial perceptions, ideas and even personal thoughts evaporating as he gently kissed my shoulder. And when I fell asleep, it was wrapped in his arms.

By morning my phone was filled with countless messages and texts from both Zara and Hayley. Some of which required proof of life and assurances that I knew what I was doing, while others were filled with emojis. I'll let you guess what was from who.

Jagger kissed me, tapping me lightly on the ass before pulling me into the shower. And those texts were something I'd all but forgotten by the time we'd loaded into his car and driven back to my apartment.

"Don't be late," he warned, leaving the engine still running as I lingered with one last kiss.

"Geeeez, one time and all of sudden I'm profiled." I rolled my eyes as I gently pulled away. "I'll see you at the theater soon, just need to change my clothes."

In a perfect world, we'd have drunk mimosas while we devoured french toast and sweet pastries. Then—holding hands and gazing lovingly into each other's eyes—we'd have ambled into the theatre together. But it was Jagger Hartley we were talking about and unless I had a magical, fairy vagina that could transform him, that scenario wouldn't be happening. He had an affliction to public displays of affection, add in the place where he expected respect and authority—yeah, there'd be less than zero chance. Still, he was a complicated man, and I was under no delusions I'd slept with Cuddly McCuddleson.

So with another quick goodbye and a wave, I watched as he left. My heart fluttered a little as I watched his taillights get farther, feeling slightly idiotic standing on the sidewalk. "Just don't pretend it didn't happen," I whispered, even though the only person who could hear it was me. "Please."

There was no guarantee that our hot and sexy night would be something that would continue. And while we'd both had an amazing time, and expressed mutual appreciation for each other, there was no way of knowing what was going through his head. If he'd scratched that itch finally and would move on like it'd never happened, or if he'd become insecure and get suddenly cold and distant. Or a third and final possibility, if he decided he wanted to have a relationship with me and we actually dated. Not like normal people or anything—please, not unless he was possessed by aliens—but something that would fit within our definition.

The possibilities tumbled into my head as I tried to stop them. I had a tendency to fall too fast too soon, and I couldn't let myself do that with Jagger. Not because I didn't want all those things. The relationship. The romance. Spending my nights curled against his ridiculously hot body. But because deep down I was worried I was setting myself up for a fall. I'd never really cared before, blindly following my heart. But for some reason, this one felt different. And that made me a little scared.

Shaking my head and promising myself I wouldn't over-think it, I rushed upstairs to my apartment, glad to see the place was empty. Zara and Lincoln were already at work being lawyer-ly and responsible, which meant I didn't get the double prosecution cross examination on entry and could get back out the door before I was late. Jagger's warning about not being tardy wasn't a joke, and I didn't need extra complications.

I'll admit I did go to a little extra trouble making myself look good, smiling to myself as I locked up my apartment and headed to Brooklyn with plenty of time to spare. I wasn't going to be overtly flirty with him at work or anything, that wasn't my style. But if I happened to look good and accidentally turned him on while simultaneously being brilliant, well that was just an occu-pational hazard, now wasn't it.

About half the actors were already there when I arrived. Chase—the male lead—was chatting to Joe the assistant director. We'd met briefly but he'd been more preoccupied with getting face time with Serenity and the directors than to worry about a lowly understudy like me. It used to bother me, the bullshit pecking order that dictated that somehow, we were less talented or important. And sure, I got that they were the "big stars" but it didn't cost anything to be humble and polite.

"Belle." I turned at the sound of my name, a gorgeous smiling man grinning at me. "Logan, remember?"

"Of course, I remember." I elbowed him playfully. "The second string need to stick together."

He was my male counterpart, Chase's back up should he get struck down with the flu or food poisoning or if his head suddenly became too large to fit through the theatre doors.

"Right?" He laughed, glancing over at the two men deep in conversation. "You think they're discussing the script, or which is their best side? I'm rather partial to my left." He flipped around, raising a brow as his fingers waved at the side of his face. "See, total gamechanger."

"Totally." I chuckled as I contemplated his rather good-looking visage. "Maybe *that* is what Chase is discussing. That they find a replacement who is right-faced orientated." I leaned in, dropping my voice to a whisper. "I've heard rumors that some people can't go left and believe it's unnatural."

"Noooooo," Logan gasped. "Tell me it isn't so, Belle."

I nodded, selling it for all it was worth. "I wish I could, but sadly there are face-ists among us."

"Logan. Belle." Jagger's brisk, tone pierced our bubble of giggles. His impassive face studied us as we both turned to face him. "I assume you've both gone through your scripts and are prepared for today."

"Sure have, Jagger." Logan saluted. "We were just discussing the script."

He was so seamless in his delivery that had I not been a part of the conversation, I'd have totally bought it.

Jagger, however, still looked suspicious as his eyes moved between us. "Good. You're both working with Joe."

"Great," I added, wondering if he was in a regular I-hate-everyone-mood, AKA his general disposition or if he was especially prickly. I mean, he'd been fine when he'd left me at my apartment. Happy even. So I wasn't sure if he was just trying to be professional—which for Jagger meant kinda a dick—or something had happened in the time in between.

"Now would be good." He tipped his head in Joe's direction.

"Yep, thanks." I waved, refusing to react even though part of me was a little hurt. Sure, I knew he wasn't going to put his arms around me and declare to the whole cast we were a thing, but I expected . . . I don't know, a little warmth. Even just a glimmer.

Logan matched my strides as I walked away from Jagger, my cheeks feeling hot as we headed toward Joe. It wasn't so much hurt as it was embarrassment, wondering if I'd somehow hallucinated the connection we'd shared. Maybe I'd been a challenge, and after sleeping with me, the interest was gone. Or if he was just expecting me to be his dirty little secret, ignore me during the day because I wasn't a headliner and then screw me at night. And I wasn't comfortable with either scenario.

"Hey." Logan grabbed my arm, stopping us short before we got to Joe. Our assistant director was in an animated discussion with one of the set designers so not paying us any attention. "Jagger Hartley is an asshole." His voice had dropped to a whisper. "Everyone is afraid to say it because he's our boss and brilliant." He waved his hands for effect and rolled his eyes. "But an asshole nonetheless."

And didn't that make me conflicted, because of course, yes, it was mostly true, but I'd also seen a softer side. A more vulnerable side. A tiny piece of Jagger very few were lucky to see. And that part, *that* part was most definitely not an asshole.

A long breath blew out from my lips, knowing that whatever position I was in wasn't entirely Jagger's fault. He hadn't clubbed me over the head and dragged me to his lair. And truth be told, I wasn't exactly surprised. Or maybe I was, thinking that even though he clearly had baggage and trust issues, that it would be different with me.

"I know." I shrugged, figuring it was better to agree than pretend otherwise. "It just stings a little to be put in your place."

And even though Logan probably assumed I was talking about the production, it meant so much more to me.

Vowing to not let it ruin my day or my opportunity to show everyone exactly how talented I was, I forced a smile. "Lucky for us, we don't have to see him for the rest of the day." I looped my arm around Logan's elbow. "Now let's show Joe how amazing we both are."

And with an award-winning smile, Logan shot me a wink as we continued to our "post."

"Good, I want to go through the scenes with both of you." Joe looked up at us, giving us a half-smile. "Now let's start from the beginning."

It was easy to forget everything when I was on stage. Even if technically, I wasn't on a stage but in a corner. I just loved the way it made me feel. Like I could shelve whatever problems were weighing on my mind and just explore something else, *someone* else. So it was a surprise when Joe called a break, telling us we'd been working for two hours straight. It had felt like ten minutes, but I was glad for a moment to catch my breath.

"Great work." Joe nodded his approval, looking surprised we'd needed minimal line cues.

Funny how we hadn't had a problem learning the script when we hadn't been busy maintaining a "high profile" or chatting to our publicist. Sure, it was slightly catty but I wasn't saying it out loud, so it was allowed.

"Why don't you guys get some lunch, and we'll pick up where we left off after that," Joe offered, frowning at his empty coffee cup. "I'm going to get a refill. Be back in thirty."

While larger productions often had elaborate craft services, Jagger was still small fry in Broadway terms. Which meant we had the basics—coffee, pastries, sandwiches that looked edible—but not the kind of spread that evoked excitement. So when Logan suggested we go get something to eat at a café close by, I couldn't say yes fast enough. And yeah, part of me figured it would illustrate to Jagger that I wasn't going to wait and be at his beck and call. Because fuck that.

Logan was sure to let Joe know we were stepping out as he grabbed my hand and led me outside. We both squinted, our eyes needing a minute to adjust to the sunlight after being in the darkness of the theatre.

"What do you think our chances are?" he asked, chuckling as he closed the door behind us. "Both Chase and Serenity are claiming they're *never* going to miss a show."

"It's a short run, I mean, it's plausible." I shrugged, knowing there was a very real chance I'd never get to show the world my Lilith. "But there's always hope."

He shook his head, swearing under his breath. "You're ten times the actress she is. And have you seen the way she flirts around Jagger? Could she subscribe anymore to the stereotype? Can you imagine if they slept together?" He laughed, seeming to be amused. "Like anyone would ever take her seriously again."

My blood ran cold.

Not because Serenity was possibly flirting with Jagger—that would be a footnote in a low-key therapy session on jealousy at most. But because of what Logan said. He had no idea that *I* was the one sleeping with Jagger. And if that's what he thought about her—who had a fairly impressive IMDb page and credits to her name, then what would he think of me?

Shit.

Shit.

Shit.

"You okay?" he asked when I didn't respond. At least I hoped that was what prompted him, and none of those *shits* had been actually vocalized.

"Look Logan, I'm not her biggest fan but trashing her isn't my style either. Especially since we have no evidence to know that's what's happening."

"O-kay." Logan's eyes widened, clearly not expecting my response.

"And considering if it were Chase, and the director was female, everyone would be high fiving him." I blew out in frustration. "You know, the double standard is honestly disgusting. Who cares who she sleeps with? She is clearly talented, unless you think she slept with every director she ever worked with. In which case, I'm surprised she doesn't need a freaking nap instead of a Tony."

"Belle." Logan's hands gently took my arms. "I'm sorry. You're right. I was trying to make you feel better, in the process I acted like a pig. It's honestly not who I am."

And to his credit, he looked genuinely apologetic. But he was just one guy, one person in the sea of many who probably thought the exact same thing.

I shook my head disappointed, annoyed, angry and wanting to rage against the machine all at the same time. Oh, and I was hungry too which just made things infinitely worse. "It's fine," I dismissed, not wanting to make him feel bad when he wasn't really the problem. "I just really get pissed off. It's hard enough for us to get taken seriously in this industry. To be taken on merit instead of what we look like. And that kind of attitude, no matter how much you think is a joke, doesn't help us. Can you imagine if it were me?" I asked, the truth finding its way into my question. "If they said that about *me*?"

"Belle, no one would ever accuse you of that." He gasped, looking shocked. "You're sooooooo nice."

Ahhhh, right. I was nice.

Not sure what that meant, but it wasn't reassuring.

"Belle, honestly. I'm sorry. And while I know it doesn't make up for it, let me buy you lunch. Better yet, let me take you out to dinner. So I can show you exactly what kind of guy I am."

There was no innuendo, no flirty undertext. And I could tell he was genuinely trying to make amends. "I'll let you buy me lunch." I nudged his shoulder. "But we should hurry, I don't want to get back late."

Agreeing we'd make it quick, we ducked into a small deli and grabbed a couple of sandwiches rather than a café. And while "sandwiches" were technically on offer back at the theatre, they weren't *delicious made-to-order ones filled to the brim like they were going to burst on freshly baked bread* like we got. We made small talk in between bites, sitting on the theatre steps as we finished our lunch. And while I was no longer angry at Logan, what he said weighed heavily on my mind.

Jagger looked up, his lips thinning into a tight line as we reentered the space. No one else seemed to care, busy enjoying their inferior lunch or spending quality time on their social media.

"Ahhh, good, you're back," Joe called from behind us. "You ready to pick up where we left off?"

"Of course." I smiled, ignoring Jagger who'd not taken his eyes off me since we walked in. "We're ready, aren't we, Logan?"

"Ready, willing and able," Logan added, snapping to attention by my side. "Want us back in our corner?"

"No," Jagger answered before Joe had the opportunity, prompting us all to turn our heads.

He was his usual calm, devoid of anything that would even give a hint as to what was going on in that beautiful, complicated and infuriating mind of his.

"Errr, everything okay, Jagger?" Joe asked, clearly not in with the change of plans.

"Everything is great." Jagger gave a curt nod that did nothing to reassure anyone anything was great. "But I'd like to see Belle and Logan on the main stage. Serenity, Chase—you'll be with Joe for the rest of the day."

"What?" Serenity coughed out, who was clearly not cool with being taken out of the spotlight. "But Jagger, Chase and I—"

"Will continue to work with Joe." He cut her off, leaving no room for discussion. "Belle, Logan. On stage."

Low murmurs echoed through the space as eyes swung our way. And while I wasn't sure it was a good thing—were we being called to the principal's office?—I wasn't going to let it shake my confidence. Besides, Logan and I *knew* our lines. We were prepared. So if Jagger wanted to see if either of us was screwing around, he was out of luck. And I maybe—not so quietly—was glad to have my moment to prove what I was capable of.

Serenity and Chase didn't even try to hide their displeasure or disapproval, the death stares heated as they stepped off the stage and moved to Joe's corner where we'd been working previously.

And with the stage vacated, Logan and I took our marks and waited for his direction. My heart was beating so loudly I was surprised no one else could hear it, Logan's gaze catching mine and giving me a "what the fuck" I couldn't answer.

"Take it from the fight scene." Jagger sat in his usual seat, front row and center as he gave us his full attention.

The fight scene was what I'd used for my audition, so I knew it incredibly well. And even though it was further along in the play than we were supposed to be, I wasn't going to let the lack of order unnerve me.

I nodded to Logan, signaling I was ready. The dialogue was heavy in my favor but if it's one scene I knew inside-out and back-to-front, it was that one. And I wasn't sure if Jagger was testing me, putting me through my paces, or wondering if I'd slacked off. Whatever he was thinking, he best buckle up because I was going to blow him away and anyone else who doubted I had the right to be on that stage.

Taking a breath I started, falling quickly into the headspace of the anguished, tortured Lilith who was misunderstood and underestimated.

Like I was in a trance, I delivered my lines, grasping at Logan as his character told me I'd never be more than a whore. It wasn't a rehearsal for us, the energy so intense that it felt like it was a sold-out opening night.

"You think you can change people's thoughts, Lilith? You think they care anything about you?" Logan spat out as he sneered at me with distaste. "That I care?"

"You can pretend you don't care." I lifted my chin, defiant, giving it everything I had. "But you do. They all do. Because if they didn't, why would they even notice me?"

I felt the power of those words as I spoke them, wondering if that's how Jagger felt. I wondered where the motivation for such a strong, resilient female character had come, and how in the end, she would be the one who would triumph. It was so startling how I'd never really noticed before, or given that much thought to the subject matter, his Lilith so beautifully complicated and damaged all at the same time.

I wasn't sure if Jagger had asked me to stop, or if the scene had ended the way it should. My soul feeling like it returned to my body as clapping filled the air around us.

My eyes blinked, aware that everyone—even the technical staff—had watched us, their hands unanimously applauding our effort as Logan pulled me in for a huge hug.

"Way to go, rockstar," he whispered in my ear. "That was amazing."

My eyes prickled with tears as I blinked them back, everyone looking at me with awe and adoration.

Me.

The understudy.

They were clapping for *me*.

With my fingertips, I wiped my damp eyes and started to laugh. It was ridiculous I'd become overwhelmed, it wasn't like it was the first time I'd been on stage. Or applauded. But for some reason, it just felt like more.

"Thank you." I chuckled, giving a little curtsey before turning my attention to Jagger. "Do you want us to move on to the next scene or did you want something else?"

He looked around, eyeing his two headliners before turning his attention back to us. "Next scene. Keep going. Everyone else, back to work."

And with a wave of his hand and a well-choreographed look, he dismissed our makeshift audience and dispersed the crowd.

Serenity and Chase were visibly annoyed, shooting us heated glances as they went back with Joe. Things were sure going to be frosty after, but I had bigger problems to deal with.

Like Jagger.

And what the hell happened from here.

I finally found a guy I really liked, and it could seriously screw my career.

For a smart girl, I sure could be dumb sometimes.

Crap.

Chapter 18

Jagger

She was fucking brilliant.

The kind of talent where words truly weren't enough.

And I could watch her for hours and never get bored.

It was no surprise that both Chase and Serenity wanted to meet with me after rehearsal. I'm sure they both wanted to vocalize their displeasure, when really they were probably pissing down their legs.

Maybe not Chase.

Logan was adequate, and certainly held his own. And had he not had his hands all over Belle, I might have liked him a little more. Not sure what the hell was going on there, but if she was trying to make me jealous, it was fucking working. Me, the guy who couldn't barely work up a fuck about anyone, wanted to rip the guy's hands off and stuff them down his throat.

See, who says change isn't possible.

But Serenity had to be worried. Even with her inflated ego and million-follower support group, she wasn't blind. And like it or not, Belle was the better actress.

"Jagger, I'm a little concerned with the changes you've

made," Serenity started, Chase by her side, ready to fire off his round next. He wasn't brave enough to go first of course, his rumored "big balls" were just that. Rumors. And if he could hide behind a woman and still get what he wanted, then he was all for it. Dick.

"What changes?" I asked drily, watching as the rest of the cast and crew packed up for the day. Belle was still talking to Logan, her smile wide as he joked about something. And I wanted to choke him out.

"Jagger." Serenity sighed, clearly not happy with the level of attention she was getting. "Come on, you pulled us from the stage."

I blew out a slow breath, knowing I couldn't say what was on my mind which was, *"fuck's sake, it's one fucking rehearsal. I haven't replaced you even though I probably should."* That was the second time I'd shown restraint in the last few hours, pity I wasn't going to get the recognition I deserved.

"I didn't *pull you from the stage*, Serenity." My eyes moved reluctantly from the woman I wanted to the one I was speaking to. "I wanted you to do some more in-depth character development with Joe. Which I heard went well. Logan and Belle need to be ready to step in if either of you guys are sick. I can't have them being tossed in like ring-ins at the community theatre."

Part of that was true.

Chase and Serenity did need to work on their character development. And Joe was a better people person than me. And even though I'd told Belle she was going to be working with someone other than me, I couldn't help myself. Sue me, I fucking lied. And it was one fucking time. Sure, part of it was to see what the hell Logan's issue was, because clearly I'd regressed to a fucking child. But more than that, I wanted to see her. Work with her. Watch her. Not in a fucking creepy way like a stalker, but because she awed me.

"They're not even going to be needed." Chase finally found his sack and decided to speak up. "Short of a disaster—"

"Oh, so you can predict the future now?" I scoffed, quickly losing my patience with both of them. Seriously, since when was any of this shit open to debate? "There is a reason you have a supporting cast, which includes understudies. And I'm going to run this show the best way I know how, which is what's best for the show. Now, if that doesn't align with you or you have a problem with the way I do things, I'll agree to let you break your contracts." I eyed them both hard, letting them know I wasn't screwing around. And as they saw for themselves, I wasn't going to have a hard time filling their slots. "But this isn't a democracy."

Serenity opened her mouth like she was going to say something but closed it quickly. And while I doubted it was the end of the discussion, I was positive it was the last I was going to hear about it from her. She'd have her manager or agent, or possibly her lawyer, intervene on her behalf. And I'd tell them the same thing I told her. I might have needed her initially to secure the investors, but I wasn't going to be held hostage by anyone. I'd cash in the trust fund I hadn't touched before I gave away my integrity, and would bankroll the whole thing myself.

"Well, as long as things haven't changed." Chase stood up straighter, the idiot actually believing he'd somehow come out of the conversation with a favorable outcome. Well, I guess he had, I hadn't fired anyone, and they were still my leads.

"Go home, read your scripts because I'll be working with you both tomorrow." *Unless you piss me off and I toss you back to Joe.*

They nodded like good children who'd been chastised and walked off together. I was sure to be the topic of conversation and how much of an asshole I was, but I didn't care, turning my attention to where Belle had been and noticing she was gone.

My assistant director was standing in the space now vacated, talking to someone else I didn't really care about.

"Joe, where's Belle and Logan?" I looked around, the prick noticeably absent too.

Joe's head lifted, nodding to the door. "They left together a few moments ago. Did you need them? I can probably have someone try and catch them."

Keep a handle on it, asshole. Just because they walked out together didn't mean they're doing anything.

Sure, they went out to lunch together.

Seemed really fucking chummy when they came back.

And who could forget that heartwarming hug the cocksucker gave her on stage.

Stop. It.

"No, it's fine. I'll catch them both tomorrow." I did my best not to sound as pissed off as I felt.

"They were pretty great today, though, huh?" Joe clearly didn't get the read that I wasn't in the mood for a chat, smiling as everyone left. "Belle is really something special. Whoever snaps her up to be their lead is going to be in for a treat."

No shit.

"Yep, she's talented." Which was about a tenth of what I felt about her.

"Thank Christ, you gave her another chance." Joe chuckled. "Can you imagine if you'd let her walk out the door all because of your pride?"

Really, Joe?

Really.

I leveled him with a look that clearly communicated I wasn't interested in continuing his dissection on my pride or my casting decisions, flipping him off discreetly. "You done? Because if I need someone to give me shit, I can call Dane."

Joe barked out a laugh. "Ha! True that. Okay, well if we're done, I might head out. I promised the wife I'd take her out to dinner."

"Go." I nodded, pointing to the door. "You better hurry too before Gabby wises up and realizes she's too good for you. I'm about to leave myself."

"Yeah, well she hasn't left me yet and she knows the company I keep." The bastard had the nerve to smirk. "Maybe some of us just get lucky."

With a wave, Joe disappeared through the door, and I'd waited exactly three seconds after he'd gone to pick up my phone and call Belle.

Voicemail.

It didn't even ring, going straight to her bubbly, sing-song voice telling me to *leave a message and she'd get right back to me*. Which I didn't of course because I'm an idiot and I hate talking on machines.

Which meant I had a choice to make.

Did I go home, try to call her later or better yet, hope she called me.

Or did I go to her apartment, turning up on her doorstep like a stalker.

Decisions, decisions, and fuck me if I didn't hate both of them.

"Fuck," I cursed under my breath, getting into my car and heading to Greenwich. And really, like I was going to go home and sit in my apartment and twiddle my thumbs. Especially after last night. Sure, there was nothing I could do when we were at work. That was for her benefit more than mine. But I wasn't and couldn't just forget about her.

Could she?

Wait.

Waiiiiiittt.

Was she fucking done with *me*?

Refusing to accept the bullshit that was churning around in my head, I drove to her apartment like a man possessed. I hadn't really thought about what I was going to do if she wasn't there, or worse, if she wasn't alone.

Not able to find a parking spot close, I had to leave my Lexus almost a block away and then double back, trying not to sprint as I made my way to the front of her building and pressed her buzzer.

"Yes?" An impatient, curt female voice responded, and I knew immediately it wasn't Belle.

"Zara?" I took a guess, figuring it had to be her sister.

"And you are?" She gave her noncommittal rebuttal, not confirming or denying or identity until I gave her mine.

"It's Jagger. Jagger Hartley." I figured clarifying was redundant since she probably remembered me from the other night at the karaoke bar. Or from the one drunken night I'd spent in her sister's bed. But it was a habit, and she seemed like the type of person who'd appreciate the clarification

"Really." It was more a statement than a question, and held even less enthusiasm.

"Was hoping I could come up and see Belle." I looked around the street, not liking the feeling of being so exposed.

"Well, that's nice, but Belle's not here. I'll be sure to let her know you stopped by. Thanks, Jagger." The intercom popped, reinforcing the conversation was concluded, whether I wanted to or not.

And while I had no idea if Belle was up there and just refusing to talk to me, or if she was genuinely not there, short of breaking in, I didn't have a lot of options.

Fuck.

Deciding loitering on the street wasn't a good look or productive, I jogged back to my car and drove myself home. Of course I couldn't stop thinking about her the entire ride, dreaming up every worst-case scenario imaginable as I parked my car in its usual spot. Annoyed, and remembering the last time I'd been in my apartment was earlier that morning with her. I didn't bother checking my mail as I went straight to my door.

"Belle?"

Her back was to me, a bobby pin in one hand and a credit card in the other.

"I was trying to break in," she admitted, shrugging as she put her inadequate lock picking instruments back in her bag. "One of your neighbors let me up, but I figured sitting on your doorstep would look suspicious."

"And you assumed breaking and entering was better?" My grin was automatic, unable to hide how ecstatic I was for the potential crime. "Your sister would be horrified."

"I—"

She didn't get to finish, my mouth claiming hers as I cleared the few feet between us and took her in my arms. I didn't care I'd been pissed five minutes ago, or jealous, or fucking irrational. Or that I was getting in deep too fast with someone I barely knew. I wanted her, and she was there, and I wasn't wasting time asking questions.

"Jagger." She moaned against my neck, her body undulating against mine.

If she'd wanted me to stop, she sure wasn't acting like it, pulling me closer as she grabbed my ass.

"Inside," I whispered against her lips, wanting her naked and on my bed right the hell now.

Reaching behind her, I unlocked what she couldn't, throwing open my door and lifting her off the floor. I carried her through, kicking it closed behind us and tossing my keys.

My hands both needed to be on her, palming one of her breasts as I toed off my shoes and walked us into my bedroom. "I want you." I ground against her core, lowering her to my mattress. "I want you so badly."

Her hands lifted to my waistband getting busy undoing my pants while I concentrated on getting her naked. It was quick and uncoordinated, a flurry of arms, legs and hands desperately tearing at clothes until we were both bare.

Fuck she was beautiful, her skin so soft and smooth that I wanted to lick and kiss every inch of it.

But she didn't let me admire it for long, clawing at my neck and bringing me back to her, her tits pressing against my chest as I settled on top of her.

It wasn't how I'd planned it, wanting to go down on her first and at least taste that sweet pussy of hers even if I didn't make her come. But she seemed impatient, her delicate fingers wrapping around my cock and giving me a firm, slow stroke.

"Jesus, Belle," I breathed out, moving my mouth to her nipple and sucking on the tight pink tip.

My hand found her core, already slick and needy for me as my thumb circled her clit. Her body responded, lifting her hips and rocking with each sweep, a low and desperate moan spilling from her lips.

"Fuck me," she demanded, the curse word sounded even hotter coming from her pretty little mouth as she writhed underneath me. "Jagger, I want you in me, I don't want your hand."

And while I usually liked to be in control, assertive Belle was a surprising new turn-on. "What do you want, Belle? What part of me do you want in you?"

I wanted to hear the words, watch as those plump sweet lips asked for my cock as I rubbed it against her center.

Her head fell back in a moan, her hand dropping to my balls and giving them a squeeze. "Your cock, Jagger. I want your cock in me."

"Fuck, Belle." It was irrational how much I wanted her, how desperate I was to give her exactly what she asked for, which was why I didn't hesitate, plunging into her in one long thrust.

"You feel so good." I supported my weight on my elbows, careful not to crush her as I drove in again. "Perfect."

She was tight, her body needing a minute to adjust as I continued to move. Her lips kissed me hard as I thrust in again, lifting her legs so I could get deeper.

"You're going to make me come like that, Belle," I warned as she lifted her ass. She was fucking me right back, making me need a minute to lift off so I could watch my cock bury itself inside of her.

It was the hottest thing I'd ever seen, covered in her slickness as I pulled myself to my knees and drove in deeper.

With the larger gap between us, she lifted her beautiful, toned legs to my shoulders, pressing them against my chest. My lips kissed them as my fingers ran down their length as I bucked against her.

"Harder," she moaned, one of her hands fell between her legs touching herself as I pushed in deeper. "That's it, Jagger. Right th—"

She didn't get to finish, her pussy pulsing against my shaft as she came undone. My name was separated by gasps as her body trembled, the sensation of her coming enough to tip me over the edge.

"Fuuuuuck," I breathed out as I spilled into her, my body feeling electric as I—

Oh.

Fuck.

"I'm not wearing a condom." I pulled out, which is something I should've done earlier considering the circumstances. "Fuck."

I'd never had unprotected sex.

Never.

Even when a woman swore she was on birth control and we'd been dating awhile, I always wore one. Because, you just didn't know. And the last thing I wanted or needed was to be responsible for another human being, or worse, be used as a meal ticket.

But apparently years of being careful went flying out the window when I met Belle, because it only took a day and I stopped using my goddamn head.

Her inky lashes widened a little as she glanced down between us. "If it makes you feel any better, I'm on the pill."

If it makes *me* feel better?

What about her? Wasn't she pissed I'd just fucking come inside her without fucking permission? Or hell, worried about the consequences.

"Belle, I'm sorry." I rolled off her, trying to think of anything reasonable to say. But everything either sounded like a stupid excuse or contrived. "I should've known better."

"Hey, I could've stopped you, you know." She gave me a weak smile. "If you're worried about me, you don't need to be. I've got Zara as a sister and a best friend who had an unplanned pregnancy, I'm more regimented with my birth control than charging my phone. And I don't usually have unprotected sex. I mean, well, I haven't in a really long time."

"Well, that was a first for me. So . . ." *Yeah, still not sure what to say.*

"Wait! Like ever?" Belle's eyes narrowed turning to face me as I laid down on my bed. "As in *never* ever?"

Not sure if that was surprise or disbelief, but I wasn't comfortable with either.

"Yes, Belle, never." It was a little harsher than I meant it to be, regretting it the minute it had left my mouth.

And I was just about to apologize, when her lips curled into a beautiful smile. "Thank you for trusting me." She nestled in and rested against my chest.

Of all the things I was expecting, being thanked wasn't one of them. But it was more than that, like she knew the significance of what it meant. And as much as I wanted to pretend, things with her were different. *I* was different with her.

"I do trust you." It felt like the most natural thing to say, and yet, I could never remember saying it. Even at work I had trust issues, not fully believing people had my back.

I turned to face her, looking into her beautiful light brown eyes. And as much as I'd been fighting this feeling, there was no denying this was more than a fling.

She was more.

And I wanted it.

Wanted her.

"I trust you, Belle. More than I've ever trusted anyone." It fell from my mouth before I could stop it and then I kissed her.

I still had no idea what she felt, or if she wanted someone more like Logan, but I wasn't just going to walk away. Nope. I wasn't that considerate. And while I had to be distant on set, make it seem like I didn't give a shit, when we were alone, there would be no one else but her.

There was no other choice.

Chapter 19

Belle

"**B**elle, stop pacing." Zara grabbed my arms and forced me to sit down. I'd never been so relieved she was currently working from home, needing someone to talk to in the worst way. "Just tell me what happened. It can't be that bad."

"That bad? *That* bad?" I almost hyperventilated, feeling more panicked than I had in a long time. "Zara, this is a catastrophe. I'm so incredibly fucked." My head fell back against the couch, my chest still struggling to breathe.

Yesterday, after rehearsal, everything had been so clear. If I wanted to continue to work for Jagger, I needed to break up with him.

I mean . . . *were we even dating?*

We'd slept together once—okay a couple of times but it was only *one* night, at least it *had* been—and maybe that was all it was going to be.

But as much as I liked, and *really* liked spending time with him, it would hurt us both if we continued. Well, he'd probably be okay, but I'd be branded a Broadway harlot with no real talent. And he'd tried to tell me from the very start, and me, like an idiot hadn't listened. Because, stupidly I wanted to believe that the only reason I was attracted to him was because he was dark, mysterious and really freaking sexy.

Dumb.

I was so dumb.

"Belle!" Zara shook my arm. "Talk to me. You said that you were going to end it, right? That it would be too big a risk to your career and that if anything was going to happen, it would be better after the production ended. Isn't that why you went to see him?"

Sure, that had been the plan.

If my day had shown me anything it was that I wasn't built for being ignored and treated like some dirty secret side piece. Not that I expected him to declare his undying love for me or give me any special treatment. But some warmth would've been nice.

A secret gesture.

Hand signal.

TikTok challenge.

Anything to give me some indication it wasn't just going to be a one-time thing and maybe he felt more.

But I'd never—and yeah, I'm freaking saying *never*—been with anyone who could turn it off like Jagger.

Like I was nothing.

"So, I went over there," I started, figuring if I said it out loud it might make more sense in my head. "And one of his neighbors let me in. Side note, that is such a bad practice and I'd be pissed if I were him."

Zara rolled her eyes. "He came here looking for you, by the way."

I sat up, surprised because he hadn't mentioned it. Well, not that we'd done a lot of talking yesterday, but he hadn't told me he'd been to my apartment.

"Relax, I didn't tell him anything." She raised her hands. "I hope you appreciate how hard it was for me to bite my tongue. I was so wanting to give that asshole a piece of my mind."

"Thank you." I relaxed, gently breathing out a sigh of relief. She might not be happy about it, but I was grateful Zara was letting me sort out my own mess.

"Okay. You were over there, waiting for him . . ." She waved her hand, urging me to continue.

"And then he kissed me."

I didn't mention I'd been trying to break in because, really, it was highly irrelevant. And make her an accomplice after the fact—who said I didn't pay attention. What was important was that I'd gone there, clear picture in my head about sitting him down, telling him that I thought we should keep it strictly professional.

Platonic even.

Completely a working relationship only.

I'd rehearsed the speech possibly a million times, even gone through it with Zara on the phone in the Uber on the ride over. And every single time I imagined it, it ended with both of us agreeing it was for the best and parting ways amicably.

There was no reason to be enemies. And who knew, maybe after the play wrapped, we'd pick up where we left off. Then it would be some adorable meet-cute we could talk about at dinner parties. Not a salacious side-whisper on set.

But he kissed me.

KISSED me.

"And it was a good fucking kiss," I continued, the ghost of the memory still on my lips as goosebumps covered my skin. "The kind that makes you lose your breath and mind, and all sense of time and purpose. Because when he finally lifted his mouth from mine, the only thing I could think of was going into his apartment and letting him kiss me more."

"Belle," Zara groaned, shaking her head.

"I know, I know," I argued, knowing exactly what she was thinking. How could I have been totally derailed by a kiss. But she wasn't there, she didn't see the way he was looking at me and the way it felt when he pressed against my body.

"Anyway." I decided to spare her the dirty details of how fast he made me come and how much I wanted him to do it again and again. "We didn't use protection, and then he said he trusted me, and you don't understand what that means for a guy like that, and now I can't leave him because I think I might love him." The words came out in a rush.

"Whoa! Belle!" Zara stood up, shaking her head. "One thing at a time. Firstly, you *didn't* use protection?"

"I know, I know," I repeated, because I was aware of how careless it was. "But I take my pill every single day religiously and you can set a Swiss timepiece to my cycle."

"Uhhhhh what about diseases, STDs, do you need me to go on?"

"That's just it, Zara. He's never had unprotected sex." I joined her on my feet. "He said he's never done it, and because he's freaking paranoid and suspicious of everyone, I totally believe him."

He had given me something he'd never given any other woman before.

Trust.

And as much as I wanted to be flippant and pretend he'd just got caught up in the moment and it was his dick talking, my head was telling me different. Jagger would never let his guard down and randomly give anyone the upper hand without intention. So subconsciously, deep within the recesses of that beautiful mind, he knew it was safe. That *I* was safe. And there was no way I could walk away from that.

No way.

"Zara, I know it was stupid, careless, reckless—throw in all the adjectives to illustrate it wasn't the wisest of choices. But it felt so right. And I don't regret it."

No way.

Instead, I wish I could do it again, see the way his body relaxed beside me and the way it held me all night. I wanted to relive the way he looked me in the eyes and told me that he trusted me. And how I intuitively knew those words meant more to him than saying I love you.

"Belle." Zara blew out a breath, no doubt trying to choose her words carefully. "I love you, and I'll support your decisions no matter what. But if he breaks your heart—"

"It will be okay, I promise." And I honestly believed it, knowing there was no way Jagger would intentionally hurt me. My ever-cautious sister was just trying to protect me like she always did.

"Now what?" she asked, which was exactly the same question I'd been asking myself since I'd left Jagger's. He'd dropped me off, kissing me gently before needing to head to the theatre. I was going in later, rehearsal for the cast not starting until midafternoon. Which gave me the whole morning to obsess and overanalyze everything. Especially since I'd planned to be walking into rehearsal today minus any complications.

"I don't know," I answered honestly, not really sure what I was going to do. "But I know that I want to be with him, Zara. And I think . . ." I paused, shaking my head as I continued, "No, I *know* that I have feelings for him."

That was a lie.

It wasn't just *feelings*.

It was love.

And sure, I'd probably said I'd been in love like a million times before, but this was different. And I knew deep down this was what *real* love was supposed to feel like. All those other times had been infatuation, lust, even seriously intense like—but not love.

Never like this.

"It's going to be totally fine."

And I wasn't sure if that was the second lie I'd told my sister, because honestly I didn't know.

Rehearsal had been tense.

Both Serenity and Chase were in a mood since their public sidelining the day before and were actively posturing. They were dominating most of Jagger's time, tossing everything they could into their performance like they knew they could no longer coast.

Jagger was predictably the same.

Professional but distant, limiting his interactions to those that were absolutely necessary. And while previously it had hurt—his indifference and seemingly cold behavior—I understood it a little better.

He trusted *me*.

But not *them*.

And he would never let any of them into such a private part of his life, even if most people would hardly notice if he gave me a smile.

"So do you forgive me?" Logan handed me a coffee and a napkin-wrapped cinnamon bun. "I am really sorry for what I said about Serenity yesterday, I'm not usually that much of a jerk."

I took the coffee *and* the cinnamon bun because I was hungry and it felt like an eternity ago since I'd eaten. "Of course I forgive you." I gave him a warm smile. "Already forgotten."

And I had for the most part. Except for the small part of my brain that told me all of that would be said about me and probably worse if anyone found out Jagger and I were sleeping together. At least Serenity was sort of famous, or at least had built a name for herself. I didn't have that luxury.

"Good." He sat down beside me, his own coffee and pastry balancing in his other hand. "Because I think you're really special, Belle."

Oh.

No.

"I have a boyfriend," I blurted out awkwardly. "I mean, I know you're not hitting on me or anything," I quickly added since it was fairly presumptuous to think he was interested in me in *that* way. But I didn't want there to be any mistake, even if technically I wasn't even sure if I *could* call Jagger my boyfriend. Even in abstract. "I just want to make it clear because—" I shook my head, trying to think of a legitimate reason for declaring my relationship status unprompted. "Sorry, we're just in a really weird place."

His smile hitched a little at the side as he took a small sip from his cup. "I was totally hitting on you. But not in a creepy, I'm-going-to-stalk-you kind of way. I totally respect boundaries," he added. "Guess I should've figured someone as wonderful as you would already be with someone though. That was my bad."

"Actually, it's sorta new." I shrugged, feeling weird talking about it, even cryptically. Not like Logan knew who I was talking about. And it would probably be more suspicious if I didn't talk about it, considering I'd been so willing to volunteer it earlier.

"New and already in a weird place?" He raised a brow. "Doesn't sound promising."

"Honestly, it's not like that." I tried not to sound as defensive as I felt, taking a minute to choose my words carefully. "His family makes things complicated."

Family complications happened all the time, right? There was no way anyone could hear that and connect it to Jagger. I mean, if I'd said work or something similar, then sure, maybe. But family issues was a long, broad stroke. And besides, half the guys I dated had family issues. It wasn't like it was an affliction that was exempt for the middle class.

"Ahhhhh." He nodded, making up a scenario in his head. "Well, that does make it complicated. My last girlfriend's dad hated me. Assumed because I was an actor, I'd be unemployed or some kind of loser. Like we couldn't possibly be productive members of society." He scoffed. "In the end, it was too hard, ya know? She had to be one person with them and then another with me. It gets to a point, you're not even sure who you're dating anymore."

"What do you mean?" I asked, the circumstance eerily similar even though the situation was totally different.

Logan looked around, making sure we were alone and not in Joe or Jagger's firing line. "I mean, she loves her family, and if it really came down to it, she's always going to choose them. She was supportive, told me how proud she was when I'd land an audition or if I was lucky enough to get a part. But whenever we were around them, she'd make a big production of telling them I'd found a job waiting tables or selling shirts at The Gap. She'd laugh every time her dad cracked a joke about me finally growing up and being a real man. Then we'd get home and she'd be all normal again. Total mindfuck."

"Well, she sounds terrible," I spat out, knowing I'd been lucky enough to grow up with a family who fully supported my career choice even if it wasn't traditional. "I'm sorry they made you feel that way."

He shrugged, resigned to it. "Meh, it's okay. But it made me decide that I'm not doing that again. If what I do or who I am is something they feel they need to hide, then it's a hard pass. Plenty more fish in the sea." He chuckled.

"Yeah."

Not sure why every time I spoke to Logan, it felt like a therapy session, and it wasn't in a positive way. Instead I was questioning all my current life choices and feeling confused and conflicted.

I'd tried to quit Jagger, and it hadn't stuck.

But I knew it wasn't going to be easy.

Were we going to have to be secretive in public or just when we were at the theatre? Was dating going to be a thing? Or were we just going to meet at his apartment, have sex and then pretend we barely knew each other when anyone else was around?

We'd been together.

Even kissed on the dance floor.

But I guess that was technically before I'd signed my contract.

Fuck.

"Where did you go?" Logan laughed, waving his hand in front of my face. "I asked if it was his mom or his dad giving you a hard time."

"Oh!" I quickly recovered, not realizing I'd been completely lost in my own thoughts. "His mom," I shot out, figuring it was probably the most plausible.

"Knew it." Logan winked. "No way was his dad seeing a beautiful woman like you and having an issue. Now, the mom, she's probably assuming you're just going to mooch off her little boy and get him addicted to 'the crack.'" He made little air quotation marks with his fingers.

I covered my mouth stifling a laugh as Jagger and Joe looked over. "You're going to get us both in trouble. And I don't need to add unemployment to the list of disappointments."

"Ha! Like they'd ever fire you." Logan shook his head, unapologetically. "You're the most talented person in this place."

"Working hard I see." Jagger looked between us with his usual level of coolness. It still stung a little, even if I knew why.

"Yes, we are." I lifted my chin, trying to be as unaffected as he was. "Would you like us on the main stage again? Or are we going to continue working with Joe?"

I was trying.

Trying to do it his way where I pretended I didn't want to wrap my arms around his neck and kiss him.

Trying to pretend that my body didn't want to be nestled up next to him.

And trying to pretend, that as much as I didn't need his approval or acceptance, I liked it when he gave it to me.

"With Joe." He tilted his head to his assistant director who was still working with some supporting cast. "Unless there's something you think needs my attention?"

It was so out of character that even Joe turned and looked at him strangely. Maybe it was the first time Joe had seen him act semi-human instead of the stoic machine he usually seemed to be.

"Ummmm," I stumbled, wondering if it was an opening. Was he giving me an excuse to interact with him? Or was it a test? "We're fine."

It wasn't what I'd wanted to say, desperate to make some convoluted reason to speak to him privately just to have a minute alone with him. But it was a risk.

"Logan?" He turned, facing my acting partner.

"Yeah, all good here, Jagger," Logan added, probably wondering if our director hadn't been taken down by some weird fever.

"Good, then you're with Joe. I'll let him know you're waiting for him." And with a curt nod, he disappeared back to the main stage.

"Well that was fucking weird." Logan's face pulled into a grimace as Jagger walked away. "It should feel comforting that he cared enough to ask, yet all I feel is unsettled."

"I know the feeling. Do you think he is trying to be nicer?" I asked, hoping my concern wouldn't arouse any suspicion.

"Not sure anyone could accuse Jagger of being nice, Belle." Logan shook his head. "More likely he saw we weren't some B-Grade wannabes yesterday and is attempting to keep us happy. You know Rittenborough is casting. Bragging how he wants fresh blood. Unknowns."

"What?" I spun around, surprised to hear there was a new production looking for actors and I hadn't been aware. Granted, I'd been distracted since I'd met Jagger, so I guess it made sense.

Logan leaned in, lowering his voice. "Yep, and just between you and me, I'm thinking about it."

"You would leave?" I squeaked out.

"He doesn't have the same prestige as Hartley, and the script probably isn't as good. And let's face it, the money would be less too. But, there's a chance to be a headliner, instead of a backup." He moved his hands up and down like he was weighing his options. "Tough call."

"But what if you don't get it, and then you've left," I argued back, trying to convince him to stay. Not sure if it was for Logan's benefit, Jagger's or my own, but I didn't want him to leave.

"So I audition, keep it hush and then if nothing happens, I'm no worse off."

It made sense, even though I knew it would infuriate Jagger if he ever found out. It wouldn't take a rocket scientist to know he'd take it as betrayal, and Logan would probably never get cast in another Hartley production again.

"You should come with me," he suggested, watching as Joe finished up and turned to walk in our direction. "Just feel it out, see if it's something you might want to do. After all, Serenity said she's never sick, so the chances of you being on stage are slim to none."

"I can't," I argued, knowing I had maybe a minute before Joe was in ear shot. "Hartley would *kill* us."

Not literally, but professionally.

Especially me.

God.

He'd never recover from that stab in the back, he'd not only hate me but probably make sure I never worked again.

"Just do me a favor, at least let me talk to you about it. We'll meet tomorrow away from here where we can discuss. Okay? No obligations?" Logan hurried, turning just in time as Joe arrived. "Hey Joe, Belle and I are ready. Which page?"

"Good." Joe clapped his hands. "Let's go from page ten. Belle, your scene."

"Great." I smiled at Logan as he shot me a wink. "I'm ready."

But I was so not ready.

Chapter 20

Jagger

It didn't take a genius to work out that the lack of structure and boundaries in my childhood was the reason I mainlined it in my adult life. While growing up with a dad who smoked weed and painted naked sounded like a good time, it had its own set of challenges. And while Dane had turned out 'just fine' I often wondered if that was because he wasn't gifted our defective DNA.

Okay, that was a little harsh. My parents weren't completely terrible, and they'd been far from abusive. But they were incredibly selfish and self-absorbed, and if that was what a relationship was supposed to look like, it was no wonder I wanted none of it.

But Belle, well, she was making me question everything.

Firstly, I hated Logan.

Hated the way he looked at her, the way he hugged her, the motherfucking way he made her laugh. And while I knew this new feeling was jealousy and apparently normal, I didn't like it. And most of all, I didn't like the irrational, uncontrolled way it made me feel. Primal. Like I wanted to beat a man to death with nothing but my bare hands.

The structure and boundaries I fucking got off on, fucking

torched as I tried to figure out what the fuck I was doing and how the hell was I going to stop myself from screwing it up.

Assuming the worst had been my first instinct.

Because of course she'd be fucking someone else.

But when I'd found her at my doorstep instead of in the arms of that asshole, all I wanted to do was kiss her, hold her, and take her to my bed.

It was such a caveman thing to do—drag her into my cave and bury myself inside of her. But since those feelings were new to me and I had zero idea what the hell I was doing, I didn't bother arguing with myself.

So, since Belle was giving me no reason to believe she actually wanted to be with the cocksucker—Jesus, I really didn't like him—I wasn't going to risk looking like an insecure dipshit and bring it up.

They were coworkers, no more. And while it was normal for actors, especially those closely partnered together, to form a relationship, that was no reason to expect it was anything more than that. Proximity. Friendship. Mutual respect and admiration.

Oh, he wanted her, that I knew.

I could see the way he looked at her, that bullshit smile as he rolled his eyes over her body like an unwelcome pair of invisible hands. But as long as she was uninterested, he could fucking look until his eyeballs shriveled and he needed a vat of Visine just to be able to blink.

And work, well that was harder than I thought.

I wanted to touch her.

To kiss her.

To claim those smiles as my own.

But more than any of that, I wanted her on my stage, giving life to the scenes I'd fucking written. To capture the soul of my words and take them off the page so everyone could see them, showing the world exactly how amazing she was.

Screw Serenity. She didn't give a tenth of what Belle did, and holy hell did Belle deserve it more than the woman who currently had top billing.

That was twice I fought against my initial instincts and played nice.

I deserved some kind of an award for sure.

"Mmmm," Belle mumbled in her sleep, curled up beside me as I lay in bed awake. Ordinarily I'd have been up hours ago, gone for a run and eaten an egg-white omelet like I did every other Saturday. But a week of having Belle in my bed, waking up with her warm soft skin plastered against me, made it hard to find the motivation to leave.

"Mmmmmmmmmmm." She nestled in closer, her beautiful full lips pressing against my torso.

Great.

Because I wasn't already hard, I needed to be thinking about her fucking mouth.

And hell, if she mumbled again, I was probably going to kiss her. Because it was simultaneously the most adorable and sexiest thing ever, and my balls were fucking aching.

"Jagger?" Her fingers swirled on my chest as she reached up, her voice thick from sleep. "You're so sexy."

Not an animal, I reminded myself.

You.

Are.

Not.

An.

Animal.

"Is that your hint for me to go get you breakfast?" I asked, willing my balls to chill the fuck out. As much as I wanted to have sex with Belle again, it had been pretty much the only thing we'd done in the past few days.

Work.

Eat.

Fuck.

Sleep.

Repeat.

I was working almost every spare second, killing myself trying to get the show put together since we opened in the next two months. So, when I wasn't in rehearsal with the cast and crew, I was in meetings, dealing with marketing, reassuring investors, playing nice with the press blah, blah, blah. Which meant I didn't get a lot of time to see Belle during the day *unless* she was at the theatre.

And when I was done, I wanted nothing more than to eat, be with Belle, and fall asleep with her in my bed.

But I also wasn't a moron who thought that would cut it, or that a woman like Belle would be happy with that kind of existence. Which is why instead of taking that beautiful mouth and making her come three times, I was going to take her out to breakfast. Maybe a walk in the park. Or whatever else it was normal couples did.

Her hand inched lower, dangerously close to my cock that was not on board with my amended plans for the day. "You're going to get me breakfast?"

Not.

An.

Animal.

"Mmhmmm," I almost groaned out, ignoring the pain in my balls. "Better than that, I'm going to take you out for breakfast."

She shot up, almost headbutting me as she kicked off the covers. "Out, out?" Her voice hitched in excitement. "Oh my God, where are we going to go?"

And if I needed any other validation that she'd wanted more than what we'd been doing, there it was. "Where would you like to go?" I asked, brushing the hair back from her eyes as I shuffled up against the headboard. "I have the entire morning free and can take you anywhere you like."

Being out in public was a mitigated risk. Sure, there was a chance someone might see, but unless I was accompanied by my illuminated last name, no one really recognized me. And as for the cast, I assumed they were either sleeping until noon, curating their social media accounts or so self-absorbed with their own existence, they didn't care about strangers on the street.

"You're working this afternoon? But there's no rehearsal." A flash of disappointment passed through her eyes.

"No, no rehearsal. But I've got to meet with Dane, it's his birthday."

Every year he had a big flashy party. Not nearly as over the top as what our parents would've thrown but nothing I wanted to be a part of. Instead, Dane and I would meet somewhere in the afternoon, have a few drinks so I could celebrate his day without the sideshow.

"It's Dane's birthday?" She had another burst of excitement, the disappointment gone and in its place a mischief I wanted part of. "Jagger, why didn't you tell me. Of course you have to go to his birthday."

"No, not like that," I corrected her. "His party is this *evening*. I'm not doing that, which is why I'll get to spend it with you."

I hadn't asked if she had plans or wanted to do something with her friend, Hayley, or sister. But I was hopeful. Besides, even if she did want to spend time with them, she had to go to bed eventually, and there was no reason why that couldn't be with me.

"No, no, no." She shook her head. "You *are* doing that. He's your *brother*. It's his *birthday*. You are going to his party."

"Belle." I blew out a breath, loving her excitement for basically anything but not sharing the sentiment. "This isn't new. Dane understands. Besides, I'm sure he'd rather celebrate with his friends."

"I'll go," she offered, giving me a big smile. "Oh, it will be fun. We've been working all week and a party sounds amazing. Unless you're not allowed to bring a plus one? Or would you rather I didn't come?"

"Assuming I was going—which I'm not—of course I'd want you to come." I kissed the top of her head. Hell, if I were to go, having Belle there would be the only thing that would make it more bearable.

"So let's go." Her smile widened, completely ignoring the fact I'd said I wasn't going or wanted to go, and basically had never gone or intended to in the future. "It will be so much fun. Is it fancy? Should I wear a cocktail dress? Oooooooo I need to buy a present."

She kicked off the covers, leaping from the bed.

Of course that just reinforced how naked she was, her lithe, delicate body stretching in a way that I was positive wasn't supposed to be erotic. Not that my cock got the memo. And wow, was she stunning, her beautiful, toned body dancing in front of me with her blinding gorgeous smile.

Not sure how I was supposed to think straight, let alone have a discussion which might have well been her plan.

"Belle, Belle, Belle." I tried to ignore the beautiful lines of her body as I focused on her face. "I know you heard me say I wasn't going, right? I wasn't just talking to myself."

"Jagger." She folded her arms across her chest, pushing up her tits in what I could only describe as a tactical maneuver. Because there wasn't a man alive who could be in front of that and say no. "I know you don't want to go. But he's your family. And while I know yours is complicated, you love your brother. Going to his birthday, doing something even though you know you might hate it—for someone else, for someone that you love—is how you show them that you care."

It was the stupidest thing I'd ever heard. How could making myself miserable and doing something that I hated, prove I cared? "That doesn't even make sense, Belle. He *knows* I don't want to be there. It will just ruin his night."

She threw her hands in the air. "Why would it? Are you going to sulk in a corner? Demand he talk to you and only you? Put Ipecac in the appetizers?"

"No, of course I wouldn't." I rolled my eyes.

"Good, because as much as you say he understands, I bet it would literally make his day if you turned up." She moved back on the bed, straddling my body so her tits were now just inches away from my face.

Jesus.

Christ.

She was diabolical.

"And if I say no?" I tried to argue, the words getting stuck in my throat as she moved closer.

"Then I'll go by myself," she whispered in my ear. "I'm sure Dane won't mind if I go and help him celebrate. We are friends after all."

I swallowed, knowing she wasn't just making idle threats. "You'd do that? Just turn up to Dane's birthday party?"

"Yep." Her mouth popped off the p as her finger bopped my nose. "And I'll be wearing something fabulous. Such a shame you'll miss it."

"Fine," I gritted out, not sure how much longer I could've held out. As irrational as it was to get jealous, there was apparently no controlling it either. Great. "I'll go. A couple of drinks, we see Dane, and then I'm leaving, Belle, with or without you."

"Yay!" She threw her arms around me, peppering my face with kisses. "We're going to have the best time. I want all the details. Oh, on second thought, why don't I just call Dane and get them myself. I wouldn't want there to be any confusion on where this party is or what time it starts." She eyed me cautiously.

"Whatever, can we go have breakfast now?" I asked, my hands settling on her hips. I had about five minutes before I gave up on trying to be decent and fucked her like I'd wanted from the start. No one was perfect, my resolve wearing thinner the longer she was naked.

She clapped her hands, dropping an enthusiastic kiss on my lips. "Yes, breakfast."

Shuffling back off the bed, she swayed her hips as she walked to the bathroom. The sexy look over her shoulder had me joining her whether I wanted to or not. And even though I was trying to be a good boy and do more with her than just have sex, the temptation of a wet, naked Belle was too much even for me.

So after shower sex, my promise of breakfast had turned into lunch before we left my apartment and walked to a local café. It was the first real "date" we'd been on since we'd became a couple. And while I didn't subscribe to everyone's definition of what a relationship should look like, I wanted to do it with Belle.

"Oooooh what's good here?" Belle turned over the menu, reading it while I was looking at her. "I'm starving."

God I loved looking at her.

Studying the lines of her face, watching her animated expressions change a thousand times, seeing the edges of her eyes crinkle when she laughed. There was a warmth that emanated from her from the inside out. So inherently good, pure and honest that it almost didn't feel real. But she was. She was the realest person I had ever met, and I wanted to get lost in both her flaws and perfection.

"What are you doing?" She laughed, noticing I'd been staring. "Is there something on my face?" She self-consciously rubbed at her check at invisible marks that weren't there.

"I'm just looking," I answered honestly, holding back exactly just how much I was looking and how much I liked it.

Liked her.

Liked us.

Liked this.

She leaned in, dropping her voice to a whisper as her lips pulled into a grimace. "Well, that's kinda creepy."

"Stop acting surprised, Belle." I fought the urge to smile, loving how unintimidated she'd always been by me, unapologetically speaking her mind. "You knew I was creepy when you met me."

Her shoulder lifted in a small shrug. "True, but I hate that I can never tell what's really on your mind. You always have this expression." She gestured to my face. "It's like a mask and I have zero idea what you're thinking."

I guess I'd done it so long, the mask she spoke of, I didn't really know how to turn it off. Or if I wanted to. "If there's something you want to know, Belle, you can just ask."

It was my compromise, my way of letting her know that if she wanted in my head, she could have access.

She flopped the menu down, her hand curling to a fist that she rested her chin on top. "Anything?"

"Anything, what?" I asked, not sure where she was going.

"I can ask you anything and you'll just answer?" she clarified, losing interest in ordering food even though apparently she was *starving*.

"Sure, ask me anything." I relaxed into my seat, being surprisingly okay with the uncertainty. Maybe there was hope for me yet.

Her eyes darted left and right as if scanning for possible eavesdroppers. "Are we dating?"

"Huh?" I coughed out, wondering if she was being comical or was genuinely asking. "What do you mean?"

"I mean," she continued, a small puff of air slowly escaping past her lips, "is this a relationship? Or are we just, you know, bed buddies?"

Those thoughts I had, about her and Logan, came back in a rush, heat prickling my neck like a woolen sweater that made me itch. "What would you like it to be?"

"No." She shook her head, refusing to answer. "You said you'd answer, you don't get to hedge your bets. What is this to you, Jagger? What am I to you?"

Thankfully the waitress picked that exact moment to ask us if we were ready to order. And while Belle would've asked for another few moments, I needed the reprieve.

"I'm good if you know what you want." I picked up the menu, pretending to look at it even though I was well aware of what I was going to order. "I'll take the turkey sandwich, side salad, sparkling water."

Belle didn't even bother looking back at the list of options. "I'll take a burger, fries and a Coke, thank you."

"Any particular burger?" the waitress asked, her pen mid scribble on her order pad.

"Surprise me." Belle smiled. "I've yet to meet a burger I haven't liked and doubt today will be that day."

The waitress shrugged and shoved the order pad in the front of her apron. "I'll go grab your drinks."

"So?" Belle asked, waiting until the waitress had disappeared. "You didn't think I was just going to forget because we were interrupted, did you?"

I was hoping.

"No, of course not." I cleared my throat. "Yes, Belle, I want a relationship with you. We're not just *bed buddies*."

My hand reached across the table, touching hers. "I want you, and only you."

"As your girlfriend?" she clarified, closing any potential loopholes.

"Yes," I answered without hesitation. "As my girlfriend."

Her eyes shone with excitement. "Good, because that's what I want too."

The relief was immediate, feeling like the metal cage around my lungs had been magically unlocked. "I'm glad. And I meant what I said, Belle. You and only you."

It was probably assumed I meant exclusively, but if she wanted to take care of loopholes then so did I. And while I trusted Belle, I was well aware my newly titled 'girlfriend' was ridiculously beautiful and could have any man she wanted.

She laughed, either enjoying my insecurity or the serious expression on my face. "You're so adorable."

"Not really what I wanted to hear." My brow rose, wondering if she was going to make me ask.

"Jagger, I'm not and would not date anyone else. Even if all we were doing was sleeping together." She rolled her eyes like it was something I should've already known. "Besides, we've barely been apart since—"

"Since you tried to break into my apartment," I finished for her, remembering what it had felt like to find her there.

"But I *didn't*, and anyway, look how wonderful it turned out." She laughed.

I loved that sound. The unrestrained melody of her joy, the way the sound tingled up my spine and warmed my soul and I couldn't help but smile back.

"Anything else you want to know before the waitress comes back with your mystery burger?" I squeezed her hand, wishing we could forget Dane's party and whatever else we had planned for the day and just sit in that moment.

"Well . . ." She bit her lip, her nose wrinkling as she hesitated.

"Go on, what is it?" I chuckled, wondering what she was going to ask next.

"Serenity has pretty much said she's going to crawl in half dead if she has to, and isn't going to miss a show." She took a breath, getting serious.

"Is there a question in there? Because if you're wondering if I think you're talented enough to carry the lead, Belle, I absolutely do." Even though I knew it could potentially bite me in the ass, I couldn't lie to her. Or have her believe that she was somehow less deserving. "You're amazing on that stage, Belle. Amazing. One of the best I've seen."

"Understudies, you mean. Best understudy, not lead."

I shook my head. "Best, period."

I wanted to tell her more, confess the bullshit politics that dictated me relegating her to second chair, but it wouldn't be helpful. But I didn't want there to be any misunderstanding as to her talent. And not just because I was sleeping with her.

"Belle," I leaned closer, "you're amazing. And trust me when I tell you that your time is coming. You're going to be bigger than Serenity, more sought after than Hayley, and I'll be able to say, I'd cast her when."

It was a small consolation, being the first runner-up when you wanted that win, and I knew how it felt. How even being the very next choice still stung of rejection, especially when you knew you could do it 'better' than the person who won.

And more than anything, I hated that I was part of the reason she felt that way.

"Thanks." A small smile edged out her lips. "I'm not usually needy. I guess I was just hoping I'd have a chance. Even if it was one show."

"Hey, you still may. It's almost unheard of for an actress to get through a whole run without at least one or two breaks. She's not a robot." Sure, we didn't have the kind of dates a huge production did, with bookings months and months in advance. But unless it was a one-night-only situation, even a two-week engagement used their understudy at least once.

She waved her hands, dismissing the idea. "It's fine, it's fine. Let's talk about more interesting stuff. Like what am I getting Dane for his birthday? And what am I going to wear?"

While I knew she was playing it off, not willing to admit how much she wanted to be the star, I wasn't going to push the issue. Because if anyone knew about wanting to move on when they didn't want to talk about shit, it was me. "You don't have to buy him a present. I've got him a nice bottle of scotch and a tie."

"You got him scotch and a tie?" She gasped, horrified. "He's your brother, not your eighty-year-old grandfather."

"It's expensive scotch and the tie is Hermès," I corrected. "And my grandfather passed away years ago."

"I'm sorry about your grandpa." Belle quickly apologized. "But I still think your present sucks. Tie, scotch—boring."

"And what would you suggest since you know him so well?" I folded my arms across my chest, waiting for the brilliant suggestion I had no doubt was coming.

"Oh! Why don't you get him tickets to something? For him and a friend." She raised her eyebrows suggestively. "You know, he asked for Hayley's number when you guys met us at karaoke. They've been texting."

While I knew he'd wanted Hayley's number, I didn't know they'd been texting. Not that I usually interfered in my brother's dating choices unless you counted when he'd hit on Belle. "I'm happy for them. But not sure organizing a date for him is something he'd want or needs. Dane is more than capable of doing that all by himself."

When it came to getting women, Dane was definitely the Casanova of the Hartley brood. Not that he was an asshole about it, but he sure as shit didn't need me.

"You're no fun." She sighed, shaking her head as our waitress brought our food. "Give him your boring present. I'm still going to think of something else that's just from me."

I didn't bother arguing because as beautiful and captivating as Belle was, she was also impossible.

"Great, can't wait to see what it is."

Chapter 21

Belle

Apparently I liked complicated.

Because not only had I *not* broken up with him, but I was now officially Jagger's girlfriend. Which should've been awesome because I really, really liked—okay, maybe even loved—him. Except we were in this weird place where we weren't going public with our new relationship status, but we weren't hiding it either. At least, I was *fairly* sure we weren't going public with it. Or maybe we were, just not at work? All I knew was, at the theatre I was just another member of the cast, someone he barely acknowledged, but when we got home he couldn't keep his mouth—or his hands—off me.

And while labels and definitions had never really bothered me before, it irked me more than a little that I had this amazing man I was apparently dating, but couldn't really talk about.

"You asked him?" Hayley's eyes widened, carefully keeping her voice down even though Bobbie had a sleepover with her mom, and we were alone. "And he said he wanted you to be his *girlfriend*?"

"Way to make me feel better about this." I tugged her arm,

pulling her down onto her sofa. "I came here for reassurance, and hype, not more doubt and skepticism. I have Zara for that."

Hayley sighed, turning to face me. "And what did she say?"

"That she'd support me but thinks *it's an epically bad idea.*" I repeated my sister's words almost verbatim. "She didn't come right out and say I was making a mistake, but I always know with Zara. She gets this look, and then the careful silence . . . in some ways, she's kinda like Jagger. Except he's broodier. And sexy. And obviously, I don't want to sleep with my sister." I shivered, not really having noticed the parallel before. Huh, I wonder if that was why I was so attracted to him, because like Zara, he was an amazing person but you just had to get past that hard, skeptical exterior.

"Well, Zara does know you pretty well, and if she's telling you to be careful—"

"I think I love him, Hayley." I cut her off, the feelings in my chest so overwhelming I felt like I might explode. And I needed to tell someone, and I trusted Hayley with my life. "No, no I don't *think*, I *know*. But even though I'm deliriously happy, I feel like I'm walking a tightrope. If the wrong person finds out." I shook my head, resting it in my hands as I contemplated. "It could be so bad for both of us."

I hadn't forgotten about Logan's "gossip" or was naïve as to what it would look like. Didn't matter that I'd earned my place, and had talent, everyone would just make assumptions.

"Fuck," I cursed out, lifting myself from Hayley's sofa and starting to pace. "Why does this have to be so messed up?"

"Well . . ." Hayley took a breath, and like I knew when Zara was thinking something I didn't like, I could tell with my best friend as well. "You *could* walk away."

Sure.

I finally find the man I fall in love with, and I will just walk away.

Annnnnnnd, not only that, but in his own way, I think he loves me. At least he seems to. He definitely trusts me when usually he trusts no one, so not only will it break both our hearts but probably send him into therapy for the next year or so too.

My head shook, the idea of leaving Jagger not something I even wanted to contemplate. "I've been down that road, and I couldn't do it. And now, I'm in too deep."

"No, not leaving Jagger, leaving the production."

Hayley's suggestion was so crazy that I audibly gasped. And not for dramatic effect, but because the idea of walking away from the opportunity was insane.

"Walk away? Walk away? I stuttered, wondering if she had a better, more sensible idea she was going to give me next. "Hayley, I fought my ass off for this part. I literally hijacked the man and thrust my audition on him. I can't just turn around and leave it." Not to mention that parts in paying productions weren't easy to come by. Sure, I'd done some T.V. work, occasional voice-over stuff and even modelling if I needed to make sure the bills were paid. But my heart belonged on the stage.

"Yeah, you can," she insisted, making me believe my earlier diagnosis of insanity wasn't so hypothetical anymore. "Didn't you say Logan was auditioning for Rittenborough? I hear he's adamant he gets new, fresh faces."

I'd confided in Hayley about Logan's audition because basically I hated keeping secrets and I needed to tell someone. We'd both agreed Jagger would curse Logan's household for sixteen generations and he would never get a part in one of his productions again. Because, loyalty. But we—Hayley and I—never—not once during that discord—discussed me auditioning. Because I didn't need a curse on my household, or to betray the man I loved.

"You can't be serious." The breath expelled from my lungs in a rush as it came to my attention that yes, she was very serious. "Do you not remember what we discussed? How Jagger would launch a medieval vendetta?" I scoffed, wondering if the sleep deprivation from being a new single mom wasn't affecting her reasoning capabilities. "When I said I couldn't walk away from Jagger, I didn't want to be dumped either."

Because that was what I was looking at.

I'd lose *both* Jagger and the part in a double fudge sundae of misery.

"Belle, you said he trusts you. And you know, maybe you should trust him." She broke out her *mommy* voice, which while new, was seriously effective. "He'd be reasonable, understand that the best thing for both of you would be to separate your personal and professional relationship. Then you would be free to really see where this all goes."

Made sense.

But.

"I feel light-headed." The room suddenly felt smaller, the air heavier and harder to get into my lungs. Was I having a panic attack? Oh my God, was I going to die?

"Belle, take a deep breath," Hayley encouraged, rubbing big circles on my back. "You're overthinking this."

"Oh, Oh, I totally am!" I gasped, trying to get that big breath I was instructed to take. "I'm supposed to be going to Dane's birthday party, with Jagger. And while it might not seem like a big deal, the enormity of what it means is not lost on me. He's doing it for *me*, because I'd asked. And then what? I turn around and stab him in the back?"

And as if I'd summoned him, my phone buzzed with a text from Jagger, reminding me he was picking me up at eight. I'd insisted he still have his traditional birthday drinks with his brother to give me time to scout a present and get myself birthday party presentable. Of course, that was before I was having my existential crisis, which would undoubtably need more time.

"It's not stabbing him in the back if you tell him. Just be honest, Belle." Hayley's hand continued to rub my back, trying in vain to calm me. I will say, she'd really embraced the whole mom thing though. Not twelve months ago she'd have suggested us doing shots until we worked out a solution. The deep breathing and comforting were a welcome change.

And that's when I realized.

We'd both changed.

The drive to succeed was still there, and neither of us wanted to walk away from a job we both loved. Just not at any cost. For Hayley, her daughter gave her that perspective, and me, well I'd found the first man I could honestly see a future with.

Not just dating.

Not just for now.

But forever.

And hell, maybe love—*real* love and *real* happiness—was just as important as making it on Broadway.

"I'm going to tell him," I breathed out. The choice made by my heart before my brain had even really weighed in. "I can't be in the shadows, pretending I don't love him for the next few months while we work together. And maybe if he sees what I'm willing to give up, he'll know how much he means to me. That or he'll hate me forever and break my heart."

I still wasn't sure how it was going to go. For all Hayley's assurances that he'd be reasonable and professional about it, I still knew that underneath that tough, prickly exterior was a man who just wanted to be loved. Loved for *who* not *what* he was.

Hayley pulled me into a hug. "You can do this, Belle. And I promise you that whatever happens, I'll be here."

And with my new resolve, I straightened my spine and gave her a huge hug goodbye. I still had a birthday present to wrangle and make myself party ready, oh and think of a way to tell Jagger I was in love with him, which was why I had to quit a role I was honestly dying to play.

With a promise to call her later, I headed back home where I found Lincoln working on a case at the kitchen table.

"What's the asshole done?" He eyed me suspiciously, watching as I tossed my handbag on the floor and my keys on the side bureau. "You know what, better you don't tell me. Just perhaps leave me his schedule for the next week and we'll just take it from there."

I guess I really did wear my heart on my sleeve, or on my face as the case were, not realizing how incredibly bad I was at hiding my emotions from the people I loved. And even though Zara and Lincoln weren't married yet, he was the best brother-in-law I could ever ask for. Because not only did he love my sister fiercely, but he'd do anything for her and in turn, me. I wanted that, and deep down, I knew I could have that with Jagger.

"It's not what you think," I started, holding my hands up in defense.

"Says everyone always when it's exactly what I think," Lincoln shot back. "And whether or not you believe there's an explanation for his assholish behavior, it's irrelevant."

"Ughhhh I just went and fell in love with him," I huffed out, exasperated. "And not only have I not told him, but I need to quit as well. Oh, and hope he feels the same way and doesn't hate me for walking and going to work for someone else."

His eyebrow rose, closing his laptop as he stood. "Have you spoken to Zara about this?" Then he shook his head, answering his own question. "Of course you haven't."

Oh, Zara knew I had feelings for Jagger, but I'd been adamant it was all going to be okay. Reassured her that I totally had it under control, and I wouldn't get hurt. Not so sure anymore though, was I.

"It will be fine," I lied, making assurances I knew I couldn't back up. "I'm going to go to Dane's birthday, tell Jagger later tonight and I'm going to see how unnecessarily worried I was." I'm sure I was trying to convince myself more than I was him, but both would be a benefit.

"And if it's not fine, you're going to call me." It wasn't a question, rather another reassurance, only this time from Lincoln.

Gahhhh, if all these feelings weren't making me emotional. Without warning, I threw my arms around Lincoln, crumpling his expensive business shirt in a hug. He responded, gently holding me as he whispered, "Just make sure it's me you call instead of Zara. I'd rather not have to dispose of a body this evening *and* establish alibis."

"You're the best," I added, knowing the clock was ticking and Jagger was going to be there soon to pick me up. "Now

I've got to go get ready for this birthday party. Make sure Zara doesn't work too late, go drag her butt home if she doesn't leave the office in the next hour or so."

Lincoln laughed because he knew as well as I did, Zara would come home when she was good and ready, and no one was dragging her anywhere. And secretly I was a little relieved she wasn't home, knowing out of the two of them, Lincoln was the safer option to answer the door when Jagger arrived.

Disappearing into the bathroom, I quickly showered and threw on my makeup before slinking into my bedroom and choosing a dress. I'd decided on a present, which thankfully I didn't have to leave home for, leaving all the valuable moments I had to decide on what I was going to wear.

There was a knock on my bedroom door just as I was applying my lipstick, my signature candy pink generously lashing my lips as Jagger entered before I could turn around and answer it.

"Wow." His eyes rolled up and down my body, the sparkly rose gold dress clinging to my curves like a second skin.

It was probably a little over the top, but I didn't care, preferring to be over dressed for Dane's soiree than turn up looking like I was heading to a BBQ. Besides, from what I saw when I crashed the Hartleys' anniversary party, they liked to do fancy. At least *most* of them.

"You like?" I spread out my arms, letting him get a better look as I twirled. "I didn't get a chance to call Dane myself, but I assumed cocktail attire given the time."

His body moved against mine, not giving me time to appreciate the beautiful lines of his immaculate tailored black suit. His shirt was popped at the collar with no tie in an understated effort to not look too formal. "I don't like it, Belle, I love it. Then there probably isn't a lot you could wear that I wouldn't love. Or not wear." His lips spread into a cheeky grin.

I loved him like that, playful, relaxed, unguarded.

There were glimpses, especially when we were alone. But I cherished the moments that I knew were preciously unshared, reserved just for me.

"Oooooooo, you'll have a chance to take it off me later, Hartley," I teased, smiling seductively. "But we need to go to this party first."

Jagger sighed, cursing under his breath. "I still can't believe you talked me into this. I hate these things."

"Did Dane have a heart attack when you told him you were going to his party?" I played with the lapel of his jacket. "Or was he already bored to death after he got his scotch and tie?"

Jagger playfully squeezed my hip. "He was shocked but grateful, and I'll have you know he loved my presents."

"Sure, sure, lying to preserve the feelings of your sibling isn't even a thing." I laughed. "Anyway, my present is more than going to make up for it."

"What did you get?" Jagger asked, looking worried.

My fingers reached down to my nightstand, picking up an envelope. There was no card inside unfortunately but after raiding Zara's stationery, I managed to whip up a pretty note and enclosed the voucher I'd printed out. "Circus school! A whole day playing on the trapeze. Fun, right?"

Jagged eyes widened as he coughed out. "Trapeze? You've met Dane, right?"

I rolled my eyes, wondering if maybe I should've gotten circus school. "Relax. It's indoor rock climbing. Not as fun, but apparently very popular right now in corporate circles. It will totally give him more street cred at board meetings."

His lips spread into a grin, inching me in closer. "That's actually a pretty cool gift."

"I told you so. When it comes to presents, I'm really good." I beamed, hoping I'd soon be able to give him a gift too. Maybe opening night, even if I would be sitting in the audience instead of the stage wings.

He leaned closer, brushing his mouth against mine in a kiss. "You're really good when it comes to more than just presents."

It was so easy like that.

Just the two of us, in a bubble where nothing else mattered. But I wasn't the kind of girl who could live like that, separated from everything and everyone. Even though I loved our moments.

"Come on, we'll be late." I tugged at his arm, both anxious and excited. "And I know you're just looking for an excuse to not go."

Chuckling under his breath, he took a much-needed step back, kissing my knuckles as he locked our fingers together. "We'll go. But I hope Zara and Lincoln aren't expecting you home later, because I'm going to need you in my bed tonight."

I hoped he still felt like that later.

"I'm all yours," I declared, meaning every single word of it. "I won't leave until you ask me to."

His voice lowered, the words so gently spoken I almost didn't hear them. "Well then, you'll be around for a while."

And God, I hoped he meant that.

Chapter 22

Jagger

I could probably sit through anything if Belle was with me, wearing that dress. Hell, she wouldn't even need the dress, she could just give me that smile of hers and that would be enough.

And while I wasn't a fan of crowded public gatherings, it was nice to be able to be in public with Belle. We'd had to play it cool at work, but Dane's friends literally couldn't care less about me and who I was dating. With most of them trust-fund babies, with fat bank accounts and full social calendars, they had more interesting topics of conversation to gossip about. Although I didn't really enjoy their company, I was grateful for the opportunity.

It was a date.

Something we'd barely done since we'd met, and I was hoping to show Belle I was willing to meet her halfway and do things that were important to her.

Dane had rented a penthouse apartment in Manhattan with a huge balcony overlooking the city. He figured it was easier since most of his friends lived in New York, opting for a more scaled-down version in Connecticut with Mom and Dad later. It was a family tradition to have more than one celebration for a birthday. A tradition shared by everyone except me, who preferred one quiet and understated gathering, if anything at all. It wasn't that I didn't like parties, or my birthday, I just wasn't into the self-indulgent circus that accompanied them. Which was why I avoided Dane's. Or at least I did. Past tense.

Belle was a ball of excitement, her light brown eyes shiny as she bounced on her heels, almost giddy as we made it to the door. Not even a hard-ass like me was immune to her infectious elation, finding myself not dreading the gathering as much as I thought I would.

"Well, well, as I live and breathe." Dane mock gasped, taking a step aside so we could enter. "Not sure I'd ever see the day Jagger Hartley willingly came to a family event, and yet here we are."

I smirked, raising an eyebrow as I put my arm around Belle. "No one said I was willing."

Dane laughed, punching me lightly in the arm. "Yeah, well I'm just glad you're here. Fairly sure this is the first birthday you've attended since I was sixteen."

"Eighteen," I corrected. "It was at that godawful dive bar in Queens that didn't care they were serving a bunch of minors. I was the one picking up the tab and giving them a hefty tip so they'd overlook your inability to handle your liquor when you vomited on their pool table."

"Ahhhhh yes, of course." Dane winked at Belle. "Best big brother anyone could ever ask for. Feel free to get messy and allow me to repay the favor. There's no pool table, but there's a pretty impressive baby grand piano in the living room."

"Happy Birthday, Dane." Belle moved from my hold on her hip and wrapped her delicate arms around my brother. "Thank you so much for having us."

Dane accepted her hug, the smile on his face getting even wider. "Are you kidding? It's always a pleasure to see you. And I don't know what you had to do to get him here, but keep doing it. You guys look good together."

While I wasn't sure how *good* we looked together, I would agree that I'd never been happier. Things were still complicated at work, and it was a balancing act, but I was doing everything I could to not fuck it up.

"Can I have my girlfriend back now?" I asked, pretending to be bored.

Dane's eyes widened, releasing Belle as he took a step back. "Wow, did you say *girlfriend*?" He grabbed his chest dramatically. "Is one of New York's most-eligible bachelors off the market? Someone call *People* magazine, stat."

I flipped him off discreetly, rolling my eyes. "We're not going public just yet." Not that Dane was the kind of guy to talk to the press but I didn't need him telling our parents either. They'd find out eventually, but at the moment, I wanted to keep Belle all to myself, away from the convolution that was the Hartley family.

"Oooooooooooo." Dane lowered his voice. "Well, your secret's safe with me. Enjoy your night." And with a quick wave he disappeared to mingle and network, something he excelled at.

"So what does that mean exactly?" Belle asked, her smile dropping a little.

"About not going public?" My brows knitted in confusion. "I thought we agreed that it wouldn't be a good idea until the end of the season. When the show is over, it won't matter anymore."

Granted it wasn't ideal, but I wasn't exactly hiding her away in the basement either. I wasn't some huge celebrity that press followed, so being seen on the streets wasn't really an issue. After all it was New York City, and most people didn't give a shit. But I wasn't going to be advertising it either, knowing that even though I'd be careful to make sure there was no impropriety, it still wouldn't look good. It was a compromise, something most people didn't assume I was capable of.

She looked around, no one paying us any attention. "Aren't you worried? What if someone sees? Oh, so that's why when we're out you barely touch me. Plausible deniability?"

I shook my head, not blaming her for not seeing that it wasn't the same thing. "Yes, and no," I tried to explain. "Here, no one gives a shit. But I'm not the kind of guy to kiss you on the street either. I'm not denying anything, Belle, I'm just not advertising we're together. It's not the same thing."

"You kissed me at the club," she pointed out. "And then out on the street after karaoke."

She was right, I'd done both of those things and if she wasn't careful I was going to kiss her in front of all these people too. "It was different, no one knew who we were. I don't regret it, Belle, I'm just trying to do what's best for both of us."

Her head bobbed in a slight nod, but I could tell she wasn't convinced. Or maybe she assumed it was my way of keeping her my side piece, happy to fuck her senseless in the shadows but not proud enough to have her on my arm. It was bullshit, and if only she knew exactly *how* much I cared about her. "You have to know that this isn't about my feelings for you. If things were different—"

"I quit." It shot out of her mouth in a rush, but there was no mistake it hadn't been what she'd intended to say. "I'm auditioning for Rittenborough and if that doesn't work out, then I'll find something else."

What?

WHAT!

I'd assumed there was a possibility that I could lose her. I couldn't guarantee stage time and if someone else could give her that shot, then I'd have to respect the choice.

Business was business, and she was too talented to sit on the sidelines.

But that hack?

No. Just fucking no.

"Rittenborough?" I coughed out, convinced I must've heard her wrong even though I knew he was scouting. "The Andrew Lloyd Webber wannabe who wouldn't find an original idea if he fell into it?"

She stood up straighter, unperturbed by my assessment of her potential future employer. "He has an original script, and from what I hear it is a great opportunity."

"Let's talk about this when we get home," I bristled, my mood taking a turn and not in a good way. "You wanted to come to Dane's birthday, so let's do that."

It was harsher than I'd intended, annoyed about Belle going to work for that asshole and leaving me. And while I knew it technically wasn't personal, it felt like it all the same.

"No." She put her hands on her hips, not letting it slide like I wanted. "You said it yourself, no one here cares about us or what we're doing and I'd rather talk about it now than pretend to be having a good time."

"Belle, I do not want to do this here," I warned, not interested whether anyone was watching or not. "I said no."

She took a step back, almost shocked. "No? No to what exactly, Jagger? To the conversation or to me leaving?"

I wasn't completely stupid, and knew that while I wanted to tell her flat out she was going to go work for that piece of shit over my dead body, it would ultimately send her running there. "The conversation."

"Fine." She shook her head, a fake smile edging wider. And I knew it was fake because her eyes were no longer glassy. Instead they were fierce, a deadly glance that could kill a man from ten feet away with little effort. And had that death stare not been directed at me, I'd have been incredibly turned on.

Okay, so maybe I was turned on anyway.

"Belle." I put my arm around her, pulling her in close. "Let's not ruin the night."

It wasn't overt but I felt her stiffen, and while she was a brilliant actress, I could tell she was annoyed.

"Belle! Oh my God, is that you?"

I turned finding a dude who I immediately knew I wasn't going to like. "Jesus! It is you. Wow, how are you? Imagine meeting you here."

Without warning he pulled her into a huge hug, his hands lingering too close to her ass as he laughed. "You look fucking awesome, by the way."

Belle chuckled, her icy demeanor shelved temporarily as she welcomed the affections of the mystery prick. "Drew! Wow, what a surprise. What are you doing here?"

"It's my catering company." He pointed to the table laid out with assorted food. "Dane's an important customer, I'm hanging around just to make sure everything runs smoothly."

Not only did he completely ignore me when exactly five minutes ago I'd had my arms around Belle, but it was clear that not only did he know her, but was *friendly* too.

I cleared my throat in what was probably the douchiest most pathetic move of all time, but I didn't care, prompting them both to turn in my direction.

Belle smiled patting me on the arm, "Drew, this is Jagger, Dane's brother. Jagger, this is Drew, a dear friend."

So I was Dane's brother now? And what the fuck did dear friend even mean? They played together as kindergarteners? Dated? She donated blood when he was dying? A lot of fucking leeway.

"Oh hey! Hi, Jagger!" Every sentence met with what felt like an exclamation point as he stuck out his hand. And either he was high or didn't understand the nuances of expression. No one was that surprised all the fucking time.

Reluctantly, I shook his hand, eyeing him carefully as I kept my expression neutral. No point letting him know how much he was getting under my skin. Besides, familiarity aside, I couldn't plot the demise of every man who looked at Belle like he wanted to fuck her. Tempting as it were.

"Hey." My lips folded into a narrow smile, not giving him anything else.

His attention swung back to Belle, moving his fingers up and down her arm. "I should probably get back to work but give me your number. I lost all my contacts when I accidently washed my phone in a pair of jeans, and we should catch up."

Without skipping a beat, the cocksucker slipped out his phone and deposited it into Belle's delicate fingers.

"Sure. That would be nice." She grinned, entering what I hoped was the number for Dave's Laundromat instead of her own digits. "Oh, and congrats on the catering business. I'm so happy for you." She handed the phone back and gave his arm a squeeze. "I'll be sure to taste everything."

"Exactly what I wanted to hear." Douchebag winked. "Talk soon." And with a sly grin I didn't trust, he disappeared back to the food table, no doubt needing to readjust his balls.

Belle turned to face me, expecting I'd have something to say. But I didn't budge, biting my tongue and instead remaining completely impassive as we stood in relative silence.

I was Switzerland.

Refusing to act like a jealous jerk regardless of how justified I felt I was. And trust me, I had a lot to say, starting with are you actually going to catch up with the asshole.

"Something wrong, Jagger?" she baited, blinking innocently like she didn't know how infuriated I was.

"Nope, nothing," I lied, refusing to make a scene. "Let me go get you something to drink at the bar. I'll be right back."

Needing a minute to cool off, I stalked to the full-sized bar that had been installed in one of the corners of the room. There were white shirted dudes flipping cocktail shakers and pouring beers, giving everyone a show as well as quenching their thirst.

Belle surprisingly didn't follow me, staying back while I grabbed her something fruity and colorful and got myself a beer.

It did occur to me that she might go and cozy up to the ass-hole but at least then I'd fucking know, wouldn't I? I wasn't even sure why I was so mad, knowing her leaving made sense.

It would fuck us a little—needing to get a new understudy and get her up to speed—but it was early days, and a professional could come in and get it down quickly. It wouldn't be Belle, but she would be adequate, I was sure. And then there would be no conflict. We could see each other with no issues. But for all the intelligent parts of my mind telling me that it was potentially a good thing, there were equal parts countering.

She deserved better.

Of course she did.

But Rittenborough wasn't better.

Even if she was headlining, at best she'd get reduced to a three-sentence review in some buried article. He wasn't the messiah he claimed to be, promising unknowns their chance for their day in the promised land.

Fucking.

Hell.

The confliction bubbled inside of me as I walked back, and while she wasn't chatting to the moron, she was deep in conversation with one of Dane's female friends.

"Well, well. Jagger Hartley as I live and breathe."

I was so focused on what Belle was doing I almost slammed right into Rebecca. She arched a brow, taking a huge swallow of her tequila on ice as she straightened. "You must be dying. Because I can't think of any other logical reason why after all these years, you'd finally come to your brother's birthday."

While she was technically Dane's friend—they went to college together—we'd dated briefly. Well, not so much dated as fucked, casually hooking up and satisfying the urge.

"Not dying," I responded drily, watching as she took another gulp from her glass.

She lifted her shoulder in a shrug. "Shame, I have the perfect funeral dress picked out. I'd have looked fabulous."

A small smile crept across my lips. "I'm sure you would have." Not many women understood the brevity of a casual no-strings relationship like Becks, and for a while it worked out well for the both of us. Except she eventually wanted more and knew I wasn't the guy to give it to her.

"So who's the girl?" She tipped her head in Belle's direction. "And don't tell me nobody, Jagger. I know you better than that."

"My girlfriend." And it occurred to me that it was possibly the only time I'd said it out loud to anyone other than Belle or Dane. "We're dating."

"Dating or *dating*?" Becks arched a brow to illustrate the distinction.

When I didn't respond, she made her own conclusions. "Wow." She chuckled, shaking her head. "Must be really something special then. Congratulations."

"Thanks." I glanced over at Belle who was looking right at me. And she didn't look pleased. "I should probably go."

Becks laughed. "How the mighty have fallen. Better get back to her before she wises up."

And while I knew it was a jab—probably well deserved—I didn't care, knowing Belle could do better. She just wasn't going to get the chance, at least not if I could help it.

Belle watched curiously as I left Becks and strode toward her. "Making friends?" she asked as I handed her a cocktail. "Let me guess, old girlfriend."

I shouldn't have been surprised, Belle was probably one of the most perceptive people I'd ever met. And I wasn't going to lie to her, even if I wasn't interested in having the conversation.

"We dated. It wasn't serious." I took a sip from my beer. "Anything else you want to know?"

"Yeah, but I'm not going to ask now," Belle answered honestly. "But if you could look like you're having a better time, I'd appreciate it. Last thing I need is for anyone else you dated thinking you're miserable with me."

"Belle, I'm not miserable." I laughed, loving that she said whatever came into her head even if it sounded a little crazy. "This is how I usually look, don't pretend to be surprised now."

"I didn't say I was surprised, I just asked for you to modify it. For my benefit." Her lips twitched at the edges. "This isn't going as well as I'd hoped."

"Really?" I deadpanned. "In your head you saw this going a different way?"

She rolled her eyes, trying to hide her smirk. "Fine. But we're here until cake."

And while I wanted nothing more than to leave, take her back home and be alone with her, I knew the inevitable conversation would follow.

Not Drew.

Not Becks.

But her leaving to go work with someone else.

And I'd rather deal with hours of social interaction with people I could barely stand than hear she was walking away.

It didn't matter in what capacity.

It would hurt all the fucking same.

Chapter 23

Belle

Jagger stayed until cake.

He even managed to crack a smile from time to time so he didn't look like a hostage victim, held against his will in a YouTube video for ransom. I did notice "Becks" the woman he apparently dated-but-not-seriously eyeing us on more than one occasion.

Of course I was jealous.

Irrational, because if Jagger wanted to be with her, he would be. And considering he barely even looked in her general direction, he clearly wasn't interested.

Unless he was purposely trying to seem disinterested.

And why the hell didn't he ask me about Drew?

He wanted to, I saw the way his jaw ticked when I was adding my number to Drew's phone for a catch up I had no intention of. Granted, I'd never been romantically involved with Drew and was just trying to be friendly.

Fine, maybe I was being a little bratty opportunist, hoping to get a reaction.

Gahhh, I was becoming neurotic.

Trying not act like a totally unhinged psychopath, I was quiet on the ride home. Because for as much as I loved Jagger, I hated this version of myself where I was an insecure lunatic.

"Do you want me to take you home?" Jagger asked, even though we'd pulled up in front of his building. "You don't have to stay with me tonight if you don't want to."

"What?" I looked up, surprised the engine was still running and he'd made no move to get out of the car. "Why wouldn't I want to stay?"

"Maybe because you haven't said two words to me since we left Dane's and look like you're a million miles away." He turned to face me. "If you want me to take you home, just ask me, Belle."

"No, I don't want to go home." I shook my head knowing it would be worse if I left. I'd only obsess about it all night, creating a bunch of scenarios in my head and make myself even crazier. "But we should probably talk."

I said *probably* because I wasn't sure that was what I wanted.

Blindsiding him at his brother's birthday party hadn't been the plan. Especially when it was such a big deal trying to get him there. No, I was going to have a rational, well-thought-out discussion where I listed all the pros and cons, ultimately walking away for our greater good. Like a superhero. We'd make love and live happily ever after. Or at least that was the way I'd intended it to go.

But.

The more time I spent with him, the harder it was for me to think straight. Justifying it in my head that 'it would be okay' and chicken out. Like I did the first time where I wasn't going to sleep with Jagger again. Because that worked out so stellar. And I just knew that *this* time, I couldn't back down. Even if the timing was terrible and it made me feel like a callous and inconsiderate bitch.

Honestly, I'd have preferred to go upstairs to Jagger's apartment, have him rip my clothes off and give me three orgasms.

Push the inevitable drama aside and deal with it another day. But I'd been doing that a lot, pretending that things would miraculously fall into place if I just ignored them long enough.

"Here or there?" Jagger pointed up to his bedroom window that was visible from the street.

"There."

Bad idea. And yet, I didn't want to sit in an idling car like I was in a Taylor Swift style breakup.

"Okay." He cut the engine, popping open the door and stepped out onto the sidewalk. I did the same, meeting him there as he hesitantly put his arm around me. "Let's go."

The elevator was torture, wanting to turn into his body and kiss him. I hated the uneasy feeling, just wanting to make it better with our connection. And when I kissed him, everything felt right.

But I didn't.

Keeping my lips to myself as we made our way inside his apartment.

"Jagger," I started, figuring I was just going to say it all before I lost my nerve. And then before I could get anything else out, he was kissing me.

I hadn't started it.

I'd been strong.

But once his lips were on mine, I was powerless to stop.

"We're supposed to be talking," I mumbled against his lips, attempting to be responsible. "I can't think when you kiss me."

My body wanted to stay in that moment, to forget everything and deal with it tomorrow.

Next week.

Next month.

But I promised myself I was going to make the break tonight and I was already losing my nerve.

"Jagger. Stop." I kissed him, sending so many mixed signals I was mad at myself. "We need to talk and then after, if you still want me, I'll stay."

He pulled away abruptly, looking into my eyes. "You'd think I'd ask you to go?"

"Jagger, I know you're pissed about me leaving—"

"Belle." He cut me off, not letting me finish, his tone softening as he grazed my chin with his thumb. "You don't have to quit. It's a couple of months. And then we can do whatever we want."

And that was why I didn't want to kiss him, because when he looked at me like that it was easy to believe that yeah, sure, it would all work out.

Except we'd tried it.

And I hated sneaking around.

"I can't, Jagger. I love you." The words came out in a rush, unable to hold them back any longer. "I *love* you. And I don't want to have to hide that like it's something to be ashamed of. Like we've done something wrong. I don't want to pretend you're not my boyfriend to people at work, or be worried when we're out that someone might see us."

His eyes were wide, mouth opened as he stared at me, speechless.

"I know you think it's just a couple of months." I shook my head, unable to stop myself now I'd given myself permission to say it. "But I am not going to live a lie. It feels wrong, and I don't want that. I can go," I offered, my heart not wanting to leave him or the production but knowing I couldn't have both.

And while I didn't necessarily expect him to say he loved me too, he didn't say anything at all.

Nothing.

"Did you hear me, Jagger?" I asked, wondering if he hadn't slipped into a wormhole and had missed the part where I told him I loved him.

"I heard you, Belle." He took a step back. "Well if you want to go, I'll release you from your contract. I think you'd be wise to wait until you've been at least offered a part before you go torching your career though."

What?

225

He had heard ALL of that and was focusing on me quitting?

Not only was I crushed that my declaration of love had gone unnoticed and unacknowledged, but he was also doubting my talent. That I couldn't land another part and he'd been my savior, plucking me out from obscurity to give me my big fucking break.

Anger, hurt and a bucket of emotions I couldn't identify bubbled to the surface as I breathed out a hard breath. "Logan has already spoken to Rittenborough," a detail I might have omitted earlier, "and he has almost guaranteed me the lead."

"Oh so Logan is involved as well? I should've fucking known." Jagger's eyes flared, his body stiffening like it was made of stone. "You and Logan cook up this little mutiny while we were paying you to rehearse? Or did you meet in your own time, behind my back?"

"It's not like that," I argued back. The discussion had been more a passing comment, Logan trying to entice me, insisting Rittenborough would take us both. "I wasn't doing anything behind your back."

He scoffed, running his hand through his hair as he barked out a laugh. "Sure, because those kinds of assurances just happen. What did you promise him? Was it Logan or Rittenborough? Which one are you going to sleep with next?"

He'd barely gotten the words out when I slapped him across the face.

Hard.

And not like a 50s starlet in a black and white movie, her gloved hand barely leaving a mark. I'm talking a full opened palm with enough force to leave fingerprints on his skin making his body pitch back.

And fuck him for making me resort to violence, my fingers curling into a fist as my own skin stung.

"Don't you ever speak to me like I'm a whore, Jagger," I spat out, my little body trembling with anger even though he was double my size. "I don't care how you spin this in your head, but

I have never used my body like that. And if I did anything wrong, it was sleep with you."

My finger jabbed in his chest as my throat tightened, sick to my stomach that not only minutes ago I'd told him I loved him.

Damn him.

He didn't even have the decency to touch his cheek even though I knew it had to have hurt, his hazel eyes emotionless as he said nothing.

"Well, guess that has solved that problem." I moved back to the door, the very one I'd been so convinced I wouldn't be leaving through so soon. "I quit, effective immediately. You can let the cast know I'm moving on to pursue other opportunities." My feet stopped, looking back over my shoulder. "Oh, and in case there was any doubt, me and you are also done."

Turns out that not only could I not have them both—the production and Jagger—but I couldn't have them at all.

And how stupid was I? Spilling my guts, emotionally bleeding in front of him when he clearly didn't love me.

He trusted me.

Guess that meant he'd be okay with me having his wi-fi password and the login to his Netflix account, just not access to his heart.

My eyes stayed dead straight, focusing on the wood as I opened his front door and then closed it quickly behind me. I didn't expect him to stop me, or chase me out into the hall. That would involve emotion and he was clearly a corpse.

A living, breathing bag of muscle and bones with a chest cavity where his heart should be.

Not having any real solid plan, I stomped down the stairs rather than take the elevator to give myself time to think. I wanted to go home but knew Zara or Lincoln would probably start planning Jagger's murder and their defense, and I didn't have the stomach for either of those.

Because as much as I hated him at that moment—and trust me, I did—I still loved the stupid jerk.

"Gahhhhh." I was so mad, grabbing the handle of the external door and pulling it open.

I didn't even bother opening my phone to get an Uber, managing to grab a cab almost the minute my feet had hit the sidewalk. At least there was that, throwing myself into the back seat and giving the driver the address of where I wanted to go.

Hayley's would've been the obvious choice, she'd have not only understood but let me wallow in my misery without judgment or an I-told-you-so. But it was late, and I didn't want to wake the baby, and part of me wasn't sure Jagger wouldn't come looking for me. Maybe that was what I was hoping for, but then secretly wanting to punish him by not being able to find me.

Because that wasn't messed up.

Opting to go to the one place I knew he wouldn't look, I sat back in the cab too consumed with my own thoughts to make small talk with the driver. I'm sure he thought I was some rude princess, grunting monosyllabic sounds when he asked me how my night was.

He'd no doubt confirmed his assumption when he dropped me off at a building on the Lower East Side, rolling his eyes when I pulled out my credit card to pay the fare.

I stared up at the windows, praying he was home. I'd already established I lacked the skills to break into anything, and the apartments I was in front of were a lot more secure than Jagger's.

My nerves jangled as I pressed the buzzer, figuring that since it had been so easy to get a cab, the universe clearly was on my side. And when the crackle of the speaker broke through the noise on the street, I felt my shoulders relax as I exhaled.

"Hello?"

"Hey, Nate, it's Belle. I need sanctuary."

Nate's warm laugh exploded through the speaker. "Well, you best come on up. Must be pretty bad if Zara and Lincoln traumatized you, of all people. I'll get the eye bleach ready."

And with a loud buzz the external door popped open allowing me entry.

I almost ran to the elevator, pressing the button for Nate's floor and finding him waiting at his front door.

"Come on in." His head tipped toward the inside of his apartment. "Just don't expect therapy, Belle, you know I'm not that kind of a doctor."

Nate Baxter was one of the best humans alive.

He was magically brought into our lives when Zara met Lincoln. As Linc's best friend, we happily adopted the very single, very amazing E.R. doctor who was as talented in the medical field as he was hot. And had he not been gay, we'd have been the perfect couple. Instead, we became really good friends. And while we didn't see each other enough because of his insane work schedule, I adored the hell out of him. He was also loyal, trustworthy, and would happily bury a body for any of his friends. Not that I needed that level of commitment, but it was nice to know it was there.

"I've missed you." I threw my arms around him, pulling myself in for a hug before he'd properly closed the door. It had been weeks since I'd seen Nate, my distraction with Jagger making me miss the last time he came over for dinner with Zara and Lincoln.

He hugged me back, his big strong arms lifting me off the ground with little effort. "Missed you too, Tiny Dancer. Now tell me why you're here because as much as my ego would like to think it's for my stellar personality, your eyes are too sad."

He was always so perceptive, which was probably why I loved him so much. "Boy trouble." I sighed, feeling like I was on the brink of dissolving into a puddle of tears.

I'd been so good to keep it together up until that point, but I didn't trust myself much longer. And now that I was safely away, with no one judging me, I just knew those inevitable tears would come.

"Did someone hurt you, Belle?" He lifted my chin away from his chest, studying my face. "You can tell me."

I shook my head as my eyes started to get damp. "Not like that. But I just can't face going home right now."

He pulled me back to his chest, gently stroking my hair. "Then you'll stay here, and we'll work it out."

Not sure anything could be worked out, but I didn't have it in me to argue. "I should call Zara so she doesn't worry, but I just don't have it in me to talk to her right now."

I loved my sister, but she'd be out for blood. Want to hunt him down and maim Jagger for hurting me, but my heart couldn't cope. And deep down I knew hurting him wouldn't make me hurt any less, still in love with the jerk, even if it was totally unwarranted or smart.

"I'll handle that call. And then you can tell me what happened. Deal?"

My head bobbed, my throat feeling tight. "I'll tell you everything."

Chapter 24

Jagger

"**H**ow the hell did you let her walk out?" Dane yelled, pacing in my apartment as I sat on the couch with my head in my hands. It wasn't like me not to know what to do, but when Belle walked out, I was literally at a loss.

Did I stop her?

Barricade her in?

Fairly sure false imprisonment wasn't the answer.

So instead I let her leave, going against every instinct I had but figuring it was for the best.

"What was I supposed to do, Dane? Grab some zip ties and strap her to a chair? Being held captive is such a turn-on," I spat out, irritated at my brother but mostly at myself. Because he was right. I shouldn't have let her leave.

Not like that.

She loved me.

Loved me.

And while she hadn't been the only woman who'd ever said it to me, she was the first one I'd felt the same way.

But I didn't say it.

Too fucking up in my own head about her walking out of the production and conspiring with Logan. Basically sabotaging myself because what the fuck did I know about love and happiness.

I'd convinced myself we just needed to stick it out.

For Belle to stay with me so that when we opened on that first night, she was there by my side. Because as much as I'd never needed anyone's approval or fucking adulation, I'd really wanted hers.

It was a few lousy months. We could do exactly what we were doing and then when the show wrapped and I wasn't her director anymore, we'd tell everyone. Fuck, I'd even rent one of those billboards in Time's Square if she wanted, and I fucking hated the attention.

But I'd have done it for her.

Instead, she was scheming ways to leave, and not just go, but partner with the dude I was positive was desperate to sleep with her to go be directed by a hack.

"Fuck." I pushed my hands through my hair. "This is so fucked up."

Dane picked up my phone, handing it to me. "Call her, Jagger. Call her, apologize and tell her that you want to talk. I don't care how much you don't want her to go work for whatever his name is, you losing her over your pride is the dumbest thing you've ever done."

He was right.

And he was wrong.

The dumbest thing I'd ever done was not casting her as my lead. She'd more than earned it, deserved it, and would've been perfection on that stage. But instead I caved to money and investors, and toed the company line. Ironic I'd been fighting the same bullshit in my family but so willingly did it for strangers. Because that made fucking sense.

"I called her a whore."

"You fucking did what?" Dane's eyes widened as his voice exploded. "Jagger, have you *completely* lost your fucking mind?"

Well, that sure as shit was up for debate.

"Not exactly like that." I shook my head, knowing it was semantics and no fucking excuse. "I was pissed, and it just came out. Anyway, I got what I deserved." I rubbed my cheek, her hand surprisingly powerful for being so small.

It was unlike me to call Dane and ask for his help, especially when it involved abandoning his own fucking birthday party. Chalk it up to another shitty thing I'd done, the list proving to be quite extensive. But of course the minute I'd dialed he didn't even let me finish before he was in the car. I guess never asking for help makes the first time feel sorta urgent. Which I guess it was considering I was in uncharted territory. And while caring about the breakup of a relationship was completely new for me, as was the feelings that came with it. It was the unbearable desperation and confusion that made me the most concerned.

"I should've told her." I shook my head, wondering if it was too late.

Dane looked at me carefully, unsure what else I could've added to the conversation after accusing Belle of prostituting herself. Yeah, not my finest hour. "Told her what?"

"That I love her," I admitted, the words feeling wasted since I'd wanted Belle to hear them first. "She told me she loved me and I didn't say it back. Even though I knew I loved her and have for weeks. I didn't say it, Dane, and now I'm not sure I'll get the chance."

His lack of a response spoke volumes, because as long as he'd know me, he'd never heard me say 'I love you' to a woman. Not even when I was in a relationship. I'd duck-and-weave, side-stepping with a heartfelt "I care about you" or an "I think you're great." But I wouldn't lie, not even if it would make my life easier. And the first time it was actually justified, I chickened out.

"Why didn't you?" Dane asked, refusing to give me a free pass when I didn't elaborate. "If you loved her, why the hell didn't you tell her, Jagger? Why would you say all that other stuff?"

"Fuuuuckk," I breathed out, frustrated and annoyed with no real idea on how to fix the situation, or myself. "Because I'm a coward, Dane. Because, while I get wanting to put distance between our work and personal relationship makes sense, I feel like she's choosing herself over me." I shook my head, realizing that I sounded like a selfish bastard. "Of course, she's entitled to. She should do what's best for her. And if being with me and doing the play made her feel like she was sneaking around or living some double life, then I get it. But it wasn't forever. I wanted her with me for fuck's sake. As conceited and selfish as it sounds, I wanted her with *me*. Everyone has had their fucking moments, Dane. You with your multiple degrees and chair appointments, Dad and Mom with their fucking ridiculous eccentricities and high-profiled careers, and I wanted this to be about me."

Even saying it out loud made me sound like a spoiled little shit.

And I hated it.

Hated that I needed it and how weak it made me feel.

Poor little Jagger didn't get enough love and attention from Mommy and Daddy and now has abandonment issues. Jesus Christ, could I be more pathetic?

"Jagger . . ."

"Don't," I cut him off, knowing nothing he could say or do was going to fix it. "I don't want your fucking pity right now. Seriously, I don't think I could fucking take it."

I stared at the door, wishing I could go back in fucking time and handle it differently. Or convince her to stay. Or at the very fucking least, tell her how I felt.

"It wasn't going to be pity." Dane finally spoke, pulling my arm so I turned to face him. "But I was going to say that while I appreciate you admitting that to me, I'm not really the person you should be telling."

"No shit." I barked out a humorless laugh. "I'll just make my way over to her apartment and camp outside her door. Wait for her attorney sister and her soon-to-be brother-in-law to tally up multiple counts of harassment and stalking charges. I bet they have judges on speed dial."

"Or she might talk to you. It's happened before."

Dane and his everything-will-turn-out attitude. I swear, in a different world, he and Belle would've been soulmates. They were both clinically optimistic with an unhealthy addiction to happy-ever-afters. Except in this case, where Belle went totally off-script, and assumed the worst. Not that I'd have ever allowed that to happen, the two of them ending up together. I was so instinctively and intensely attracted to Belle that I couldn't give her up even though she'd have probably been happier with him. That was exactly the kind of prick I was.

Frustrated and angry, I grabbed my keys and headed toward the door as I let out a groan.

"Where are you going?" Dane asked, the ever-present hope shining in his eyes.

"To go get myself arrested, clearly. Have the fucking Hartley Family legal team on standby. I guess if I'm going to shit the bed on this thing, it might as well be all the way."

And with the decision made, and not wanting to talk about it anymore, I walked out of my apartment, leaving Dane inside.

There wasn't a doubt he'd offer to come with me.

To drive.

Help diffuse the situation if needed.

But I was a stubborn son of a bitch and if there was ever a need to do something on my own, it was this.

Unless that arrest wasn't so hypothetical and then, fuck, I'd take all the help I could get.

It was late by the time I got to Belle's, the day feeling more like it had been a week as I pulled onto a side street and parked my car. Knowing it was inviting trouble, I cursed under my breath as I exited onto the street and jogged to the external door of her building.

My finger hesitated for a second before I pressed the buzzer, then waited for my fate.

"Yes?" Lincoln answered and didn't seem all that surprised. Almost like they were waiting for me.

"It's Jagger, Belle's . . ." *Boyfriend? I mean, did I even get to say that anymore*? "It's just Jagger," is what I settled on, assuming they'd have already heard what an asshole I'd been.

"She's not here, buddy. Good luck."

Huh, what did that even mean? Obviously Lincoln knew *something* but I had no idea what and how much. Did she tell them we had a fight? Was she out with her sister? Because I was fairly sure that if Zara knew the circumstances, it would've been her on the other end of that speaker and it wouldn't be to wish me good luck.

"Lincoln." I punched the buzzer again, not giving a shit how desperate I sounded. "Where is she?"

He laughed, the sound crackling out of the tiny box. "Mmmm, nice try but no. But whatever you did, you best fix it before her sister finds out."

Wait.

What?

Zara didn't know? Had Belle not gone home? Where the hell did she go after she left my apartment? It was late. Where would she have gone?

I shook my head, feeling stupid I hadn't thought of it before. *Hayley's.*

Of course she'd have gone to her best friend's place.

With a quick thank you, I left Lincoln and ran back to my car. Maybe there was hope for me yet. And if there wasn't, at least she was somewhere safe, and with someone who cared about her.

I was only slightly calmer making the drive over to Hayley's, once again finding a parking spot and then heading to Hayley's buzzer. There was a huge risk I'd wake the kid but short of scaling the building and sliding in a window, there wasn't much else I could do.

My finger ultimately made the decision, waiting until I heard the pop against the speaker.

"Hello?" Hayley answered, sounding like she'd been asleep.

"Hey, it's Jagger." I didn't bother with the preamble, just needing to see Belle. "Can I please speak to Belle?"

"Belle?" There was a hesitation. "What are you talking about?"

I wasn't going to assume it would be easy, or that her BFF would welcome me with open arms. But I hadn't expected her to lie to me either.

"Come on, Hayley, I know she's here." I looked around, wanting to desperately get off the street. "Lincoln told me she wasn't home."

Confirming I was right, she pressed the external lock, releasing the door so I could go up. I didn't even bother with the elevator, taking the stairs two at a time until I reached Hayley's door.

She didn't look pleased.

"What did you do?" she spat out, pulling me inside. "Start talking, Jagger."

I looked around finding the apartment empty, the only sound coming from a baby monitor in Hayley's hand. "She's *not* here?" I asked, slightly confused. "Then why—"

"Why did I let you up?" Hayley folded her arms across her crumbled pj'd chest. "Because if you wake Bobbie, I'd have to kill you. And I'm not sure if I still need to kill you anyway for whatever you did to Belle. Which I'm sure must be pretty big, considering she's not at home and you don't know where she is."

Fair, but considering I had a bigger problem than worry about my personal safety, I wasn't overly concerned with whatever fate Hayley had planned.

"You haven't heard from her at all?" I asked, knowing how good of an actress the woman in front of me was. Not saying she wasn't telling me the truth, but I needed to be sure.

"No, Jagger, I haven't. So start explaining." She tapped her foot impatiently.

Clearly talking about my feelings wasn't a strong point for me, because had I done it to start with, Belle might not have left. Add in that I didn't really know Hayley very well, and getting me to spill my guts like I was on a talk show wasn't happening.

"Does she have another friend? Someone else she might go and see?"

Her brow rose as her lips pursed. "Are you trying to piss everyone off tonight, Jagger, or you just have a flare for being offensive?" Hayley asked, her tone dry.

Fine, probably not as tactful as I would've liked but Belle had a lot of friends, and was well-liked, so it was feasible she'd gone somewhere else, right? "Sorry, I didn't mean it like that. I just meant, maybe she was worried about waking the baby." I pointed to the baby monitor. "And gone to see another one of her close friends."

Hayley shifted on her feet, knowing I was probably right. While I'd not thought twice about disturbing two households, Belle would. "I don't know."

That wasn't what I wanted to hear.

Because if she wasn't home.

And she wasn't here.

And Hayley couldn't think of a friend that Belle—

FUCK.

She was with him.

Of course she was with him.

Logan, the very piece of shit I'd accused her of sleeping with.

"Goddamn it," I cursed out, annoyed that I'd rolled out the red carpet for that asshole. Hell, they might not have even met if not for me. I bet he was comforting her at that very moment, telling her what a prick I was and how he'd treat her so much better.

I was going to wrap my hands around his fucking neck and squeeze until his stupid Instagramable face exploded.

"Need to go." I turned toward the door, annoyed at how much time I wasted.

Was he kissing her?

Touching her?

Fucking her?

"The hell you are." Hayley grabbed my arm, stopping me from leaving. "You tell me something right now, Jagger Hartley, or I'm grabbing Bobbie and we're coming with you. Oh, and you'll be responsible for putting her back to sleep when we get back."

"She's with Logan. She quit and was going with him to—"

"Rittenborough," she finished for me. "I know, she told me she was going to audition."

Wow, so everyone knew except me, it seemed.

Well then.

"I might not have taken the news well," I offered. "She's probably gone to see him."

And that cocksucker would've been only too happy to welcome her.

Shady son of a bitch.

"Jagger, I really don't think she'd go see Logan."

She didn't think, but she wasn't sure either. And considering what we'd fought about, I'd say I was right.

There was a cry from the monitor, the kid stirring as the volume got louder. She wasn't going to be able to hold my arm and go comfort her baby, and I knew that it wasn't even going to be a choice. "Jagger, just wait for me, okay?" She let go of my arm. "I'll be two seconds and then I'll try calling her. She'll answer my call no matter where she is and what she's doing."

And give her a tip-off I was coming?

Not a chance.

"Sure," I lied, pushing my shoulders back as she took a tentative step back. "I'll wait."

And the minute she slipped out of the room, so did I.

Chapter 25

Jagger

I'd almost had to fire Joe.

Him and his thirty-five million questions about why the hell I needed Logan's fucking address when it was almost one a.m. and what was I going to use it for. Like it mattered to him. All he needed to do was to reach into that personnel file and give me the information. Oh, and start looking for another couple of understudies because apparently, we were going to be down two. Not that I currently gave a shit.

I didn't even care if I wrecked my car, driving like a madman as every single bad thought rushed through my head. Anger, no *rage*, burned through me as my skin itched, my mind trying to focus and not *fly completely off the handle* while mentally I already knew it was too late.

"Open up, Logan." My fist banged on his door. Lucky for me one of his neighbors was walking in at the same time I was, so I didn't have the confrontation on the street. Not sure he'd have let me up, and as much as it was going to suck, I needed to see Belle with him.

Why?

Because it would somehow justify this fucking mess and make me feel like I was less of a prick. Oh, and if she could say she loved me and then run off to some other guy then I guess it would answer questions about exactly how much she loved me. Or didn't.

I was sooooooo fucked up.

"What the fuck?" Logan answered, wearing nothing but a pair of boxers and a dopey look on his face I wanted to smack off. Girls might fall for his stupid act, but I knew better. "Hartley? What are you doing here? It's the middle of the night."

The surprise was no doubt genuine. After all, I had no idea what Belle had told him, if anything at all. For all I knew she'd told him nothing, seeking comfort without the side chat, and he was just as dumb as he looked.

"And you were just what? Sleeping?" I tried not to laugh, the man was a notorious party animal and the only reason he'd be in bed early was if he was with someone. Didn't even need to guess who that was.

Not waiting for an invitation, I pushed past him and moved into his apartment. Figured there was no point playing with pleasantries at the door since it had gone well beyond that.

"Fine, then come on in." Logan laughed, shutting the door behind him. "And for the record, yes, I was sleeping."

Yeah, and I believed that.

"We going to continue to play this game?" I asked, trying my best to not end up with a murder charge on my record. It was tempting, especially since I'd never really liked Logan much anyway. He'd been a decent enough actor which is why I'd hired him in the first place. Though had I known then what I knew now, I'd have passed on him even if he'd won a Tony.

He blew out a curse, pinching the bridge of his nose. "So you know? Belle told you?"

"Yes, I fucking know," I sneered, wondering when Belle was going to pick her moment to appear. Might as well rip the Band-Aid off all at once. Because while I might've gotten over her turning to the shithead while she was upset, sleeping with him wasn't something I could forgive.

He pushed his hand back through his hair and took a breath. "Look Jagger, I get why you're pissed. But it's honestly just business. It might be a smaller production, but I get to lead, dude. You can't hate on me for that."

Ha, he thought I gave a shit about him leaving? Please, it was always a pleasure when the trash took itself out. This guy was stupider than I'd thought. "I couldn't give a rat's ass about you leaving, Logan. A mediocre production with a second-rate director would probably be more on brand for you anyway." Unprofessional, but I didn't care. I mean, why stop now. "But you had no fucking right to take Belle."

And I fucking knew that she wasn't a possession and she more than likely had a say. But as much as I wanted to hate her, despise her for leaving the minute things were good with us, my stupid fucking heart held onto hope that it wasn't all her. That the dipshit hypnotized her with his dick, and he was mostly to blame.

He raised his hands defensively, which proved he wasn't completely clueless. "Look, I get you're angry so I'm gonna pretend you didn't say all that stuff. But Belle is a big girl, capable of making her own decisions. Maybe if you hadn't been such a dick to both of us, we'd have stuck around."

My fist connected before I'd even realized I'd thrown the punch, Logan stumbling back as he gripped his jaw. I wasn't going to join an illegal underground fighting ring, but I'd taken some boxing classes for fitness. And landing a right hook was something I had no problem with.

"Fuck, Jagger!" he cried out. "You fucking hit me." Disbelief dripping from his tone. "Are you insane? What the hell, man?"

"Where is she?" My fists curled at my side wanting to take another swing. "I don't give a shit about you, but I want to talk to her."

Not sure what exactly was left to be said, but I couldn't leave it the way it was. Because clearly, I wanted to turn the knife in deeper and punish myself even more. Or maybe it was some sick way of justifying my initial reaction, like saying all that hurtful stuff was actually more accurate than I knew.

Logan looked around, confused as he tested his jaw. *"Belle?* How the hell should I know? She was going to call me to set up the audition time."

"What?" I spat out, the confusion running both ways. "Isn't she here?"

"Why the hell would she be here? I know you don't really take much interest in people other than yourself, Hartley, but she has a boyfriend," he coughed out.

"Boyfriend?" The word wheezed out of me, still not sure what any of it meant.

He rolled his eyes. "Dude, we have lives outside of your fucking show. Yes, she's been seeing someone. She hasn't said much about him at work because apparently he's private, but she told me last week."

I wasn't sure what I was more surprised about, that Belle had mentioned me or that Logan had been respectful of her relationship. "You want her, I know you do."

The bastard shrugged. "Um, yeah, so what? She's fucking beautiful, and smart, and talented. And that body." He bit his lip suggestively. "But she's not interested. Doesn't mean I'm going to stop being her friend. And despite what you think about Rittenborough, Belle deserves to be a lead. He'll give her that."

Well, we agreed on one thing, Belle *did* deserve to be a lead. "Do you know where she is?" I swallowed, hating myself a little more with each passing second. "I need to talk to her."

"You think I'd tell you even if I did know after the way you acted with me?" Logan scoffed, still cradling his jaw. "Dude, you don't own us, okay. She obviously told you she's out, so you're gonna have to respect that. Like I said, it's not personal, it's business."

But he was wrong, everything about it *was* personal.

If I hadn't been dating her, she wouldn't have left the production.

And if she wasn't the understudy, she wouldn't have left me.

So whichever way you sliced it, I was the common denominator.

My head nodded, and as much as I didn't want to agree with the bastard, he was right. She was out, and I had to respect that. Even if losing her was the most painful thing I could ever imagine.

I didn't even care if she wanted to go work for someone else, I'd get over it. But after everything I'd said. The way I'd acted. She wasn't going to forgive that. And I didn't blame her, because even though in my head, I had my reasons, none of them were good enough for treating her like that.

"You're in with Rittenborough, right?" I asked, each word choking me more than the last.

"Yeah, he's cast me. I was honestly going to tell you, Jagger, we were just ironing out the contracts." Logan actually looked apologetic, which was ironic since I'd burst into his apartment and hit him.

"Good, then you better watch out for her. Because, so help me God, if I hear that he has fucking hurt her in any way or not given her the fucking dues she deserves, I'll make both your lives a living hell," I warned, more of a promise than a threat. "I'll have you and Belle both released from your contracts by tomorrow. I'll get my lawyer to get it to you."

That was assuming Logan didn't press charges in the meantime and I'd be organizing paperwork from a cell. Still, I would do it anyway. Because clearly I didn't deserve her in any capacity and the best thing I could do for her, was let her go.

"Of course I will. I'd never let anything happen to her."

With nothing left to say and wanting the night from hell to end, I turned to leave. A few well-chosen words from Logan would not only have me locked up but would also end my career, and strangely I really didn't give a fuck. Not sure what I even wanted anymore, but that desire to be the best, to fucking prove everyone wrong, didn't hold the same weight as it once did. And maybe I'd have been happy with half of what I thought I'd wanted if I'd just had the right person to share it with.

"Jagger?" Logan called after me, no doubt to let me know I'd probably be hearing from his lawyer before he'd be hearing from mine. "Is it you?"

"Is what me?" I didn't bother turning around, needing to leave.

"The guy? Belle's boyfriend?"

I shook my head, and it wasn't even a lie because I wasn't anything to her anymore. "Nope. She's too smart to end up with someone like me."

And before he could ask any more questions, I left.

I was totally done.

Chapter 26

Belle

When I woke up in Nate's bed, it took me a moment to remember where I was and why I was there. And then it all came back to me and I was sad again.

"Ahhh, more tears." Nate walked in, carrying a cup of coffee and a muffin. "I see you've been reading my anatomy textbook from med school." He pointed to a hefty hardback on his nightstand as he came to sit beside me on the mattress. "Can't say I blame you, it crushes the best of us."

A small chuckle escaped my lips as I leaned against him. "Thanks for not making this weird. I'm sorry I came here and dumped all my problems on you."

It would've made more sense to go somewhere else, home or Hayley. Or even one of my other girlfriends. But out of everyone I knew, Nate was the only person who could bring someone back to life. And even though my broken heart wasn't the same kind of trauma he could fix, there was no one more patient and caring.

"Stop apologizing, already. We're friends, you can come crash here anytime you like. Unlike Lincoln and your sister, I've not seen you naked." He waved his hand in front of his eyes. "Seen more hetero sex than I'd have liked."

I looked down at my bra and panties underneath his soft sheet, too tired to bother throwing on one of his T-shirts like he offered last night. "Is this okay? I'm not making you uncomfortable, am I?

"Belle, please." He laughed. "I'm gay, not a puritanical monk. Besides, I've seen more naked parts in the E.R. than I ever did in my apartment. I just like giving Lincoln a hard time, and have him on the hook for pain and suffering."

"Well, thanks again. It really did help being here." I gave him a hug. "I think just talking it out helped."

Nate rose a brow. "You don't have to lie to me, Belle. I held you as you cried yourself to sleep. You can pretend to be okay for Zara or the shithead who broke your heart, but you don't have to pretend with me."

He always knew the right thing to say. "Aww Nate, you're going to make me cry again." I sniffed against his shoulder. "And you're right, I haven't worked anything out."

While I knew that I still loved him, I wasn't going to go crawling back. And since I'd pretty much quit when I left, there was no real reason to see him anyway. Sure, he could try to sue me for breech, but unless you were a big name, that rarely happened. There might be some harsh words and you'd probably not get a second chance to work with them again, but usually you were let go with very little drama. Ironic, since that was literally our business.

Still, I had no idea how Jagger would handle it. Considering the things he'd said to me especially after I'd told him I'd loved him, I had no idea what he was going to do.

"Lincoln and Zara keep texting me, wanting to know you're okay and if they can come over. The shithead in question was looking for you early this morning."

"He was?" I sat up almost bumping Nate with my head. "Did they say what he wanted?"

Not that it mattered, it was over.

It didn't change anything.

But I still wanted to know.

Nate shook his head. "Nope. I didn't ask. But your phone's still on my coffee table and you have a barrage of missed calls. I assume at least one or two of them are from him."

I'd switched it to silent pretty much as soon as I got to Nate's, then I'd been too much in my own misery to even worry about it. Zara and Lincoln knew where I was so there wasn't any danger of someone filing a missing person's report. And Hayley would just assume I'd be with Jagger and would wait until I returned her call. Unless there was another emergency with Bobbie.

Shit.

"Were any from Hayley?" I asked, slightly panicked but glad to have something else to worry about. "I'd hate myself forever if something happened and she couldn't reach me."

"I didn't check, but I'll go get it for you." He stood up and went out to the living room.

My fingers anxiously knotted in my lap as I waited, ignoring the coffee and muffin he'd set next to the textbook when he'd walked in. And while I knew it was avoidance, and I desperately needed something else to focus on, I hoped and prayed I hadn't been a terrible friend in the process.

Nate walked back in, handing me my phone. "You want your privacy, or you want me to stay? I'm not going to be offended either way."

"Please stay." I tugged at his hand. "If something happened with Bobbie, it might help to have a medical professional around."

"Sure, use me for my skills." He sighed looking up at the ceiling. "Just once I'd love someone to use me for my body."

"Well, I totally would but you said hetero sex is gross." I gave him a small smile. "And I don't have a penis."

"Always something." He shook his head as he watched me dial.

There had been a large number—okay *obscene* number—of missed calls from Hayley and I was more than slightly worried. While I knew she was more than capable of calling 9-1-1 if it was a real emergency, I took my duty as Bobbie's godmother seriously and they didn't have a lot of help in the city.

The phone barely rang once before Hayley picked it up, her voice an angry whisper. "Jesus, Belle. I've been going out of my mind. Where the hell have you been?"

She barely took a breath, telling me how Jagger had gone to her apartment looking for me, piecing together our breakup even without all the details, and not wanting to call Zara since she knew I wasn't home. "I know how your sister can be, and I didn't want to set off a whole chain of events. Besides, if anyone is going to kill him, I want to do it."

It was noble so many people wanted to kill or maim Jagger at my bequest, but honestly, I didn't want him dead. Not really.

"So he came to see you *after* he went to my place?" I looked at Nate, who shrugged not having anything else to add. "And then what happened?"

Even though I shouldn't care, I very much did. Because I wanted to know, and most importantly what it all meant.

"Not sure, but I think he went to see Logan." She sighed. "Honestly, I don't care what he did, my priority is you."

"LOGAN?" I cried out.

Oh. No.

No.

Noooooooooooooo.

"He went to see *Logan*?" My hand moved to my forehead, my head having a hard time remaining straight on my spine. "What the hell!"

Firstly, Logan told me he was leaving in confidence. And while it had slipped when I'd made my confession to Jagger, it was still a shitty thing for me to do.

And secondly, while I'd confessed to Logan that I was seeing someone, more so there were no mistakes on my intentions, I hadn't told him it was *Jagger*. Hell, the whole reason I was initially leaving was so people didn't find out. If Jagger said something, or alluded to, or even hinted that we were a couple, the whole thing would've been for nothing. Well I guess *not* for nothing because clearly I was the only one who was in love, oh and a prostitute as well.

Asshole.

Gah.

I was so mad at him.

"Hayley, I know you have questions, but I'm going to need to call you back." I hurried my goodbye, ending the call to Hayley's protests. I was going to owe her one hell of an explanation when it was all over.

"I need to go." I kicked off the covers, leaping from the bed in a jeté that would've made my old ballet teacher proud. "I'm sorry, Nate, I don't mean to have a meltdown and run, but I really must go."

He grinned, picking up the coffee cup he'd brought for me and took a sip. "Go. I know you still love me."

My arms reached out giving him a hug. "I really do appreciate this, thanks for everything."

"I know. I'm amazing. Now go give that man hell, but put clothes on first."

And that was exactly what I was planning to do.

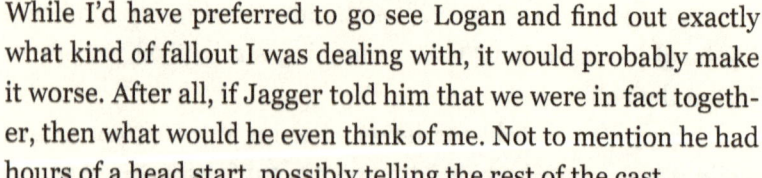

While I'd have preferred to go see Logan and find out exactly what kind of fallout I was dealing with, it would probably make it worse. After all, if Jagger told him that we were in fact together, then what would he even think of me. Not to mention he had hours of a head start, possibly telling the rest of the cast.

Fuck.

So even though I knew it was the worst of all the bad ideas I'd ever had, I caught an Uber to Brooklyn.

It had been a day.

Not even a whole twenty-four hours before walking out on him and hoping I didn't have to see him again, to waltzing back.

But it was different.

My return wasn't to forgive him or hope to rekindle whatever we'd lost.

Nope.

My purpose was to salvage the situation best I could, minimize the damage to my career, and make it clear that I might be small, but I was no pushover.

And fuck Jagger Hartley.

Okay, maybe I wasn't totally on board with the last part because as pathetic as it sounded, I really couldn't hate him. But I wouldn't allow him to know that, regardless of how much it hurt to see him again.

I couldn't press the buzzer fast enough, knowing if I hesitated or thought about it too long, I might chicken out. And I wasn't doing that, no matter how much I wanted too.

"Go away," came Jagger's clipped reply. Unsure of whether he had a security feed and knew it was me or was just being generally prickly, I instead buzzed again.

This time it was a more annoyed "what?" that barreled out of the speaker.

"I need to speak to you. Now. Let me up." I realized that there weren't any real requests in there—more a list of demands—but since he wasn't being polite, I assumed we were doing *that*. And I was all for reading the room.

"Belle?" He seemed surprised, and slightly less grumpy.

I tapped my foot impatiently, trying to not be elated that he seemed glad. It changed nothing. He was the same jerk he'd been yesterday, and I wasn't a doormat.

"Yes, it's me, let me up already."

The pop of the lock was his answer, my hands grabbing the door and wrenching it open as I gave myself a pep talk.

Find out what he said.

Tell him he's an asshole.

Leave to deal with the consequences in private.

I would *not* give him the satisfaction of a breakdown and cry in his living room though I'd wanted to before. And while everyone assumed I was fragile and would crumble easily because I was small, I was a lot stronger than I looked.

He wouldn't be what broke me.

Even if inside my heart was shattered.

Stomping up the stairs as I walked to his door—the elevator was quicker but I'd already committed to stomping, so I went with it—I finally reached the fourth floor.

He was there in the doorway, still ridiculously handsome even though he looked like he hadn't slept.

Good.

I wanted him to suffer.

No, I didn't. Not really.

Uhhhhh, maybe just a little because even good people can want vindication.

My foot almost faltered, taking the last step as I got closer. Our bodies were mere inches apart, and even though he outweighed me and dwarfed me in height, I was not going to back down.

"You." I poked my finger into his chest, hating how much I wanted an excuse to touch him. "Are a nasty piece of work."

"I am," he agreed, blinking slowly, standing there not moving out of the firing line.

And stupidly his lack of defense just made me madder.

"Why would you do that? Why, Jagger?" More finger/chest poking as I met his beautiful hazel eyes with a glare. "Do you get off on destroying people? Have some sick kink where the only way you can be happy is by making people miserable? I won't allow it. I just won't."

"Where were you?" he asked softly, completely avoiding any of my questions and countering with one of his own. He was eerily calm, but I also knew he could win a gold medal in emotional suppression.

"None of your business," I shot back, trying not to soften. I hated being angry, my soul actively repulsed by being intentionally hurtful. But I needed to protect myself too. "*I* am no longer your business."

Nothing.

No dialogue either way, just standing there, like he was willing me to continue.

"What did you tell Logan, Jagger?" I tried not to let my voice waver, pretending we were in a play, and I'd finally gotten my chance at lead. If I convinced myself it was pretend, maybe I could get through it without it hurting so much.

Because looking at him, knowing how much I loved him and how much he didn't love me, felt like I was covered in a million paper cuts.

"Nothing that wasn't true," he finally breathed out, shaking his head. "That I didn't care if he left, but you would be a big loss. That Rittenborough was a second-rate director with subpar writing, and I thought you deserved better. But I'm not standing in the way for either of you, Belle. My lawyer is drawing up your release paperwork as we speak. You're both free to go."

Free to go?

What did that even mean?

I know that I had come to see him with the intention of a fact-finding mission only, with no intention of resuming a relationship. But I'd be lying if I didn't admit I was a little hurt too.

No apology.

No trying to win me back.

No attempt to smooth anything out.

Just a release of any legal obligation and parting words that I was free to go.

Speechless wasn't normal for me, usually able to muster up some kind of a response. But as I blinked back, I honestly had no idea of what to say.

"Belle? Was there anything else?" he asked, keeping his distance both physically and emotionally.

"Did you tell him about us?" My voice was softer than I'd wanted it to be as I tried to swallow. "Does he know?"

Jagger shook his head. "He asked, I denied it. There's nothing to tell."

Wow.

Just. Wow.

It was what I wanted I guess, and I should be grateful that for the first time since we met, Jagger Hartley was finally giving me exactly what I'd asked for. Funny how ungratifying it was and felt all wrong.

"Okay, well, I guess I should go then." It wasn't a question even though I wanted it to be one, desperate to know if he was really just giving up. And yeah, I realize how stupid that sounded, and how conflicting that was. But I just didn't know how he could have turned off his feelings so easily. Guess when he didn't love me back, that should've been the tip off. "Okay," I repeated as I turned to leave.

Say something, I telepathically willed, wanting him to say *anything* that would help it make sense. It wasn't until I had my fingers on the door handle that I heard him finally speak.

"Good luck on your audition. Try and turn up on time."

Ouch.

Do not cry.

Do.

Not.

Cry.

"Thanks."

And even though I didn't think it was possible, he broke my heart for a second time.

Chapter 27

Jagger

It was the second time since I'd known Belle that I'd been drunk. The first time, it had been unintentional, those stupid Holy Waters had been stronger than I'd thought. But the current situation had been premeditated.

I knew I'd been a jerk, and selfish, and that we'd probably been doomed from the start. I'd broken my own rule—don't date the talent—and still, I'd convinced myself that it would've been different with her.

"Um, should I call an ambulance?" Joe asked when I called to tell him I wasn't going in.

"I said I was sick Joe, not dying." I tried not to slur on the phone. Last thing I needed was for him to think I was having a stroke and call 9-1-1 anyway.

"Jagger, I've known you for three years. I've never once seen you take a sick day even when you probably should. So if you're taking one now, things are probably more dire than you're admitting. This have anything to do with you needing Logan's number?"

"For fuck's sake, Joe," I groaned loudly. "I've got the flu or something. Or maybe one of those twenty-four-hour bugs. And no, it's got nothing to do with any of that. Just run through the planned rehearsal and see if you can get me some replacement understudies since ours have left us high and dry."

"Yeah, I got your email. Weird they're both going, huh?" Joe probed, carefully, like he had more to say.

And I was not drunk enough to continue having *that* conversation.

"Who cares? They wanted out, they're out. Find me replacements and I should be back tomorrow. See ya."

I'll admit if my intention was to quit being a jerk, I'd failed miserably. Wish I could work up the motivation to care, but unfortunately, I was all out of fucks.

Sure, Joe probably didn't deserve to be the recipient of my mood. But as he'd said, he'd known me for three years, he was used to me being short. And anyway, I'd clearly told him I was sick, no one was in a good mood when they're sick.

Except for maybe Belle, who I'm sure would still be trying to knit blankets for homeless people or foster stray dogs even if she was half dead.

Belle.

I needed to get her off my mind and out of my head because honestly, it was for the best. I wasn't built for a serious relationship, and obviously had more issues than I thought when it came to trust. And the last thing I wanted to be was someone's project, which is what I'd become if I told her what was going on.

What was the point anyway? She'd left, and while I didn't blame her for going, it was what I'd always expected. So, better it happened *before* I'd admitted I loved her. I still had my pride, right? So she thought I was an asshole, well guess what? So did half of Broadway.

Deciding I must be sobering up since my mood had taken another turn, I grabbed a bottle of Jack and went back to bed.

I knew I couldn't hide out forever, the show needed to go on or whatever bullshit enlightened advice was usually given. But I was giving myself a fucking day. I'd never done that, allowed myself to wallow. And fuck me if after years of watching everyone have their own pity party that I didn't deserve one too.

Turning off my phone—because who the fuck was going to call me anyway—I proceeded to drink until I no longer felt anything.

Not sad.

Not happy.

Nothing.

I wanted to live in a void of emotions.

And forget all about her.

Chapter 28

Belle

It was opening night for *Lilith*, and I had mixed emotions.

I hadn't heard from Jagger since I left his apartment six weeks ago.

In that time I'd auditioned and gotten the lead opposite Logan. It was a smaller production, and Rittenborough wasn't as good a director as Jagger, but it I was the one on the stage.

A compromise, although I wasn't sure why I'd made it anymore.

From the preview buzz, the critics were claiming *Lilith* was Jagger Hartley's "best work yet." I wasn't surprised, it had been an amazing script and Jagger was one hell of a writer and director. And I totally expected that his next show would be on Broadway proper with so many Tony nominees auditioning he could literally have his pick.

Damn him.

Because as much as I wanted to be bitter and hate him, I just couldn't.

I was glad, happy even, wishing him nothing but success. Of course I was also sad, wishing I could've been a part of that success, but I guess it just wasn't to be.

But I couldn't hate him.

I must be defective.

"Are you sure about this?" Zara asked as we walked to the front of the theatre. "You don't have anything to prove and honestly, it's probably going to suck anyway."

"You *know* it's not going to suck." I rolled my eyes. I loved my sister but knew she was just saying it to make me feel better. "And it's not about proving anything, I just need to do this. For closure."

I'd bought tickets for everyone when I was originally part of the production. Even though I knew there was a good chance I'd never step on stage—especially on opening night—I wanted them to be there and share it with me. And even though there was no reason to still go, I wanted to anyway.

"It *might* suck," Hayley added, clearly on *Team We Hate Jagger Hartley*. "He may have done a ton of rewrites and totally fucked it. Weird stuff happens all the time and you know how temperamental writers and directors can be."

"Ladies, I don't mean to be an asshole, but wouldn't this debate have made more sense *before* we got here?" Lincoln straightened his tie. "Can we at least go inside and be intimidating? I'm going to need some kind of remittance for dragging my ass here on a Wednesday night."

"I can pretend to be your boyfriend if it helps." Nate casually put his arm around me. "I was in my high school production of *Grease*. Had the biggest crush on the kid that played Danny Zuko."

"Guys!" I put my hands up to my ears, not needing anymore conflict than I was already feeling. "We're going to do this. It's going to be fine," I reassured myself more than anyone else before turning to Lincoln. "There's no need to be intimidating, just enjoy a night out with your lovely fiancée." I gestured to my sister. "And Nate, thanks for the offer, but it's completely unnecessary. He's probably not even going to see me." I gave his arm a squeeze. "And lastly, Hayley, we both know it's going to be brilliant."

With each of them suitably pacified, we made our way into the theater and found our seats. We were third row, something I'd been ecstatic about initially, but now it wasn't such a positive. There was always the possibility I'd run into Dane or his parents—awkward—or worse, someone else. Becks would've happily been his date no doubt. Curled her arm around him, while she stuck out her tits and smiled, the *perfect* girlfriend for opening night. Great for photo opportunities.

Uhhhhhhh, because I had a right to be jealous when he had every right to move on. Still, I wasn't about to hide or pretend to be in a relationship, because it wasn't about anyone but myself.

Closure.

Being the bigger person.

Moving on.

All those important things.

I may have also worn the most glamourous dress in my wardrobe—a sequin midnight-blue gown that clung to every inch of my body—because as much as I was being the bigger person, I also wasn't a saint. And the dress was beautiful and deserved a night out too.

"I'm sorry," I whispered to Hayley as I shuffled in between her and Nate. "When I originally bought this ticket, it was supposed to be for you to bring someone."

"Please." Hayley waved her hand dismissively. "I'm an unemployed actress and a single mom, my dating prospects aren't great. And besides, you're the best date I could ever ask for."

Nate put his arm around the back of my chair and leaned in looking hurt. "Wait, so you won't pretend to date me, but you'll pretend to date her? I'm a fucking doctor, Belle, doesn't that count for anything?"

I laughed, and it was the first genuine smile of the night. Because if anyone could make me feel better about going to see the production I used to be a part of, written and directed by the man I was still very much in love with, then it was my family.

And even though some of them technically weren't blood related, they were my family nonetheless.

"If it makes you feel better, I'll pretend to date both of you." I looped one of my arms through each of theirs. "Conventional romance didn't work out for me anyway, so I'm open for new things."

Not only had I not dated anyone since I'd broken up with Jagger, but I wasn't even interested in the *prospect* of having another boyfriend. The idea of another man kissing and touching me, made me physically sick. And while I knew time would probably change that, I couldn't see myself loving another man like I loved him. Perhaps the stupid fortune teller who predicted when I was a kid I'd never have that one true love was right. Granted she was a complete fraud, and had been completely wrong about Zara, but the universe was a funny place. And maybe that was okay. Because I never wanted to feel that kind of hurt ever again.

A hush fell over the crowd as the orchestra warmed up. A voice came over the PA, making the announcement for everyone to take their seats as the house lights dimmed.

I was excited and nervous, the knot in my stomach tightening with each passing second. And even though I knew I wasn't going to be seeing Jagger physically on that stage, I knew every word of it was his. It was his soul.

And as the performance started and the stage filled with familiar faces I'd rehearsed with not that long ago, I felt my eyes water. Because it was everything I knew it would be and more, brilliant in every way that mattered. Even Chase and Serenity were phenomenal, the changes to their performance probably more likely due to the skillful hand of Jagger's artful direction than anything else.

My heart was beating so loudly in my chest I was positive people would hear it over the music, constantly needing to dab the corner of my eyes to stem the stream of tears that were leaking out. And I wasn't even sure why I was crying. If it was because I was sad I was no longer a part of it, or because it was so good, or because I missed Jagger.

It was almost close to the end of the first act when I excused myself, breaking the carnal rule of sitting in your seat until intermission and shuffling out to the bathroom.

It was rude and distracting to the actors, but I didn't want anyone to see I'd been crying, and needed to get out and fix my face before the lights went back up.

I was still dabbing my eyes when I made it out to the beautifully lit foyer, grateful I was the only one there.

"Belle." I heard my name, my feet freezing in their spot.

It was him.

The voice I still dreamt about even though I'd never admit it out loud.

Doing my best to not look like a complete hot mess, I swiped my fingers under my eyes one last time before I turned around. I was an actress, and this was just one more performance.

"Hi, Jagger." I smiled, my heart breaking as I saw how amazing he looked. He was breathtakingly handsome, wearing a beautifully cut suit with just the right amount of scruff on his face. I wanted to touch him, kiss him, wrap my arms around him and ask him why he'd been so cruel. But I didn't, keeping my distance as he closed the gap between us. "You should be so proud, it's brilliant and—"

"I don't care about that right now. You're here." He sounded surprised, his eyes widening as they rolled over my body.

"Well of course, I'm here. I bought tickets. We're all here." Another fake smile, hoping he didn't get much closer.

He did.

His body inches from mine as his hand reached out and touched my arm. "I don't care about them either. Just you."

Words I'd been dying to hear, but they were weeks too late. And while I was confident in my acting ability, I wasn't about my heart.

"I should go to the bathroom before the rush." I pointed to the door. "Congrats, Jagger. It's brilliant."

Before I got to turn and seek refuge in the bathroom, his arms had wrapped around me and pulled me closer. "I love you, Belle. I've always loved you. And I'm so fucking sorry I didn't tell you before."

My mouth was on his before I'd been able to stop myself, kissing him and breaking my own rules. It wasn't supposed to be like that. He needed to grovel and apologize for weeks, dragging it out before I finally caved. But I couldn't help it, needing to kiss him even if I still walked away when the night was over, wanting to touch him even if it was for one last time.

His mouth responded, deepening the kiss as his body pressed against me. He was hard, his length rubbing against me as his hands dropped to my ass. "Fuck, Belle. It's almost intermission." He growled against my mouth in between kisses, unable to stop. "But I fucking need you."

He was completely unhinged, knowing that in minutes—possibly even seconds—that empty foyer was going to be filled with people and yet his lips stayed on mine. It was his big night, press, critics, and important people from the industry, made up a healthy portion of the audience and that we hadn't been seen already was a miracle.

"Jagger." I tried to take a step back, not wanting tomorrow's headline to be about me and him dry humping rather than the performance itself. "Not like this."

He chuckled against my mouth. "You're the one who started it. You kissed me, remember?"

"Which time?" I asked, a real smile creeping up my lips.

He intertwined my fingers with his, bringing our joined knuckles to his lips. "Every time it counted. Please don't leave, Belle. I promise, we'll talk. I'll explain. I'll apologize. And if you still want to leave after, I won't stop you. But give me one last chance even though I know I don't deserve it."

Gah.

Say no.

Say it's too late.

Say you've moved on.

I willed my mouth to tell any of those lies as I looked into his eyes. That mask he usually wore was gone, sincerity reflecting in those beautiful pools of green and gold.

"I'm not promising anything, Jagger. Even though I kissed you," I warned, knowing I'd probably do it again before the night was out. "You can't just say sorry and think it will be okay."

"I know." He nodded as the applause echoed from the still closed doors. It was intermission, we would no longer be alone. "Just one last chance, Belle."

Before I could answer, people started to spill into the foyer. I dropped his hand giving us some distance as the audience looked at us with interest. Some rushed past, making a crazy dash to the bathroom or the bar, while others were just stretching their legs and in no hurry at all.

"You should probably go backstage." I took another step back, separating us farther. "Joe is probably wondering where you are."

"Belle?" Nate appeared by my side, wrapping his arm around me. "Everything okay?" His eyes moved to Jagger as they exchanged heated looks.

"I'm fine, Nate. Thanks for checking on me. I just need a minute." I tried to reassure him, not wanting to make a scene. Being caught kissing the director wasn't bad enough, a love triangle was way over the top, even for me.

Nate nodded but not before leaning in, his voice lowered as he whispered to Jagger, "There are just over two hundred bones in the human body, and I know how to break every last one."

I shook my head, hiding my smirk as Nate kissed me on the cheek and then left like I asked.

"Your new boyfriend seems nice." The sarcasm dripped from his tone.

"He's not my *boyfriend*, he's just a friend. But he was with me the night we broke up so he's understandably protective. And like I'd kiss you if I was here with someone else." I shoved him lightly in the chest. "You're already screwing up this apology and you haven't even started yet."

It would've been easy to let him believe I was with Nate, but I wasn't that girl. If he wanted to win me back it had to be because he wanted me, not because someone else was playing with his toys.

"You're right, come with me." His hand retook mine as he waited for me to nod. Then ignoring curious eyes and cupped-hand whispers, he led me to a door taking us backstage.

"I'm jealous." He huffed out a breath. "Even though you have every right to be with someone else, the thought of you with anyone other than me makes me want to kill something."

I went to open my mouth, ready to argue that wasn't much of an apology either when he continued.

"And it's not because I don't *want* you with them, but because I *need* you to be with me. I know I fucked up, Belle. I know that I should've handled it differently. But I have trust issues, and you leaving—in any capacity—felt like a betrayal. That wasn't your fault, that was on me. Because, as Dane likes to *helpfully* point out, no one is a fucking mind reader."

He didn't stop, telling me how he was trying to do the right thing but needed me with him. How he wanted me beside him even though it required me to make the sacrifice. How he wanted me to be his Lilith on the stage and be his person off it. And not knowing how to make it work.

It was a lot.

My heart squeezing between my ribs as he spilled more of himself than he ever had.

He didn't do that.

Share his emotions.

And admitting weakness was something I knew was probably killing him to do.

"I said I loved you," I choked out, fighting the urge to hug him.

"Yeah, and I love you, Belle." His hands came around my face, his thumbs grazing my jaw. "I still love you. I'm never going to stop, even if you do. And we both know how stubborn I can be."

"Am I going to have to kiss you again?" My heartbeat quickened, my breath coming out in short bursts.

"Not a chance." His lips hovered over mine. "This time I'm kissing you."

Chapter 29

Jagger

My mouth was on hers as my hands wrapped around her body, kissing her like I'd wanted since the second she'd walked out of my apartment.

It had been weeks.

Weeks of keeping my distance because I figured it was for the best. And even though I knew deep down I'd never get over her, I had to fucking try. And the only way to do that was cold turkey.

Detox from Belle like she was a drug. Because the minute I saw her I knew I wouldn't be able to walk away a second time, and I was right.

Time had given me a much-needed perspective, and yeah, maybe I'd had some therapy as well. After Dane found me drunk within an inch of consciousness, he forced me to do what I'd been avoiding for years. Dealing with my issues so I could finally allow myself to be happy.

And while it was a process—and I swear to fucking God if I hear one more *you need to do the work*, I'm going to lose my mind—pushing Belle away had been from the fear of losing her.

So instead of giving us a chance to make it, I pulled the pin early and detonated it myself. Figured it would be easier if it had been on my terms and I'd been able to control the narrative, except it wasn't. And all I'd done was lose the only woman I'd ever loved.

Wouldn't make that mistake a second time.

Biding my time, I was going to wait until after we opened to make my move. I'd already blown off too many hours "doing the fucking" work and had saddled Joe with more than I'd have liked. I was still very much in the driver's seat, and turned up to every rehearsal, working with the team. But I'd delegated some of the less important stuff, something I was still learning to be okay with.

Seeing her in the audience was a gift I couldn't have hoped for. It wasn't how I'd intended it or thought it would go down, but hell, I wasn't stupid either. I threw out my stupid master plan and took the opportunity the universe had tossed in my direction.

Fuck it.

I needed her back.

"Should you be somewhere else?" Belle asked between kisses, her hands gripping the front of my shirt. "It's your big night."

"I'm exactly where I need to be, sweetheart, exactly where I want to be too."

There was little privacy, and I wasn't big on public displays, but I didn't give a shit if the entire cast and crew saw me kissing Belle, she was never going to be a secret again.

She giggled against my lips. "Oh my God, who is this? And what have you done with Jagger Hartley?"

"I'm right here, Belle, and if you stick around, you'll see what else has changed." My hands cradled her hips, holding her steady as I glanced down at her dress. "This is lethal by the way."

"Is it?" She grinned coyly, pretending like she didn't know she'd given every man in a two-mile radius a hard-on. "I just wanted to look my best for opening night."

"Yeah, for your *friend*? Or for me?" I asked, still not sure whether the guy she was with knew he didn't have a chance with her. Poor asshole.

Her hand batted at my chest. "Please, you think I went to all this effort for either of you? I wanted to look pretty; it was all for me."

I loved that about her, her innate sense of self-assurance, a confidence that was untainted by the thoughts of others. Man, I wanted some of that, intoxicated by her courage and tenacity, and a boldness that drove me insane.

"Whatever the reasons," my hands trailed down her body, "I like it. But it's going to make getting through the rest of tonight very *hard*."

She gasped, cupping her mouth with her hand. "Was that a joke, Jagger? Oh my God, you *have* changed."

Swatting her ass, I pulled her back to me. "Are you going to come backstage with me where you belong, or do you want to go sit in the audience? As long as you promise to go home with me tonight, I won't argue with whatever you choose."

Letting her go sit on the other side of the curtain felt wrong on so many levels, but I'd do whatever I had to. I'd learned that when it came to Belle, I didn't always have to be in control and as scary as that was, it was sort of exhilarating as well.

Belle lifted on her toes as her lips brushed against mine. "I want to stay with you, Jagger, but I need to go sit in the audience. I promise I'll be the one cheering and clapping for you after it's done, and then we'll go back to your place."

I groaned, not the answer I'd hoped but I'd already committed to not arguing. "Fine, fine, go sit with your friends." I rolled my eyes, hating I was going to have to let her go after just getting her back.

She elbowed me gently in the ribs. "Hey, this is for as much your benefit as it is anyone else's. You said my dress was lethal." Her eyes glanced down at the glittering fabric. "We both know that if I come back there, you're not going to be able to keep your hands off me."

Agreeing—begrudgingly—that she was right, I unwrapped my hands and gave her one last kiss. I wish I knew that we were okay, but there was a niggling part of me that couldn't be sure, my fingers locking around her wrist stopping her from leaving. "I know I've got a lot to make up for, Belle, and one night isn't going to do it. But all that I ask is you don't give up on me."

I hated sounding so fucking vulnerable, wishing I could just throw her over my shoulder and demand she love me. But that wouldn't work, and I'd said I'd do whatever it took, even if I had to cut myself open and expose all the ugly parts.

She squeezed my hand back. "I'm here, Jagger. I think we both know that I'm terrible at giving up especially on something I loved."

"You still love me?" It hadn't escaped my attention that when she'd said it, it was *loved*. Her feelings might've changed, not that I was going to be deterred.

Her delicate shoulder lifted as a slow smile crossed her lips. "Yes, I still do. Now go be with your cast. This is a huge night, and I meant it when I said you should be proud. *I'm* proud of you."

Never had those words meant so much.

Not from my parents.

Not from any of my teachers or professors.

Not from my friends.

But from her, they meant everything, and I guess that was how I knew she was the one.

I kissed her one last time and then let her go. "I'll see you after the show, beautiful." And then I watched her leave, her ass swaying a little more than it needed to as she walked.

Damn that woman.

She was going to be the death of me.

And I was going to enjoy every last second of that death.

We got three standing ovations.

Three.

The cheering and applause from the crowd almost deafening as the final curtain call ended.

And I had everything I wanted.

My parents had kindly offered to observe quietly from the side of the stage, forgoing the circus that usually accompanied them. I knew it had been engineered by Dane, my younger brother whisking them off before anyone saw and snapped a photo. He wanted me to have my opening night, and for it to be about no one but me.

My brother was by far my second favorite person, and no guesses on who was my first.

Belle and her party were waiting by the stage door, but they weren't wearing the same enthusiastic smile she was.

It wasn't surprising that someone like Belle had so many people looking out for her, considering how kind and beautiful her heart was. I'd never had that, but I wasn't exactly the most likeable guy either.

And Belle had obviously asked them to be on their best behavior. Because even though I could tell both Zara and Lincoln had plenty to say, they both kept their mouths shut. Hayley was less frosty, congratulating me on the show before dashing off to see some of her friends backstage. Nathan Baxter—the man I'd met briefly in the foyer—was still a variable I couldn't place, but considering the hug and kiss Belle gave me in front of him, I was going to leave that discussion for another day.

As promised, she stayed with me as the rest of them left, a few parting glares given by Zara, Lincoln and Nathan before they said their goodbyes. Hayley gave me a hug, so I guessed I had at least one person on my side.

Joe shook his head when he saw us together, slapping me on the back. "Guess this was why you were such an asshole after she left. Should've known."

"C'mon, Joe. I've *always* been an asshole." I laughed as I kissed Belle's forehead.

"True," Joe agreed. "But you were a bigger asshole after she left."

Belle chuckled. "Guess it all worked out in the end."

She was right about that, it did all work out in the end, even if I had to go through hell to get there.

There'd been not-so-subtle whispers among the cast and crew, piecing together why Belle and Logan had left. Everyone had come to the conclusion they were lovers and got sick of my shit, and I didn't do anything to dissuade the speculation. But seeing us together gave more than a few of them something to talk about, and I didn't care.

"Casual visit? Or here for other reasons." Serenity raised a brow, tipping her head toward Lacy, who had been Belle's re-placement.

It was catty, Serenity's effort to show dominance since deep down she knew Belle was a better actress. No one would deny she was talented, but if I'd had my choice over, I'd have fought for Belle to have been on that stage. Not because I loved her, but because that was where she belonged.

Unperturbed by Serenity's jab, Belle smiled, looping her arm around mine. "I'm here to support my boyfriend."

Hearing those words was everything, especially when I didn't think I'd ever hear them again.

"Lacy is a better fit," I added, both Belle and Serenity open-mouthed as they turned to face me. "Belle is born to play lead and understudy was a waste of her talent. You ready to go, beau-tiful? I have my car."

Risking pissing off my lead actress and my assistant direc-tor, I was ready to end the night. Chances were they'd have prob-ably preferred to celebrate without me, and I had some of my own celebrating I needed to do.

"I really need to teach you how to make friends, Jagger." She snuggled up close to me as we left the theatre. "Spoiler alert, that isn't how you do it."

I laughed, shaking my head. "Yeah, probably not. You better stick around then. For the good of others."

"I *am* charitable." Belle nodded. "So I guess I will."

Belle crashed into that audition, a tornado looking for her big break. But what she'd given me was far greater than any benefit I could've given her.

She was by far my biggest break, and I'd never been more grateful in my life.

Epilogue

Jagger

"**T**here was no nudity?" My father looked confused as we stood up to applaud. "Wasn't it called *Naked and Alone*? I understand the director was going for a metaphor, but he had the perfect opportunity to strip them down and give the audience a more literal interpretation."

Oh, for fuck's sake.

Inviting my parents had been Belle's idea. Her entire family was there, bursting with pride in the front row just a few seats down from us. She'd insisted mine come too in an effort to try to have a more normal and functional relationship with my parents. Of course, my parents weren't very *normal* or conducive to *functional relationships*, but I didn't have the heart to stop her. Even if it meant me listening to my dad complain about the artistic direction.

"Kirk, no one tells you how to paint." My mother chuckled. "I think Mr. Attenborough did an adequate job. Not as good as our Jagger would've done, but we can all agree, Belle was their shining star."

So much in that statement and I didn't know where to even start.

"It's Rittenborough. And yes, Belle was definitely their saving grace." It wasn't bad, per se, but the script was a little predictable, with a slant to be cliché. Not that Belle let that stop her, putting on a performance worthy of a Tony.

As for being *their* Jagger, that was also an adjustment. Wasn't sure I'd ever have the kind of relationship most people had with their parents, but I was done fighting the tide and being angry. Besides, they adored the hell out of Belle, and that was more than enough for me.

"She's without a doubt, amazing," Dane agreed. "I hope you're not going to be stupid enough to cast her as understudy again. Because, Jagger, I know nothing about Broadway and knew that was dumb."

Agreed.

"Trust me, I'm working on something big for the both of us. Now if you'll excuse me, I'm going to go kiss my girlfriend and tell her how amazing she was."

Again, something new for me, being so open with my emotions rather than grunt and let everyone work it out on their own. Not sure it was going to stick, grunting was still very much my preference, but no one could accuse me of not trying.

My mother beamed, proud that I was not only playing nice with the family but was also happy for a change. And I'll admit, I didn't hate the approval, even if I'd spent most of my life telling myself I didn't need it.

Shuffling out of my chair—the theatre was a small Off-Broadway relic and there wasn't a lot of room—I smiled at Belle's family as I made my way to the backstage area, being waved through by Rittenborough.

"She's brilliant." He grinned, the bastard knowing he'd won the lottery with her. "When Logan told me about her, I thought he was exaggerating. Surely you wouldn't have let someone of that caliber slip through your fingers. But whatever your reasons, I'm thankful."

Don't be a dick.

Do. Not. Be. A. Dick.

"My pleasure." I blew out a breath, exhausted from the effort of being so nice to everyone. "But don't get used to it. My latest script is being custom written for Belle, and this time it will be a large-scale production. After the success of *Lilith*, I finally get to sit at the grown-up table."

Okay, so I was a dick, but fuck me, you can only ask so much of a man and I was all out of patience. And besides, none of that was a lie even if it was lacking humility and decorum.

Fuck it.

"Yes, yes, I heard you got a lot of attention. Good for you." Rittenborough swallowed. "May we all have the same luck."

I was about to open my mouth and tell him luck had nothing to do with it when I saw her, literally losing my breath.

Still wearing her stage makeup, her face so animated and excited, she leapt into my arms and kissed me.

No longer caring about anything else, I kissed her back, lifting her as she wrapped her gorgeous strong legs around my waist.

Yeah.

What was I saying?

"Belle, you were outstanding." I brushed the hair off her face. "I'm so fucking proud of you."

"Awwww, Jagger." She squeezed me back. "I'm so glad you're here. I know how hard it is to take a night off, but it meant everything that you got to see my opening night."

"Wouldn't have missed it for the world, sweetheart." I cradled her body against mine. "I'll be at every single one of your opening nights. No matter what happens."

"Wow, big call." Her eyes widened. "What if there's a clash? And we both have the same opening nights?"

I didn't even hesitate, knowing exactly how I wanted to spend my future. "Then we better make sure we do as many as we can together. You want to do that with me? And not just opening nights, Belle."

She looked around, aware we weren't alone as she dropped her voice to a whisper. "Jagger, what are you saying? Because it kinda sounds like . . ."

"It sounds exactly like it is, Belle. You're my forever. And soon, I'm going to ask for that commitment in writing."

And even though I knew it was way too soon to propose, and I'd never steal the limelight for her outstanding achievement, I needed her to know what she meant to me.

Her smile exploded, showering me with kisses. "When you ask, I'm totally going to say yes. But just know I'll probably make you wait a little while just so you don't think I'm a total sure thing and predictable." She chuckled against my throat.

"There's not a damn thing about you that's predictable, and that's what I love about you the most." I kissed her again, unable to stop. "Now, go be with your cast, I'll be waiting for you when you're done."

"Are you sure?" She slid down my body, hesitating. "I hate that you have to wait around."

I shook my head, not willing to steal that from her. "I'll wait for you, for as long as it takes. Go, enjoy your moment, beautiful, you've more than earned it."

"Okay." Her smile returned. "Make sure you invite your parents back to our place. My parents are excited to get to know them better."

A groan escaped before I could stop it. I had no problem with Belle's parents and had the pleasure of meeting them just before Belle moved into my Brooklyn apartment. I think secretly Zara and Lincoln were glad for the extra privacy and space, even though they never said.

But my parents?

Hadn't I done enough for one night?

I'd introduced everyone before the show, despite my aversion to small talk, and was pleasantly surprised that everyone— my parents—was on their best behavior. Dane helped of course, mediating as always and charming over Belle's parents. He even organized a "boys" night with me, him and Lincoln. Who even was I anymore?

"Invite your parents, Jagger," Belle warned, reminding me it was not up for debate.

"Fine," I conceded, knowing there was no point arguing. "But if my dad ends up pant-less on the roof, smoking a joint, you can't complain when I say I told you so. I'm sure your dad will love that, explaining to his drycleaner why his suit smells of weed."

She grinned, having gotten her way—like always—giving me a quick kiss. "It will be fine. I promise. My parents raised me, they can handle a curve ball or two. Now, I've got to run."

And as I watched her walk away, I realized that maybe Rittenborough was right, and I had gotten lucky. Because a woman like that was one in a million, and if I had her by my side, I knew I could do anything.

Write and direct.

Deal with my parents.

Be a better man.

Yeah, I *was* lucky.

And I was done apologizing for it.

THE END

To keep up-to-date with all T Gephart's news,
appearances, and releases,
please subscribe to her mailing list
(http://eepurl.com/bws5Av).

Also please consider leaving a review
on your retailer of choice. They help the author
and future readers and we're all eternally grateful.

Acknowledgements

Lord, where to even start? How many times have I done this? And every time, I just don't think I could ever show my gratitude adequately enough.

Thanks to my family who has weathered another crazy intense writing season with me. Without you this means nothing, and I love you all with every fiber of my being. Gep, Jenna, Liam and Woodley, you are the beats of my heart.

Thank you to my extended family and friends, I feel your love and support even if we're not together and I hope you feel mine.

A million thanks to Sally Thorne and Kelly Elliott who have been my tireless cheerleaders. I'm not sure how many times you've heard me cry while I wrote this book, but I'm eternally gratefully you didn't give up on me even when I wanted to. Love you ladies HARDCORE.

Special thanks to the beautiful Gayle Williams, who will always be my person. Selfless, kind, and so remarkably considerate, it's a true blessing to know you. Thanks so everything you do for me, I hope you know how much you mean to me.

Thanks Kimberly, Aimee, and everyone at Brower Literary and Management. Thanks so much for the love and support, getting my work out in the world and being so awesome at what you do.

Thanks so much, Nichole Strauss from Insight Editing. Another book, another hot mess. I think we got through it though. I swear I'm going to get better at this thing one of these days.

Amazing thanks to MK who has kept me on the straight and narrow and always has the "good" questions. Gah, I love you and all your insight. Thank you so much for sticking with me.

Thank you Elaine York from Allusion Graphics LLC, Publishing and Book Formatting for being the most patient and understanding formatter around. I swear, one of these days you're gonna be sick of me, just not today. You always make my books look beautiful, a million thanks!

And to the AMAZING cover designer who has been with me for so long, I don't even know what I'd do without out. Hang Le, you literally worked miracles for me. So kind, so talented, I'm blessed to have you in my circle. Thank you for all you do. I promise I'll get my shit together so I'm not sending you crazy emails, thank you for yet another perfect cover.

Thanks so much to Rebecca from Rebecca Fairest Reviews Editing Services for working with me on yet another book. I know the schedule was crazy but I count on you to give my babies the last polish before they off into the world.

Much love and thanks to all my author buddies, many who I've not seen in years. YEARS. WTF is up with that? Damn this pandemic *shakes fist* I love you all and hope we can have shenanigans soon, but until then, I will cherish every message, text, call, FaceTime, Marco, and DM.

Thank you, thank you, THANK YOU to all the bloggers, reviewers, bookstagrammers, group admins and promoters who read, promote, review, and share my work. I will never take any of it for granted and am so thankful for all your LOVE and SUPPORT.

Thanks so much to Mary Dubé from Grey's Promotions.

Thank you, Liz, MJ, and Jillian at 1001 Dark Nights.

THANK YOU TO THE T GEPHART REVIEW CREW AND ENTOURAGE. Thanks for sticking with me through all these books, my crazy-ass lives, cooks, photos, shares and all the other nonsense that goes on in that group. You guys complete me.

Special thanks Pole and Aerial Divas Richmond and Pole Divas Reservoir for keeping me sane. I am so in love with being in the air—on a pole or in silks—and the community it has given me is a true gift. Love you, Divas!! #HotMessExpress #WhyIs-TinaSpinningSoFast #SupermanEndsUpSpidermanEveryTime

And as always, my biggest thanks is to YOU. How No matter how you found me, read me, or experienced this story, I am thankful. You're awesome and your butt looks fabulous, don't let anyone tell you different!

About the Author

T Gephart is a *USA Today* and International bestselling author from Melbourne, Australia.

With an approach to life that is somewhat unconventional, she prefers to fly by the seat of her pants rather than adhere to some rigid roadmap. Her lack of "plan" has resulted in a rather interesting and eclectic resume, which reads more like the fiction she writes than an actual employment history. She'd tell you all about it, but the statute of limitations hasn't expired yet. But all those crazy twists and turns have led her to a career she loves—writing romantic comedy.

When she isn't filling pages with sassy and sexy characters with attitude, she's living her own reality show in the 'burbs of Melbourne with her American husband, two children, and her fur child—Woodley.

She loves adventure, to laugh, travel, and strives to live her life to the fullest.

Connect with T

tgephart.com
Facebook (https://www.facebook.com/tgephartauthor)
Goodreads
Twitter (https://twitter.com/tinagephart)

Other Books

The Lexi Series
Lexi
A Twist of Fate
Twisted Views: Fate's Companion
A Leap of Faith
A Time for Hope

The Power Station Series
High Strung
Crash Ride
Back Stage

The Black Addiction Series
Slide
Sticks
Stand

#1 Series
#1 Crush
#1 Player

#1 Rival
#1 Lie
#1 Muse
#1 Love

Collision Series
Train Wreck
Car Crash

Hot in the City Series
Send Me Crazy
One Click Love
Not Just Friends
Between The Lines

Crazy in Love Series
My Greatest Mistake
My Biggest Break
Crazy in Love #3 (Hayley)
Crazy in Love #4? (I mean, it could happen, I suck at planning)

Standalones
The Fall
One-Night Stand-In
Viral